Rowena Summers

Dreams of Peace

CANELO

First published in Great Britain in 2002 by Severn House Publishers

This edition published in the United Kingdom in 2024 by

Canelo
Unit 9, 5th Floor
Cargo Works, 1–2 Hatfields
London SE1 9PG
United Kingdom

A CIP catalogue record for this book is available from the British Library.

Print ISBN 978 1 80436 575 5
Ebook ISBN 978 1 80436 293 8

Look for more great books at www.canelo.co

Printed and bound in Great Britain by Clays Ltd, Elcograf S.p.A.

I

4

Dreams of Peace

Rowena Summers is the pseudonym of Jean Saunders. She was a British writer of romance novels since 1974, and wrote under her maiden name and her pseudonym, as well as the names Sally Blake and Rachel Moore. She was elected the seventeenth Chairman (1993–1995) of the Romantic Novelists' Association, and she was the Vice-Chairman of the Writers' Summer School of Swanwick. She was also a member of Romance Writers of America, Crime Writers' Association and West Country Writers' Association.

For Geoff, with love as always
in our very special year

And our family:
Barry, Janet and Ann

Our clutch of grandchildren:
Nathan, Ben, Christopher, Russell, Dominic, Eleanor, Shaun,
Rowan, Daniel and Katie

And the little 'uns:
Faye and Jasmine

Chapter One

There wasn't a single dry eye in the picture-house as *Mrs Miniver* faded away into infinity, leaving that poor Walter Pidgeon sad and lonely and professing that she was still here when everybody knew that she wasn't.

After all the wartime troubles they'd been through and all, Vanessa thought, choking down a huge lump in her throat. She stumbled out of the picture-house, blinking in the daylight and praying she wouldn't be caught sneaking out of it in the middle of the afternoon, instead of being at school. Especially *crying*...Even more, praying that none of Aunt Rose's cronies would see her and report back. Lot of sneaks, they were, she thought with a final sniff, ramming her school hat back on her head and thankful that it hadn't got too creased up in her pocket. Then she forgot them as the two Americans who'd been sitting behind her caught up with her, and she quickly shoved her hat back in her pocket again.

They'd had a number of GIs billeted with them in recent months, but they had got boring as far as Vanessa was concerned, always showing off their photos of the girlfriends back home.

Right now they were "between Yanks", as she airily told the school friends who were green with jealousy that Rose Painter had opened her large house to so many of them in the cause of Anglo-American friendship.

"Say, you really got caught up in that movie, didn't you, babe?" one of the GIs said with a wicked grin. "I thought you were going to be sobbing all the way home after the Jerry planes killed off the Limeys. It's only acting, kid."

"I know. I'm not that daft," she said with a toss of her hair and trying to pretend she was a bleedin' sight more sophisticated than she felt with these two good-lookers beaming down at her.

"You're not from these parts, are you, honey?" the second one said, as they fell into step beside her as she made for the beach. It was a bit early to go home yet. The Grammar School was at the other end of the town, and Aunt Rose would be suspicious if she got back too early.

"Nah. I'm from London," she said importantly.

The GIs whistled. "Gee, I guess you were glad to get away from there when the Jerry bombs started dropping, weren't you?"

Vanessa tried to look mysterious, hoping that it would hint at a tragic and interesting past. "I'd rather not talk about it if you don't mind," she said, with no intention of letting these blokes know she had been evacuated down to Weston-super-Mare when she was twelve, and that she was only fifteen now, despite the way she knew very well she could pass for eighteen – which she longed to be.

They nodded understandingly and her heart thumped. With any luck they might even suggest they meet her at the pictures next time…Or even take her. Yanks had plenty of dough, everybody knew that. And chocolates too.

"Hey, Nessa, wait for us!" She heard a sudden shriek behind her, and the next minute two small bodies came hurtling towards her, their satchels banging against their legs, agog at seeing her with two GIs from the camp outside town.

"What you doing out of school?" Teddy shrieked. "Aunt Rose will kill you if she knows you're playing truant."

"I'm telling her," Harry chanted in unison. "Why do we have to go to school if she don't?"

"Shut up, you little snots," Vanessa shouted, aware that the two GIs were looking on with amusement now and knowing that her cover had been blown; but the boys were no longer interested in her as they saw the two Americans grinning down at them.

"It's a hard life, isn't it, kid?" one of them said, and then produced a couple of chocolate bars from his pocket like a conjuror doing his latest trick. "Here, take your sister home and don't tell on her, huh?"

"She ain't my sister," Teddy howled, grabbing the chocolate bars all the same. "My sisters are Daisy and Immy and Elsie, not *her*."

"She ain't my sister, neither. I ain't got a sister, nor a brother," Harry said, not to be outdone.

"Damn right I'm not their sister," Nessa snapped, past caring now. "We just live in the same house, that's all."

She realised the Yanks were backing away now and laughing at *her*.

"Sounds like hard luck on your auntie then! Cute kids, but you're a bit of a firecracker, aren't you?"

They had swaggered away before she could say anything more, so the obvious thing to do was turn on the little blighters who had just ruined her day.

"Well, thank you *very* much! So are you going to tell?"

Teddy Caldwell hitched his satchel over his head again and stared her out. He was ten years old now, and Aunt

3

Rose was his *proper* auntie, and he had no intention of being ruled by two evacuees, just because they all lived together, Nessa with her smart talk and Harry with his dozy Bristol accent. Teddy knew it was pretty well the same as his own, but since Harry was a couple of years younger and from a poor part of the city, he felt that much superior.

"Might do," Teddy replied now, his head on one side. "It depends."

"On what?"

"On whether you take me and Harry to the flicks on Sat'day morning – *and* pay for us," he said, after a moment's thought.

"'S right," Harry said eagerly, admiration for Teddy shining out of him.

What a twerp, Nessa thought, seething, but then the little creep put his hand in hers – out of sight of Teddy, of course – and against her better judgement her heart melted a little, because he'd been bombed out and orphaned too, same as she had, and this mixed-up family was the only one they had.

"All right then, but you'll both swear to say nothing about seeing me with the Yanks. Swear on Aunt Rose's Bible when we get home."

At the thought of the Saturday-morning pictures ahead, they agreed quickly enough. They were too daft to realise she'd never be able to get the Good Book under their noses without Aunt Rose seeing and asking what was going on. (Aunt Rose always said the words as if they started with capital letters.)

Anyway, Vanessa holding a Bible in her hand was a sight that was rarely seen, even though she did a bit of praying now and then, especially when the sirens sounded, and they all dived for cover in the cellar that was their make-shift air-raid shelter. She shivered for a minute, sending up a tiny prayer of thanks to God or Jesus or whoever was Up There (just in case), that now that the Jerries were raining bombs down on everybody, she wasn't in London anymore.

Immy was, though.

Vanessa had an awful stitch in her side now. She chased after the boys as they raced along the seafront before turning up the steep roads leading to Rose Painter's large rambling house overlooking the town and the Bristol Channel. She wondered what it was like in the Smoke now, with half the city destroyed, and looters everywhere by all accounts and black marketeers doing their stuff...

For a second Vanessa felt a surge of nostalgia, not seeing anything wrong in that, and only the thrill of it all. Being in London now could be fun as well as dangerous, *and* selling any goods you could get hold of on the black market and making a packet. Such things didn't bother her. Plenty of folk she knew had done it, even before there was a war on, on street corners and the back streets where stuff had conveniently dropped off the back of a lorry...She'd only been a kid at the time, but she knew all about it.

Get-rich-quickers, her old gran used to call them with a sniff and a spit, but she'd had plenty of respect for their nerve, always ending up by saying: *and good luck to the buggers.*

"What you crying for?" Teddy said uneasily when he and Harry paused for her to catch up. "We said we wouldn't tell."

"I'm not crying, dummy. The wind got in my eyes, that's all."

She'd loved her old gran, long gone to the market in the sky, as far as she knew, but now she couldn't help thinking about Immy, Teddy's oldest sister, who would never do any dodgy looting, but who was in the thick of it in London, driving around some posh army geezer. They hadn't heard from Immy lately, not since the last letter saying how worried she was about her fiancé, James Church. He was driving tanks somewhere in North Africa, and he was an officer too.

Nessa thought they were all getting far too posh. She'd been born in the East End and couldn't abide people who spoke with plums in their mouths – not that these Bristol and Weston folk did, she admitted, but when you were around such people for a long time, their talk rubbed off on you.

Take Elsie now. When Bristol had been in the middle of the blitz Elsie had taken her kid and gone to live in Yorkshire with her husband's family, and the last time she'd paid them all a visit, she'd looked like a proper farmer's wife, fat and apple-cheeked and waddling. Of course, she'd been six months pregnant with her second kid at the time, so it was understandable. Elsie wasn't posh, but she was definitely starting to talk like them Yorkshire folk.

"It's nice to see you come home from school cheerful for once, Vanessa," Rose remarked as the smile still lingered around the girl's mouth.

It was a bleedin' good thing she wasn't a mind-reader, Nessa thought, because right then she was wondering how the dickens Joe Preston ever heaved himself over his wife's belly to do the business.

The upper-form girls had just had their red-faced biology mistress giving them a lesson with diagrams to explain reproduction, which had caused plenty of giggling behind the bike sheds and some snide looks at the brawny boys on the far side of the playing field.

"Maybe she ain't been—" Harry began, and got a huge kick from Teddy to make him howl.

Teddy's sights were firmly set on a free ticket to the pictures on Saturday morning now, as well as wondering how long he could prolong the blackmail of catching Nessa out of school *and* with a couple of Yanks, and he wasn't about to let this little squirt ruin things.

"What did you do that for?" Rose said, diverted for the moment by Harry's hopping around the room. "You're getting to be a bit of a bully, Teddy, and I won't have it. You can all behave yourselves, anyway, because Mr Penfold is coming for tea. And get that silly smirk off your face, Vanessa."

She didn't have to ask twice. The last thing Nessa wanted was to sit here being polite to the vicar with his moony looks at Aunt Rose. It was disgusting for a couple their age – not that Aunt Rose even seemed aware of it – but ever since Uncle Bert had walked straight into a lamp-post in the blackout and died a year ago, Aunt Rose had got religion, and that old fart Penfold had set his sights on her, that was for sure.

Vanessa's vivid imagination already had them all decamping to the vicarage and singing in the choir every Sunday, done up like dogs' dinners, and there was no way she was going to do that. She'd run away once before, and she'd do it again if she had to…

"One of the girls in my class has invited me to her house for tea," she invented quickly.

"Which girl?" Rose said at once.

"Thelma. Thelma Jeffries. I told you about her."

She could see the boys making faces at her behind Aunt Rose's back. Little toe-rags, she seethed, probably thinking she was going to meet the Yanks, when all she wanted to do was get out of having tea with the vicar.

Before Rose could probe a bit more about this Thelma Jeffries, whom she was quite sure she had never heard of before, the telephone rang. She went to answer it, and, when she came back, she was smiling.

"That was Daisy, and she's coming home for a few days tomorrow. You can help me get her room ready, Nessa. Now then, about this Thelma Jeffries—"

"Oh, it doesn't matter. It wasn't a proper invitation anyway."

It would get too complicated to explain away the imaginary tea invitation, anyway...and she was far more interested in seeing Daisy again, even though she had never got on with her at first. It must be awful being a nurse and doing all the horrible jobs she had to do for the wounded servicemen who were sent to the military hospital near Chichester where Daisy worked now. She had been on the hospital ships bringing the wounded back from Dunkirk too, and that made her a real heroine in Nessa's eyes, knowing she could never do such a thing. She felt faint at the sight of blood, and always had done. It was her one weakness, and she was savage to know that she even had one.

Nurses had to attend to the patients' *personal* bits too, Nessa had often thought with a wicked little thrill, and with her newly acquired knowledge of the theory of reproduction, as their po-faced biology mistress called it, she had every intention of asking Daisy what they were like. *They* being men's bits. She was used to bathing Teddy and Harry – although Teddy was starting to object now – but in her sketchy and embarrassed manner the teacher had managed to convey that men were different. Men had different bits from little boys – or at least they worked differently. One or two girls in her class had bragged that they knew all about that already, having older brothers, and even knew about *it* as well, but Nessa was flipping-well sure that every one of them was as ignorant as herself.

And she wanted to know about *it*. Not just how and where the man *put* the bits, but what it felt like.

"Vanessa, what's wrong with you this afternoon?" she heard Aunt Rose say crossly. "That's the second time I've asked you to go and get ready for tea, and please check that the boys wash their hands before Mr Penfold arrives."

She fled upstairs, before she could start letting her mind dwell too much on the two people uppermost in her thoughts right then. Aunt Rose and Mr poncey-vicar Penfold…imagining *them* getting hitched and doing the business. It was enough to make anybody throw up.

She couldn't help watching them all through tea, though. There was no doubt the old boy was itching to get his feet under the table, even if Aunt Rose seemed perfectly unaware of it. The boys didn't seem to mind him coming to the house now, which was probably the old sneak's way of easing himself into the family favours, Vanessa thought cynically.

She could still remember the procession of uncles who had come and gone from home when she was a kid, and how her mother had done herself up for them. At least Aunt Rose had been a widow for nearly two years now, and the vicar was a bachelor…and the thought set her off giggling again, wondering if he knew how to do it, or if she should offer him the notes from her biology lesson.

With a torch beneath the bedcovers, she read them again in bed that night and, despite her curiosity about it all, she gave a small shudder. She liked boys all right, and she liked flirting with them, but she wasn't too sure about doing *that* with them after all. She supposed plenty of people did. They had to. You couldn't get babies without doing it.

She would definitely ask Daisy about it – which made her wonder if Daisy had done it with her boy yet. Only fast girls did it before they were married, but these days you never knew if you were going to live that long, so...

"Vanessa, are you still reading in there?" she heard Aunt Rose's voice call out, knowing her usual habit.

"No. I'm asleep!" she yelled back, switching off the torch at once, and snuggling down beneath the bedcovers.

–

Daisy Caldwell hadn't heard from Glenn for a while. It had been wonderful when he was stationed near enough to Chichester to phone her fairly often and get down to see her on her days off. She knew all about the daredevil raids the RAF were making on German cities now, and her heart leapt every time one of the successful raids was reported on the wireless or in the newspaper.

"They don't report the less successful ones in any detail, though, do they?" she pointed out to her friend Naomi. "They mention a few losses, as if it's nothing more than losing a slipper under the bed or something just as trivial."

"We all know darn well the reason for that is to keep up morale. But since Glenn's family is in Canada, he's registered your name as a contact to advise if anything happens to him, so as long as you don't get a telegram, where's the sense in worrying needlessly?" Naomi said with infuriating logic.

"You wouldn't say that if he was your young man – or if you even had one!"

Naomi flushed. "I've given up that lark for the duration. Love 'em and leave 'em is going to be my motto from now on, and anybody with any sense would do the same. But you shouldn't let it get to you, Daisy. The Brylcreem boys lead a charmed life. You've said it often enough yourself."

"I said it about Cal too, and look what happened to him."

She tried not to flinch as she said it, remembering that beautiful young man whose plane had been blown to smithereens out of the sky.

"Well, you know the old saying, don't you?" Naomi said, trying to boost her flagging spirits. "Lightning never strikes twice…"

But everybody knew that it could, and it did.

"Anyway, you'll feel better when you get out of this place for a few days' leave. Go home and visit your family, the same as I'm going to."

"Unless you want to come home with me?" she added. "You know my parents are always glad to see you, sweetie."

"Thanks all the same, but no thanks," Daisy said with a smile. "I need to let them all know I'm still alive. Portsmouth and Southampton are getting the brunt of it, and I'm sure they think Chichester is practically next door."

"That's because it is, as far as Jerry's concerned," Naomi said drily.

Daisy thought about the invitation all the way home on the crowded trains to the West Country. By now Naomi would have been picked up by the family chauffeur – God knew how they always managed to have petrol for these excursions – and whisked off to her family's mansion in Hertfordshire. Not that she would have changed places with her, she thought loyally. Home was where the family was, and where your roots were, and for her that was both Bristol, where she had been born, and Weston, where she had moved in with Aunt Rose and Uncle Bert after her mother's death. Strictly speaking, home was still Vicarage Street in Bristol…but it was no longer the same Caldwell home that it had once been.

Then, it had belonged to her father and her adored mother, Frances, and the five of them, Immy, Elsie and herself, Baz and young Teddy. It was all so different now. Her mother had died before the war and knew nothing of the heartache that had followed; Baz had drowned at sea after Dunkirk; Elsie had married Joe Preston and gone to live in Yorkshire; Teddy had been taken in by Aunt Rose and Uncle Bert, and she had followed, to start nursing at Weston General. Immy had joined up, and now the only people who occupied the old family house were her father and his second wife, Mary Yard.

Daisy took a deep breath, not begrudging her father his happiness, but wishing, for one aching, impotent moment, that time could be reversed, and for them all to be together again, just once more.

"Look out, miss, we all want to get home," she heard an impatient voice say, as the train lurched and crawled towards Temple Meads station.

The beginning of July was hot and sticky, and on this long journey the smells from some of her fellow passengers had been none too sweet. She was being jostled and pushed by a group of burly soldiers now, all trying to get towards the carriage doors. Their kitbags banged her shins and she bit her lips, aware that she hadn't been paying attention to anything but her own misery.

"Sorry," she gasped, squeezing herself against the window for them to pass by. She was half-tempted to get out here as well, but she had already arranged to spend these precious few days in Weston, and just to break the return journey in Bristol to spend a night with her father.

Aunt Rose had said how excited the boys would be at seeing her. Daisy wasn't so sure about Vanessa. But reunions were always joyful times, and once they had passed on their mutual information about other members of the family, and the small boys had goaded Daisy into telling them as much gory detail as she would about her nursing duties, they tired of all the questions. Especially as Vanessa had flatly refused to listen to any talk of operations and blood, blood and more blood, and stalked out of the room before Teddy started bragging about how he might be a doctor one day, or a farmer, or a grocery boy on a bike. His ambitions changed frequently, and Daisy was still laughing at him when she went upstairs to unpack her things.

"That boy is starting to remind me too much of myself," she said to Vanessa, as she paused by her open bedroom door.

"I can't think why," Nessa said, without bothering to move from her supine position on her bed, arms clasped behind her head.

Daisy went inside. "Forever chopping and changing his mind is why, which is just the way I used to be. So what's up?" she went on bluntly. "Or shall I guess? It's all this talk of blood, isn't it? I remember a time when you cut your finger on the bread knife and nearly passed out—"

"Shut up, for Gawd's sake! If they hear you, they'll never let me forget it!"

"All right, it's forgotten."

Daisy eyed her thoughtfully. Vanessa had always been destined for beauty, and she was growing up fast now, all curves and softness where she used to be gawky. "Have you got a boyfriend yet?"

Nessa went a dull red. "*No.* I'm not sure I want one either."

"Tell that to the bees," Daisy said, grinning until she saw how serious she was. "Why ever not? I thought it was your mission in life to plague the life out of the GIs you had billeted here a while ago."

Nessa sat up scowling. She hesitated, but the thing that had been uppermost in her mind for the past few days was too strong to be ignored. It was daft to feel so bleedin' tongue-tied all of a sudden, since she had been counting on Daisy to tell her more; but now she was faced with saying it, she couldn't do it, so she did the next best thing.

"This is why not," she said, pulling her school rough book from under her pillow, and thrusting the open pages in front of Daisy's startled eyes.

"Cripes," Daisy said, gawping at the diagrams, "is this what they're teaching you at your grammar school these days?"

"Is it true?" Nessa demanded, feeling about as infantile as Harry. "We were shown all these stupid pictures about rabbits and stuff, but it's supposed to be the same for...well, for..."

"For people," Daisy supplied. "Well, of course it is. How do you think you got here if it wasn't for your mother and father…um…" She knew she was tackling this the wrong way, and she had got herself into a tangle already.

She was amazed, anyway. Vanessa had always seemed so worldly-wise, streets ahead of her age, but it seemed that in intimate matters, she didn't know a thing; and what was more, she was scared stiff at the whole idea of it.

"I think Aunt Rose may have some of her old nursing books that will give you a better idea than what you've been told," she said at last. "I take it you'd rather I found them for you than ask Aunt Rose yourself?"

"If you like," Nessa mumbled. "Thanks."

"And in case you were wondering," Daisy went on delicately, "I don't know any more about it than you do, except in theory."

Chapter Two

"You could have knocked me down with the proverbial feather," Daisy told her friend Alice Godfrey on the beach the following day. "I'm hardly a Mother Confessor, am I? But, surprising though it might seem, the poor girl seemed genuinely disturbed about it all, so I had to do what I could to explain things."

"From your limited experience," Alice observed.

Daisy laughed. "If that's an obscure way of asking the question, then no, of course I haven't. Glenn's a gentleman, and that's all I'm saying on the subject. So what's been happening around here in these last few months, apart from air raids?"

"My mother says her guess is that your Aunt Rose and the vicar will tie the knot eventually," Alice said.

Daisy stopped walking so quickly that Alice was two steps ahead before she turned round for Daisy to catch up. Alice's mother was a prize gossip, she thought furiously, and it wasn't true. It couldn't be true.

"You're crazy. Aunt Rose would never marry anybody else. She and Uncle Bert were as close as Siamese twins. You shouldn't say such things."

Alice was visibly cross at her response. "Don't be so childish, Daisy. Your uncle's not here anymore, is he? And life goes on. You of all people should know that. You fell for Glenn after Cal was killed, and you always said how devoted your father was to your mother, but it didn't stop him marrying again, did it?"

This wasn't the kind of conversation Daisy wanted to hear. Her thoughts whirled the way they so often did when she was in one of her quick-thinking moods: like a camera shutter going off at high speed, her father used to say, laughing. She wasn't laughing now.

Yet, if she was totally honest, she supposed the thought of Aunt Rose remarrying wasn't as upsetting as all that…and it *was* nearly two years since Uncle Bert had died now…but if she married the vicar, he would surely want her to leave the lovely old house she had known all her life and move into the blessed vicarage…and that would mean disruption all over again. For the boys, for Vanessa, for *her*.

"Surely you wouldn't begrudge your auntie a second chance of happiness, would you, Daisy?" Alice persisted.

"Of course not. I just don't like the thought of her being the subject of speculation and gossip, that's all," she snapped.

Alice linked her arm through Daisy's again and gave it what was meant to be a comforting squeeze. "Oh well, perhaps it will never happen."

And perhaps it would. It was hardly something she could ask Aunt Rose, but she could always quiz Vanessa about it, providing she was subtle. If anybody knew what was going on, it would be Vanessa.

Daisy gave a faint smile. The thought of ever enlisting Vanessa Brown – Vanessa *Caldwell*-Brown as she called herself now – to be her secret spy, was as unlikely as pigs flying; but since the possibility of this totally unsuitable marriage would cause a drastic change in everybody's circumstances, it needed to be done.

She flagged suddenly. What on earth was she thinking about? It was no business of hers what Aunt Rose did. Alice was right. She was being completely stupid, and as childishly possessive as Teddy used to be. Next thing she knew, she'd be clinging to that beastly little dog George as a kind of security blanket!

"Oh, darn it, Daisy, I've upset you now, haven't I?" Alice said next. "I didn't mean to, honestly."

"You haven't upset me. I'm an idiot, that's all. Let's talk about something else. How is the gorgeous Iain Bailey? That was his name, wasn't it?" she asked innocently, just as if she could forget it, since Alice's letters were always full of glowing reports about the GI who had swept her off her feet – or as much as he could with a busted shoulder.

"Still gorgeous," Alice said. "He's on clerical duties at the base now, and I don't think he likes it too much, except that he can see me often, of course. Actually, I had something important to tell you, Daisy, only you haven't let me get a word in edgeways yet."

Her face flushed, and Daisy had a sudden horrible feeling inside. Everybody knew the mad saying that was bandied about regarding the Yanks: *Overpaid, over-sexed, and over here.* She couldn't imagine Alice doing anything foolish, but she also knew how crazily she had fallen for Private Iain Bailey.

"You're not – oh, Lord, Alice, you're not – don't tell me you have to marry him, do you?"

It was Alice who stopped walking now, glaring at her friend.

"Well, if you mean, do I *want* to marry him, then yes I do. And if you mean, are we going to get *engaged* on my birthday and do things perfectly properly, then yes, we are. But thanks for spoiling my lovely surprise!"

"Oh, Alice, I'm sorry! You know how my tongue sometimes runs away with me. But how wonderful. How absolutely, spiffingly wonderful!"

Alice's face cleared at once as she hugged Daisy.

"It is, isn't it? And we're gloriously, spiffingly in love. My parents love him, and since Iain will most likely be based here for the duration, we've got plenty of time to get to know one another properly – in case you were asking!"

"I wasn't. I was just thinking how lucky you are. Lord knows where Glenn is now, and as for Immy's James, he's 'somewhere in North Africa', and that's all she ever hears. I know she worries about him—" she caught Alice's glance – "but don't let's talk about that now. Imagine you marrying a Yank and going to live in America. Didn't you once tell me he lives in Hollywood?"

"Yes. A scream, isn't it? You once had ambitions of being a singing star and it's me who's going to live among the stars – in a manner of speaking," she added with a grin.

"Those days are long past…"

"And you're such a Methuselah, aren't you?" Alice mocked. "Don't you ever fancy taking it up again?"

Daisy shook her head. "I'm happy enough just going round the wards leading the carol-singers at Christmas."

She was thankful to have changed the subject from the disturbing one of Aunt Rose and the vicar, but she knew Alice was right. Her father had found happiness for the second time; and so had Daisy herself. Why shouldn't Aunt Rose do the same? Remembering Vanessa's awkward broaching of the subject of men's *bits*, she knew she was as reluctant to think of any such *goings-on*, as they said, as the girl herself; but since she was only here for a few days, she wasn't wasting her time worrying about something that was no concern of hers.

Tomorrow she was going to cycle over to the Luckwell farm to say hello to Lucy's parents, as she always did when she was home on leave. To her surprise, Vanessa asked if she could go with her.

"Good Lord. You can come if you like, though I thought you'd prefer to keep well away from farming and all those animal smells."

"That's just where you're wrong then, ain't it?" Nessa said, with the familiar toss of her head. "They've got a couple of girls from Bermondsey there now, and I go over there to see them sometimes."

"More evacuees, do you mean? Where's Bermondsey, anyway?"

Nessa gave a superior snort. "Don't you know *anything*? Bermondsey's a district of London, and Bet and Shirl are land girls."

"Oh, I see."

"No you don't. It's not just because they talk the same as me instead of having hayseeds growing out of their mouths," she added cheekily. "It's because I thought I might join, if the war goes on long enough. Do you think it will?"

Daisy felt her nerves tighten, seeing right through her. The little beast, she thought, virtually *wanting* the war to go on long enough so that she could wear the land girls' uniform with the trousers and the jaunty hats.

"I hope not," she snapped. "It's already been on nearly four years, and they all said it would be over by Christmas in 1939."

Vanessa looked at her slyly. "Bet you wouldn't come to see Madame Fifi in town, to see what she predicts about it then," she challenged.

"*Who?*" Daisy said, starting to laugh.

"Madame Fifi. She reads palms and tells the future. A couple of girls in my class have been, and she told them all kinds of things about themselves."

"And I bet they told her half of it in the first place. These people have a way of getting information out of you and then pretending they're telling you. If they were that clever, they'd already have predicted when the war will end, and nobody can tell us that. You can't trust them – and besides, Aunt Rose would be horrified, to say nothing of Mr Penfold. The Church doesn't hold with that kind of thing."

She paused for breath, aware that Nessa had folded her arms, and was looking at her through narrowed eyes.

"You're scared, aren't you? You think Madame Fifi might tell you something awful about your airman. But she might tell you something good!"

"Stop it, Nessa. I don't want to hear any more."

"I'm going, anyway. Tomorrow, on the way back from the Luckwells."

It wasn't a good idea. In fact, Daisy knew it was a very bad idea. Trying to look into the future was tempting fate. Trying to change it was even worse. She knew Aunt Rose would say it was tampering with God's plans…even though Daisy also knew she had been to one or two seances after Uncle Bert had died. Mr Penfold was adamantly against such things, and now that she was so thick with the vicar, Aunt Rose no longer went to the meetings. Daisy had no intention of telling her that she *might* go along to this Madame Fifi's with Nessa, if only to see that the girl wasn't being cheated. At least, that was what she told herself.

That night, the German planes came over as usual and the town reverberated to the barrage of guns and falling masonry, and they all spent the night in the cellar while the house shook above them. They eventually came upstairs when the all-clear sounded, to find the contents of the larder spilled over everything.

Dishes and plates were in smithereens; tins and packets were strewn about everywhere; drawers had been flung open and cutlery was all over the floor. In the middle of it all was an unholy mess of sugar and flour into which the jug of milk had crashed, and two precious eggs had smashed. Their feet crunched on broken china; even Aunt Rose's stoicism was stretched to the limit as they set to work to clean it up, and they were all close to tears by the end of it.

The one thought that kept infiltrating into Daisy's mind was that if this Madame Fifi had any inkling at all as to when this nightmare would end, it was her patriotic duty to reveal it, but first she intended spending a little time with Lucy's mother at the farm while Vanessa chatted with her new-found friends from Bermondsey. It was always hard, as well as a comfort, to be here where she had spent so much time with her friend before Lucy had died from TB at only seventeen. She would have been twenty-one now, the same as Daisy, and sometimes Daisy tried to imagine her grown up and probably with a young man of her own, or already married to a neighbouring farmer. Or still winning trophies at the horse-riding that she loved.

"I asked how you're getting on with your nursing now, Daisy." She heard Mrs Luckwell's warm and comfortable country voice penetrate her thoughts.

"Oh. The same as ever, you know."

"And you still like it?"

Like? Daisy wasn't sure that was the best word to apply to it. Once you had got beyond the first traumas of all that being a nurse entailed, especially in wartime, it seemed to her that few people ever left nursing; but this nice woman was waiting for an answer and so she smiled.

"Oh yes, I still like it."

Mrs Luckwell nodded in satisfaction. "I knew you would. Me and Lucy always said so, from the day you fixed her ankle when her horse fell heavily on her. We both said you were a born nurse, my dear."

"So you did, Mrs Luckwell," Daisy said, her throat thick.

"And how is that nice young man of yours?" the farmer's wife went on more briskly. "Still doing his bit for the RAF, I daresay?"

Without waiting for an answer, Mrs Luckwell was looking out of the window now, to where Vanessa and the land girls were chatting, the girls busily stooking the corn while Vanessa draped herself over a fence.

"That young 'un seems to like it down here. I wouldn't be surprised if she don't decide to join up with them land girls, if the war goes on that long."

"I'll believe it when I see it, but she's barely fifteen, Mrs Luckwell. I hope it'll be over long before she leaves school!"

She shivered as she spoke, because that day was only a year or so away, and as yet there was no respite in the beating Hitler was giving the Allies. Even the advent of the Americans hadn't stemmed the tide as everyone had hoped.

"We all hope for that, maid, and I keep sayin' it'll be all over by Christmas – *again* – but some days it don't seem very likely, do it?"

Daisy didn't know how to answer that, and by the time they left the farm she was feeling more restless than before. Mrs Luckwell was usually cheerful, but she didn't seem so today, nor did she echo Mr Churchill's words, who was constantly telling them all to be of good hope and never despair. Daisy sometimes wondered vaguely if he had ever lost anyone close to him…

"What's up?" Nessa said chirpily. "You look as if you've lost a shilling and found a tanner."

"I was just making up my mind whether or not to visit your flipping Madame Fifi with you," she snapped.

"Knew you would," Nessa said airily.

—

When they entered the small premises in a side street, a bell tinkled over the door, and they blinked in the dim and gloomy atmosphere inside. These places were always like this, Nessa hissed in Daisy's ear, as if she had inside knowledge. Moments later a plump, ordinary-looking woman came through from a curtained-off back room. For a moment Daisy felt cheated, realising she had half-expected some exotic creature in flowing robes to appear, wreathed in perfume and exuding an air of eastern mystery – which probably came from reading too much of *Arabian Nights*.

"Good afternoon, young ladies," she said, motioning them to sit down at the table where a crystal ball had pride of place, and pushing a box prominently in front of them with the words: "Consultancy one shilling" marked on its side.

Nessa quickly pushed a coin in the slot in the box and nudged Daisy to do the same. As she did so, Daisy pushed down the urge to giggle. It was all so theatrical, so badly theatrical…

Madame Fifi gave her a sudden piercing glance.

"You find it amusing, my dear. Well, let's hope that fortune will smile on you, and that your future will be happy rather than sad."

Daisy hadn't been aware that she was even smiling, but it was Nessa who giggled with nervous excitement now.

"We just wanna know when this bleedin' war is going to end," she burst out.

"Ah, a young lady from London, I believe. And one who has been sorely troubled, and perhaps lost a family member. Or even more than one."

Daisy clamped her lips together. It didn't need a clairvoyant to recognise Vanessa's accent, and to guess by her age that she would have lost someone in the blitz. As Vanessa muttered that it was true, Daisy vowed not to give anything away; and since they were here together, she waited to hear that she was a Londoner too, and had lost someone…

Before she could say or do anything, however, Madame Fifi caught hold of her hands, closed her eyes for a moment and then looked deep into the crystal ball.

"But you're different, aren't you?" she said in a softer voice. "I feel healing in those hands. They've helped many and will help many more. But I fear there will also be those that you will be unable to help. Those that are close to you."

Daisy snatched her hands away as Nessa gasped in awe.

"That's right. Daisy's a nurse—"

"Shut up, you idiot!"

Madame Fifi smiled sadly. "It's all right, my dear. I understand your reluctance to believe that anyone can see

26

what fate has in store. Many disbelieve, but what's written in the stars cannot be unwritten, and I hope you'll be given the strength to deal with whatever catastrophe lies ahead."

"Like a war, I suppose," Daisy said sarcastically.

"Like the victims of a war," the woman intoned, seeming less ordinary now, and more prophetic.

"What about me?" Nessa said eagerly, holding out her hands to the woman.

Madame Fifi went through the same procedure, telling the girl she saw good fortune ahead of her, a new life and good people to care for her. At which Nessa was clearly delighted, and by the time they left the stifling little room she was elated and buoyant.

"See? I told you she'd be good!"

"I told you she's a charlatan," Daisy said, raging. "She should be locked up, scaring people like that."

"She didn't scare me!"

"She didn't tell you people close to you were going to die, did she?"

"She didn't tell you that either. Not exactly."

They continued to glare at one another as they cycled home. It was midsummer, but Daisy's heart felt as cold as winter, and she couldn't rid herself of the feeling that the clairvoyant's words had been directed very personally at her. She had already had enough suffering in her life through the deaths of her mother, her brother Baz, Uncle Bert, her best friend Lucy, her army friend Molly – and her beloved Cal – but she couldn't help the feeling that this had been a warning that there was more in store for her. For *her*, Daisy Caldwell, who hadn't yet suffered enough. Nor had she, compared to many families, she thought painfully.

It was *the gypsy's warning…* except that Madame Fifi hadn't looked in the least like a gypsy – more like one of the ordinary housewives in their headscarves wrapped around their heads like turbans, queuing endlessly for food.

"You've really got the hump now, ain't yer, Daisy?" Nessa said uneasily. "She prob'ly didn't mean anything, and she could prob'ly guess you're a nurse anyway, because of the smell of carbolic."

"I do not smell of carbolic!" Daisy said indignantly; then after a few minutes she began to laugh when she saw that Nessa was teasing her and trying to jolly her out of the bleak mood she had dropped into.

"Come on, I'll race you home. Last one there has to do the washing-up," the girl yelled, and tore off up the hill on her bike at a fair rate.

By the time they reached home, Daisy had such an ache in her chest she thought she would probably drop dead there and then from a heart attack, and that would solve everything; and the thought was at once so ghastly and so comical that it somehow settled everything down into its rightful place.

Of *course* she was likely to see many more gruesome sights before this war was done, and of *course* some of them would affect her. Caring for a severely wounded patient for even ten minutes affected her, creating a special bond between nurse and patient that those who had never experienced it could never even begin to understand.

"So how was Lucy's mother?" Aunt Rose asked as usual. "Still prophesying it'll be all over by Christmas, I suppose?"

Daisy and Nessa looked at one another, and burst out laughing, while Rose went off muttering that young people these days were becoming far too insensitive and finding the most outrageous things amusing.

As always, days at home were both familiar and strange. Distance in time and space did that to a person, and even spending the last evening at home in Bristol had the same effect. Daisy was realising more and more that her father was content now, and she was glad for him. The sweet ghost of her mother would never die, and Frances's legacy was in her children; but Quentin's life was now with Mary, and she gave them both a special hug before she left to return to Chichester the following morning.

"Please take care of yourselves," she begged. "No heroics, Daddy, and Mary – you keep the home fires burning...or something."

They all laughed, creating a complete unit with their arms around one another, but there was a small note of desperation in Daisy's voice. If there was even the slightest chance that Madame Fifi's words were true, then she was going to lose someone else from her world.

The hell of it was that it was so damnably logical to suppose so. She hated the woman for putting the fear in her mind, thinking of every one of the people she loved, and wondering *who*...

"You look after yourself too," Quentin told her. "And give that young man of yours our best wishes the next time you see him."

"Our prayers go with you, Daisy," Mary added softly.

Too much emotion was starting to make her feel claustrophobic, and she extricated herself from the circle of their embrace with a small, shaky laugh.

"Goodness, you'll make me feel as if I'm in the front line in a minute. I'm just doing my job, the same as everyone else. And I had better find my way to the railway station, or the train will be leaving without me."

"I would drive you there, Daisy, but—"

"Save your petrol, Daddy. I can easily take a bus if one happens to come along. Or I can walk. It's downhill most of the way, so it won't kill me."

Besides, it gave her a chance to see for herself how the city had fared and was still faring. The blitz here had been short-lived in its intensity, but there had been many more indiscriminate air raids. The loss of human life went on, and the damage to a once-proud city from those raids was heartbreaking. Buildings and churches still tottered obscenely on skeletal structures, and dust still lay over piles of rubble like a grey pall, since each time the rescue workers and demolition experts removed some of it for safety, the choking pall rose again.

Here and there, the remnants of someone's personal possessions still lay pathetically exposed to public view: a prized book, its pages charred and fluttering in the breeze; a child's shoe; a broken doll; remnants of clothing clinging to masonry. Someone had once bought all those things, loved them and cherished them, never thinking that a demon from the sky would tear them apart.

"My God, it's Daisy Caldwell, isn't it?" she heard in a jeering voice. "You keep popping up like a bad penny, don't you?"

With all the sights she was seeing and those that her too-vivid imagination was supplying, her eyes were burning with the effort not to cry. She was filled with a huge longing to be away from here. Anywhere. She glowered at the brash young man barring her way.

"Do I know you?" she said shrilly, resentful that he wasn't wearing a uniform, that he looked so chipper and cheerful, and that he was *Welsh* in a city that belonged to Bristolians. She knew who he was all right. Elsie had confided that Immy had been fond of him once, and perhaps even more than fond…

"Morgan Raine," he said in that sing-song voice they all had, and which annoyed Daisy even more right now, even if some thought it was attractive.

"Not in uniform yet then, Morgan Raine?" she asked pointedly.

He laughed, looking her up and down in a way she didn't like, his dark eyes full of something she couldn't fathom, his black curly hair giving him an untamed look. Oh yes, she thought to her furious annoyance, I can see how anyone could fall for him – even Immy.

"I'm busy enough reporting events for the newspaper, and besides, the army wouldn't take me. I told you once before, I've got a heart murmur, and right now it's going nineteen to the dozen, just looking at your pretty face. Here, feel it. Wouldn't you say I need some urgent nursing attention?"

Before she had any idea what he was going to do, he had grabbed her hand and placed it over his chest. As it was midsummer, he didn't wear a jacket, and she could feel the warmth of his skin through his shirt. She snatched her hand away at once, not bothering to resist rubbing away the contact on her skirt.

Hateful, hateful man…

She could still hear the sound of his mocking laughter as she continued making her way to Temple Meads station, her eyes smarting. Thank God Immy had managed to end her association with him. Thank God she was engaged to James now – James, who was still driving tanks somewhere in North Africa. Last year it had been

El Alamein, and no one had heard from him for weeks until General Montgomery and all of them had emerged triumphant after beating Rommel and been covered in glory.

As James's name came into her head, a cloud passed over the sun and, despite the warmth of the day, Daisy shuddered, as if struck by a premonition.

Refusing to look at any more of the chaos all around her, she virtually kept her head down until she reached the railway station and didn't fully relax until she was safely on the crowded train out of the city.

Chapter Three

British raids on Germany had started in earnest in 1943 – and not before time, some said. There were those who scoffed at such a cavalier statement, especially those who had lost friends and family members long before. Casualties were heavy on both sides, but even the German propaganda minister Josef Goebbels had told the German people to follow the example of British civilians, presumably to straighten their shoulders and show the world that they could take it too...

"It's all just a lot of talk, whichever side it comes from," Quentin Caldwell snorted to his wife as they listened to the nightly bulletins on the wireless, to the accompaniment of the regular bombardment outside.

Mary had taken to staying in the house during the raids now, since the smell of damp earth in the shelter made her claustrophobic. It was even worse when she had to be in there by herself while Quentin was out firefighting.

"If a Jerry bomb has got my name on it, then I'd rather be blown up in my own bed than try to crawl out of that horrible smelly shelter like a rat caught in a trap," she declared obstinately.

"You can hardly call it that. Think of the poor devils who go down to the London tube stations every night, sleeping next to God knows who. They're no more than those what-do-you-call-'ems – people who live in the dark – troglodytes."

Mary started to laugh, refusing to flinch as the sound of a bomb blast shook the house, followed by a roar of retaliating gunfire.

"Have you swallowed a dictionary or something?"

"Mary, please go down to the shelter," he said more tensely. "It's time I left, and I don't want you to stay in the house alone."

"I'll be more alone down there. At least I've got the wireless or the gramophone to listen to in comfort indoors. And I can read without my eyes going all funny from the smoke from the paraffin lamp. Please don't fuss me, Quentin. God will keep me safe."

"Now you sound like our Rose," he said gruffly, resisting the thought that God hadn't kept Bert safe, no matter how much Rose had believed in the Almighty. He wasn't an atheist, but he didn't have womenfolk's blind faith either. He had seen too many horrific things during the past few years to accept it.

"There's nothing wrong with Rose," Mary said mildly. "And having *anything* to believe in is better than believing in nothing, don't you think?"

"Would you mind repeating that, old girl?" he said with a grin. "And anyway, I do believe in something. I believe in you, my love."

"Then *go!*" she repeated, before her eyes got all moist. "And providing the telephones are still working, I'm going to call Elsie and see how things are going. You never know, there may be good news by the time you come back in the morning, and you'll discover you're a grandfather for the second time."

"You'll be a grandmother too," he told her. "How does that feel!"

"Wonderful," Mary said softly. "Because then I shall really feel as if I belong in this family."

He looked at her in astonishment. He knew he should be leaving, and his workmates would be wondering why he wasn't reporting to his post as promptly as usual, but a few more minutes weren't going to make any difference to the outcome of the war, and this was something that needed sorting out.

"I think you'd better explain that, Mrs Caldwell. When did you ever think that you weren't part of this family?"

As his arms folded around her waist, her eyes blurred because she didn't want to hurt him, nor remind him of things that might still be painful; but he was waiting for an answer, and she knew he wouldn't budge until she gave him one. So she spoke quickly and awkwardly, saying all the things that were in her heart before she lost her nerve.

"Quentin, you and Frances had a long and happy life together. You raised a lovely family long before I came on the scene, and a second wife is always – well, must always be in second place, at least to your children. I don't resent that; I just state it as a fact of life. And when Elsie had Faith, I wasn't even your wife, but now I am, which means I'll be a proper grandmother to her new baby when it arrives, not just a sort of added-on one."

"Good God, woman, what rot you talk," Quentin said, but his voice was rough with affection. "Has anyone in the family ever made you feel less than welcome? Any of my daughters, for instance? Because if they have, by God, they'll have me to deal with!"

"No, they haven't, really," Mary said, starting to smile at his defence of her. "It's not them, darling, it's just me; I'm being rather foolish, aren't I?"

A crash like thunder shook the house again, and they clung together more tightly for a moment.

"You're being foolish in not going to the bloody shelter and making sure I've got a wife to come home to," he said shortly.

"Well, you just go and do what you have to do, and I'll think about it."

He knew this was as far as she would go. Stubborn, he thought savagely. She and his sister Rose were two of a kind, though Rose was prickly, while Mary was just, well, stubborn! Which still made it amazing that they got along so well.

"I promise you I'll be here when you come back," Mary went on steadily. "And with any luck, I'll have some good news for you from Elsie."

They both knew that if there had been any news of the new baby's arrival, they would have heard by now. But not necessarily. Communication was frequently cut off as the telephone lines went down, and there was nothing more Quentin could do tonight than let his wife have her way while he went out into the burning streets of the city to do his job.

–

The US Ninth Army had massed in Somerset prior to what everyone hoped was going to be the big invasion, though when it was going to happen was anyone's guess. This year, next year, sometime, never...

In Weston-super-Mare, American guns and army vehicles covered the golf course near the Grammar School and spilled out on to the beach lawns, making the whole of the town look like an arsenal, and American airmen were now fully ensconced in RAF Locking.

Many local people objected to what they saw as the ruination of their gracious town, but since it was all aiming towards everyone's dreams of peace, such dissenting voices went unheard. In any case, much excitement and entertainment were caused by the sight of amphibious vehicles plunging into the sea from the beach to test their waterproofing, to the cheers of watching civilians, especially schoolchildren. Some of them reckoned it was better than the flicks.

"And it's bleedin' obvious they're planning something big," Vanessa said to one of her cronies after school. "They ain't doing all this just for our amusement. My Aunt Rose says it's all to do with the invasion and that it's bound to happen very soon."

"Your Aunt Rose knows everything, I suppose?" her friend jeered.

Nessa tossed her head. "Well, we listen to the wireless a lot in our house, which is more than you do, Hilary Dobbs. Aunt Rose and the vicar are pretty thick as well, and I reckon he gets a direct line from God, 'cos he always seems to know what's going on."

"If God was organising this war, he'd have ended it by now," the other girl said flatly. "Then my brother wouldn't have been killed at Dunkirk, and your family wouldn't have been bombed out in London either."

"My brother was killed at Dunkirk as well," Nessa said defiantly, even though Baz Caldwell hadn't been her real brother, and she hadn't even known him – not that these girls knew that; but she had shared in the Caldwell family's sorrow when they heard how he'd died.

She shivered, because when his body had finally been found, the details had been reported back to his father. Although Baz had drowned, it was the force of him hitting the water from the deck of the ship that had caused his rigid life jacket to snap his neck. Nessa shivered again. Why the hell did they have to explain it in every gory detail anyway? But they probably wouldn't have done so if Baz's father hadn't insisted on knowing. Ghoulish, she called it. She didn't fancy being killed like that, nor the way her own house had been blown to smithereens by a German bomb, killing everybody in it. Since she hadn't been home at the time, she'd been lucky, if you could call that lucky.

The thought of all that blood – well, even the tiniest amount of blood, really – was enough to make her want to puke. The thought of drowning was even worse, and just about choked her up.

"What's up with you, Nessa?" Hilary said now. "You've gone all pasty."

"Thanks. That makes me sound so bleedin' attractive," she muttered, and then pulled a face. "Oops, slipped again, didn't I?"

"We should get a swear box for you; then we'd have enough to go to the pictures every week. Still, I don't really mind if you swear," Hilary said generously. "It just makes me feel more saint-like."

Nessa hooted, recovering herself quickly. "Saint-like! You're just as bad as me for giving them Yanks the eye. Come on, let's go and see if we can spot any of them on the beach before we go home."

–

Like everyone else, by the late autumn of 1943 Imogen Caldwell was very aware that invasion plans were in the air – perhaps even more so, since Captain Beckett was well informed, and trusted her discretion in whatever he told her. In any case, you didn't have to be a genius to know that this was the only way Hitler was ever going to be conquered. He had ruthlessly marched through so many countries now, and his threat was getting ever nearer to England.

There had to be a counter-attack – not only from the air, where the RAF was doing such a magnificent job, nor from the Royal Navy, whose contribution was every bit as heroic; there had to be a land invasion of France, in order to drive Hitler back where he belonged. Everyone knew it had to happen. The only thing was: when? The whole country was in a state of tension with that one question on everyone's lips: when?

There had been news from James at last. He was still somewhere in North Africa, but at the beginning of September he was due for ten days' leave. He planned to go home to Bristol for a week, but he would spend the weekend with Immy in London, if she could arrange some leave at the same time.

"I know you hate all this hole-and-corner stuff, darling," he said on the telephone, his voice tinny with distance. "But it's been so long since we've been together, and I can't bear to share you with everyone else—"

"James, you know I feel the same as you do," she cut in. "I'm just so glad to know you're safe – and I couldn't get more than a forty-eight right now anyway."

He didn't ask for reasons. Few people did, knowing of the secrecy that surrounded everything these days. The ludicrous advertising posters saying that there might be a spy around every corner, infiltrating into everyday life, didn't seem so crazy anymore.

"So I suggest we meet at the same hotel as before – providing it's still standing, that is," he said, attempting to make a joke of it.

"That will be wonderful," Immy said softly, because if you couldn't remove yourselves from the daily problems of war to make time for yourselves now and again, you might as well give up right now. There had to be time for love…

Her heart soared. They had been apart for months while James had been in North Africa, and sometimes she realised it was hard to picture his face – which was frightening. People who were engaged to be married should be spending time together, getting to know one another slowly, because the promises they would make had to last a lifetime, and you had to be sure…

She *was* sure, of course, just as he was, but this constant separation wasn't the way things should be. So many partings, and so much anxiety, and added to that, the knowledge that James would marry her in a heartbeat, if only she would say the word. Still she resisted, keeping the silly thought, like a talisman, that while they still had their marriage to look forward to, he would be safe.

In the sight of God, they were married now, and perhaps after all, she was being foolish in not agreeing to it. She remembered Elsie's decision to marry Joe…and now she had Joe home all the time. Joe, and Faith…and it was so wrong to feel resentful of Elsie's luck – and so awful to even think of it as luck.

But Elsie *had* been lucky. She and Joe had got married just before Joe had enlisted, so that when he was discharged, wounded, he had had Elsie to come home to.

She wasn't stuck in Bristol in the worst of the blitz, while he was sent home to be cared for by his mother. Joe had had a wife to come home to, and a child…and it was awful to feel jealous of her sister, but she did, she *did*…

Unable to keep her feelings to herself any longer, she discussed it with Captain Beckett, who was quite willing to take on the role of substitute father when required.

"What do you think I should do, sir?" she asked.

"Whatever your heart tells you to do, if that isn't too sentimental an answer from an old fogey like me," he said with a smile.

"You're not an old fogey," Immy replied, "but you're very wise…"

"Good God, that makes me sound like Methuselah!" But he saw how serious she was being, and his face softened. "Imogen, there's a very simple answer to this. Why don't you and your young man get a special licence, so that you can be married on this weekend you're going to spend together?"

She drew in her breath. The thought of it was dazzling, but all the same: "I couldn't do that. We've already had one secret marriage in the family, and I don't know how they would all take another one. Besides, James wouldn't be able to arrange it. He won't be home in time—"

"My dear girl, there are only two people involved in a marriage, and it doesn't matter a damn what the rest of the world thinks, including your families. As for arranging it, I can set the ball rolling. There are always ways, you know. We'll go to the Register Office together as soon as you've discussed it with James. Unless you think he'll have any objections."

"I know he won't! I'm the one who's been holding back all this time."

He patted her hand in a fatherly gesture.

"Then don't hold back any longer. And don't let any stupid superstitions stop you from doing what you want to do. How much longer am I going to have my favourite member of staff living in sin?"

Immy felt her face redden with shock until she realised he was gently chaffing her. He had never thought any the less of her for knowing that she and James had shared several leaves together as man and wife, and she knew that.

"You really think it can be arranged?" she said doubt-fully.

At his superior smile, she knew she needn't have asked. He was a whizz at arranging anything, and she felt a sudden surge of excitement, throwing all her previous anxieties to the wind. If James agreed – and she knew he would – they would be married on his forthcoming leave.

But would they tell the family? If not, could she really do as Elsie had done: turn up at home and announce that she was now a married woman? If her mother had been alive, she knew how Frances would have been shocked and hurt that she hadn't been told of her daughter's plans.

James's own words came into her head, and as quickly as the euphoria had arrived, it dwindled.

I know you hate all this hole-and-corner stuff, darling…

"Please don't do anything until I've spoken to James again," she said to Captain Beckett.

"I wouldn't dream of doing so, Imogen. I only offer my help and support."

"And I thank you for that."

If she'd dared, she would have kissed him, but he was still her superior officer, and she never overstepped the mark.

James managed to telephone her again that evening, and she said what was in her mind without any preamble.

"James, do you still want to marry me?"

After the tiniest pause, he laughed. "What sort of crazy question is that?"

"Well, I know you do, of course. But I mean now, on your next leave, if we can get a special licence."

She realised her hands were shaking, thinking for one wild moment that he might not agree to it at all.

"Immy darling, *yes*, of course!"

"But I don't want to do it the way Elsie and Joe did. I want to let the families know in advance. They won't be able to be with us, except in spirit, but it's important to let them share our day, don't you think?"

"I couldn't agree more, but, in the circumstances, I think you should badger that captain of yours to let you have a longer leave, and then we could go home together for a few days. He'll do anything for you."

"I'll try," Imogen said, excitement starting to bubble up inside her again. "And I'm sure I'll be able to wangle it somehow."

"I'm sure you will, too. But I'm stuck here for the time being, darling, so it will be up to you to get things organised."

"I know. And I know Captain Beckett will help if I ask him."

"Isn't that what I just said?" James said.

--

A few days later Quentin held the telephone away from his ear as his eldest daughter poured out her latest news.

"And Daddy, I'm sorry we're not coming back to Bristol for the ceremony, but we don't want to waste any of our precious leave in travelling before we actually get married. We hope to come down to see everyone for a few days afterwards, though. Please say you understand."

"Of course I do, Immy. It's a bit of a shock, though, since you were always so adamant in waiting until after the war."

"I was. But we want to be together now, to feel that we truly belong, just in case – well, just in case."

"Don't even think like that, my dear. James has got a charmed life – he must have, to have survived the desert campaign and come out of it unscathed."

One successful battle didn't make a war, and it wasn't over yet, and although neither of them said it, Immy guessed it would be what they were both thinking; but she wasn't going to allow such passing clouds to spoil these precious moments.

"Please let everyone else know for me, Daddy," she went on. "I've just about used up all my telephone time here, and there's always a queue waiting to use it. And tell them I'm sorry to do them all out of a big party!"

When Quentin related the news to Mary, she wasn't in the least surprised. "I wondered how long she would hold out," she said with a smile. "As for disappointing the rest of the family, well, a marriage is for two people, isn't it?" she said, unconsciously echoing Captain Beckett's words. "The ceremony is only the outer trappings and knowing that you truly belong to one another is the only important thing."

"When did you learn to be so perceptive, my love?"

"When I married you, of course."

–

Elsie was enchanted at the news. Daisy secretly planned to get to London from Chichester to be at the Register Office at all costs if she possibly could, and so did James's sister Helen, who contacted her to suggest it. None of the older members of either family could make the long journey to London for just one day, and besides, the couple promised to spend the rest of their leave in Bristol.

They wouldn't stay with either family, though, nor in Weston. For these first few days of being man and wife, James booked them into a hotel overlooking the Avon Gorge, but not the one where Immy had once rounded on Joe Preston's cousin Robert, after his attempt to seduce Helen. Not that anyone knew of that but the three of them, thank God.

Though most people were happy at the thought of the engaged couple getting married and bringing a ray of sunshine into these gloomy and anxious days, it was Aunt Rose who showed her disapproval.

"As if it wasn't enough that one of those girls ran off to get married! At least she and Joe Preston had their marriage sanctified in church, but now Imogen, who I always thought would have far more sense, is going to marry James in a *Register Office*!" She said the words as if they were something Satan himself had invented.

At the end of the evening's choir practice, when Rose and Vicar Penfold were having a welcome cup of tea in the vicarage, Freddie cleared his throat mildly. Rose was certainly a firecracker, but he admired that in a woman, just as he admired the three Caldwell sisters for their spirited natures. However, there were some things that had to be handed delicately, as far as Rose was concerned.

"The place really doesn't matter all that much, Rose. What's important is that they love one another, and the vows that they make to one another."

"And you a vicar! You're the last person I'd have expected to think that a *Register Office* is a fit place for a religious service. I thought only rushed marriages took place there. You know the kind I mean," she added darkly.

"All marriages have God's blessing, Rose, whether or not they are rushed, as you call it. A war always hastens people's desire to belong to one another – and I'm sure you're not implying that Imogen and James are marrying for any but the purest of reasons."

"Well, of course I'm implying no such thing! I would never think such a thing of any of my girls. And please get off your pious high horse! You don't need to give me a sermon, Freddie."

"Where is your tolerance, Rose?" he went on doggedly. "We've all been through a previous war to this one, and didn't you ever feel the same passion when you were young as these young people must be feeling now?"

She looked at him, this kind, gentle man who was becoming a dear friend, and who had been her strength after Bert died, understanding her grief far better than any of the young members of her family ever could. He never minded her outbursts. She was aware of something stirring inside her, and she squashed the feeling at once, because any thought of affection towards another man after Bert was completely alien to her. Except as a friend. A dear friend. And with friends, you could always say exactly what you meant without any risk of offending.

"Maybe I did," she said crossly. "I'm not a nun, Freddie. And what do you mean by asking about my tolerance!"

He laughed, and without warning, he leaned forward and kissed her cheek very lightly. "Oh Rose, you're a gem. A real gem. One of a kind, as they say."

"And you're daft," she retorted, and then laughed back, because who ever heard of calling a vicar daft!

"Anyway, what do your brood of children think?" Freddie went on.

"Oh, the boys aren't all that interested, but Vanessa's alternately saying it's mad to get married in wartime when you might be killed tomorrow, and then complaining because she thought she and Daisy might have been bridesmaids."

"That sounds about right for her," Freddie said, nodding.

–

"Do you reckon they've *done* it already?" Nessa asked her friend Hilary, as they walked home from the bus stop after school, and then roared gleefully as her friend's face went the colour of a tomato.

"You do say some awful things, Vanessa," Hilary said crossly. "My mother would have a blue fit if she knew some of the things you say."

"Good job your sainted mother don't know me then," Nessa snapped. "Besides, what's so awful about that? They say some of the girls at the dances go outside with the Yanks, and I bet that's not just to have a bleedin' chat," she added, none too pleased at being censured.

Hilary stopped walking, shaking off Vanessa's arm. "If you're going to go on like this, I'm not walking home with you. I think you've got a dirty mind, Nessa Caldwell-Brown, or whatever your name is, and, if you don't stop it, I shall find myself a new best friend. What do you think your auntie's chap would say if he knew what you were saying about her niece? He *is* a vicar, and if they get married, he'll be your step-uncle, and *then* you'll have to toe the line!"

She stalked off triumphantly, leaving Nessa in the middle of the pavement, glaring after her. What a perishin' thought! She didn't like the sound of that at all. Everything would be changed if Aunt Rose became Mrs Vicar. Their whole way of life would be changed.

Even though Rose wasn't her *real* auntie, she was the only one she had. And she was settled here now. She *liked* it here, and she had had enough changes in her life already.

But I bleedin' well won't toe the line, she thought furiously. If there's any danger of that happening, I'll go back to the Smoke, same as I did once before.

At the thought, she could almost hear old Penfold's voice in her head: *Swear box, Vanessa…*

Him as a step-uncle? Not on your bleedin' life!

Chapter Four

There was a well-known saying that was supposed to have come from a book or a play – Immy couldn't remember which. All she knew was that the gist of it totally summed up the devastation she felt: *The best-laid plans of mice and men*…come to nothing at all!

"The wedding's off," she almost wept into the telephone to her father. "James says that all leave has been cancelled, and they're sending his regiment back to the Middle East. I don't know where – it's all hush-hush, and even Captain Beckett's in the dark about it."

"I'm so sorry, darling—" he began, but she didn't give him a chance to say any more before she rushed on, too wound up to listen to platitudes.

"It's so *mean*, Daddy, just when we'd made all these plans, and it frightens me too. I feel as if I tempted fate by agreeing to get married when all my instincts told me to wait. All this time I've said no to James, and now he's being sent heaven knows where—"

"Imogen, stop it," Quentin snapped as her voice became wilder. "If you're starting to see something sinister in all this, then you're not the daughter I thought you were."

"The strong, sensible one, you mean! Well, I don't feel strong and sensible, and it's hard to live up to that image anymore!"

"You're still the same girl you always were, and the one that James will be coming home to. So you've had a little setback. We all have them, darling, and I know how disappointing this is for you, but there'll be another time."

"Will there?"

He paused, and then his voice was harder. "Now look here, Immy, don't go thinking of this as a bad omen. James is a soldier with a job to do, the same as all of us, and the last thing you must do is send him off to war with dire thoughts in his mind. He won't thank you for it."

"I know," Immy muttered. "It's just that – well, a few weeks from now it would have been my wedding day, and now I shall have nothing."

"You'll have us, and since you were coming home on leave, I hope you'll still come. It's the best thing you can do, Immy."

"Perhaps. I can't decide anything like that right now. And Daddy," she went on, more subdued now, "will you let everyone know? I can't bear to keep saying it all over again."

He promised, and she put down the phone with shaking hands. No matter what he or anyone else said, she did look on this change in their plans as a bad omen. It was also completely stupid to think she was being jilted – it wasn't James who was jilting her, and it never would be. It was the army, jilting them both. It was the *war*. Their chance of happiness was being snatched away from her at almost the last moment, and she couldn't rid herself of the thought that she might never see James again. Irrational it might have been, but such things happened in a war. She knew about the danger of tank warfare, and about James's comrades who had been blown to bits, denying their families even the chance to give them a decent burial. It had been the same with Baz…

—

"It's just too awful," Daisy said on the telephone to Helen Church. "Immy had held out for so long, and now when she'd agreed to get married, this had to happen. And we're done out of our day in London," she added as an afterthought.

"Sorry," she went on hurriedly. "That sounds awful too, doesn't it?"

"Not really," Helen said. "But listen, Daisy, why don't we let Immy know that we'd planned to be there on the big day, and suggest that we all meet up anyway, just the three of us? If we could all get a couple of days' leave, we could all get together and cheer her up, even for the whole weekend. What do you say?"

Daisy thought quickly. Helen was Immy's friend, not hers. She was also James's sister, and Daisy had a feeling that in a threesome she might soon start to feel like an outsider.

"It sounds good to me, but three's an odd number, so how would you feel about making it four?"

"You want the four of us to go on a spree in London on a forty-eight?" Naomi said, when Daisy suggested it. "I like the thought, darling, but not if your sister's going to be all doom and gloom and turn it into a wet weekend!"

"She won't be," Daisy said firmly. "Immy's not like that. I know the plan is to bolster her up, but by then she won't really need it, honestly. She always bounces back. Please say you'll come as well."

"We've got to fix it first," Naomi said, which was as good as saying yes.

Elsie Preston had other things on her mind as the day of Immy's hoped-for wedding grew nearer. The new baby was lying very heavily to one side, giving her a constant stitch and backache, and she was beginning to feel exhausted.

"Did nine months ever seem so long?" she moaned to Joe every night, as she tried every way she knew to get comfortable in their creaking double bed. "I must keep your parents awake all night long with this old bed making such a noise."

"Well, it's a sure bet they don't imagine we're doing anything else in here, with you the size of a beached whale, love," he said, grinning into the darkness.

"Joe Preston, what a thing to say," Elsie said, laughing silently, but ruefully aware that love-making was forbidden in these last weeks – as well as being impossible – which was one of the disadvantages of being pregnant for two passionate lovers; but then the thought of the parent Prestons being able to overhear anything at all made her blush.

"Oh, Joe, you don't suppose they really *can* hear everything, do you?" she said anxiously.

He cuddled her as close as he could. "Of course not. But once this is over, I also think it's time we bought ourselves a new bed. You're getting so heavy now, it's a wonder this one still stands the strain."

"Oh, you're such a pig! But I love you anyway," she said with a laugh.

"And I love you – both of you – and Faith too," Joe said, his hand resting lightly on the hard mound of her belly.

"And you're a poet," Elsie began, then gasped as a piercing pain gripped her.

"What is it?" he said sharply.

"I think it's someone telling me the time has come," Elsie mumbled.

"It can't be. There's still a week to go yet, isn't there?" There was an undeniable note of panic in his voice.

"Try telling that to the baby – and since Faith came early, this one is probably following the same pattern. You can't dictate to babies when they want to be born, but don't worry: it'll probably be hours before anything happens, and it might just be indigestion. There's no need to do anything yet."

Less than an hour later, Elsie was quite sure it wasn't indigestion, nor was this labour going to last an interminable time. It felt as if it was going to be fast and furious, and she was gasping with the contractions, and the agonising feeling of being ripped apart long before Joe insisted on waking his mother in the early hours and telephoning the midwife.

"Why don't you just get out of here and go and make some tea or something?" she ground out between clenched lips. "This is perfectly normal, Joe. Or so they tell me, ha ha," she added, with a weak attempt at a joke.

"Is it? I wonder any woman ever wants to go through it a second time then," he muttered, his face as white as the bed sheets as he pressed a damp cloth to her forehead and wiped the sweat away.

"It's not called labour for nothing," Elsie agreed, and then clamped her lips together as another contraction enveloped her.

If Faith's birth had been swift, at least she had had Daisy's amazingly comforting hands to help her, and Joe was being absolutely no good at all, she thought crossly. No wonder they never let fathers be present when women gave birth. It proved just who were the strong ones...

She quickly revised that thought, remembering how he had been wounded, and all the pain and mental agony he had gone through – and he had been one of the lucky ones. He hadn't had half his face blown away, or lost his sight or any of his limbs, and he had come home to her relatively unscathed.

Then she gave up thinking altogether as a scream of pain escaped her lips. There was no holding this one in like a martyr, and she had no intention of bloody well trying.

"I'll fetch Mother," Joe said, and fled from the bedroom.

By this time Faith was awake, and the last thing Elsie wanted was to frighten the little girl. Her wide eyes stared at Elsie through the bars of her cot, and Elsie tried to smile at her, but by the time Joe and Mother Hetty appeared in the room, all she could do was to gasp at her to take Faith out of the room.

"Our Joe will see to her," his mother said calmly. "He can take her downstairs and give her a drink and then they can get settled on the sofa. You and me have work to do, lass, and I've already sent for the midwife."

Elsie prayed that she would get here in time. It was one thing to have a stranger's hands delivering babies – providing it was what they were trained for – and even your own younger unmarried sister, providing she was a proper nurse. It was far less dignified to have your mother-in-law present at one of the most intimate moments of a woman's life.

Then she forgot all about dignity as another pain ripped through her, and she heard herself howling like an animal, clutching the older woman's hands in a vice-like grip.

"Sorry," she gasped, her face bathed in sweat now. "I'm really sorry…"

"There's no need to be sorry, my lass. You just let it out as loud as you like. 'Twill relieve the tension, and 'tis nothing that menfolk shouldn't hear. It reminds 'em of what they put we women through at such times, which can't be bad for 'em now, can it? You shoulda heard me when our Joe were born: fair raised the roof I did – and with t'other one too."

She kept on talking, and Elsie knew just why she was doing it, even down to mentioning the child who had drowned so many years before. Daisy had told her it was what nurses did to keep the patients' minds off what was happening to them.

She wasn't sure that it worked, nor how long she could hold out without fainting clean away; but if she did that, then she wouldn't know what was going on, she thought with a greedy longing for it to happen. Could you faint at will? Then came the thought that she couldn't be helping her baby to arrive in this world if she was unconscious, and it might harm the baby that she and Joe and Faith wanted so much…

The hours went on, and nothing seemed to be happening. The pains came and went, and so did the midwife, cheerfully telling Elsie that there was plenty of time to go yet, and that she had to be on call for another woman giving birth farther up the dale. It didn't endear her to Elsie at all, and by the time she had heard that the other woman had given birth to a bouncing baby boy, she felt more like screaming at the midwife than welcoming her.

At one point, Joe brought Faith into the bedroom to say good morning, since Faith was starting to fret for her mother; but one look at Elsie's contorted face and the little girl began screaming, and Joe quickly took her out again.

"Is it ever going to happen?" Elsie moaned at his mother. "I'm worried that something's wrong. I thought it would be over so quickly and it never took this long with Faith. I'm scared and I want my mother..."

The words were out of her mouth before she could stop them. They weren't even properly formed in her head. They were instinctive, incoherent, desperate.

Her mother's lovely, floaty dancing dresses seemed to swirl in front of Elsie's eyes every time a pain gripped her, and her arms thrashed about, as if trying to grab her mother's elusive hands. Her swooning senses were penetrated by the midwife's maddeningly cheerful voice saying, "Won't be long now, lass."

"I'm dying!" Elsie screeched.

"No, you're not dying! You're about to give birth to a lovely bairn. 'Tis a mite bigger than t'other one was, I reckon, but you'll come through it in no time at all now. Take a deep breath and start to push down, lass. Come on now, this babby's getting anxious to be born, and you're not helping with all this caterwauling. Do you think the first thing he wants to hear is his mother bellowing?"

"Who do you think you are to order me about?" Elsie roared.

She was normally so mild-mannered, but right now she could have strangled the woman with her bare hands.

She heard her genial laugh. "My my, we are in a right old mood, aren't we, Mother? Never mind, you and me have got work to do now, and you can holler all you like, but let's get this babby born."

Elsie concentrated on what the woman was saying, knowing that now that the final stage of labour was here at last, it would soon be over. At last she was able to push with all her might, ready for the ecstatic final moment when the baby slithered out of her body and into the world…and she was almost delirious with anticipation when it finally happened.

"You've got a lovely baby girl, Mrs Preston," she heard the midwife say as the baby screamed her way into the daylight. "And she's got a fine pair of lungs on her too."

"A girl?" Elsie panted, still trying to recover her breath. "Are you sure?"

When she and Joe had been so certain it would be a boy this time, and he had wanted a boy so much…

The woman laughed. "Well, unless I've been mixing them up all these years, I'd say so, lass. But you'd better take a look for yourself."

Wrapped in a towel, the baby was placed on Elsie's chest, warm and moist and wonderful, her eyes blinking against the light, her head a mass of red Caldwell hair, damply clinging to her head above her delicate features, looking exactly like Faith when she had been born. Elsie carefully pulled the towel aside, to gaze down at the perfect little body, and fell instantly in love as the tiny hands flailed about, and the fingers caught and held her own.

"She's so beautiful," she breathed, her throat dry from her exertions through the night, but her eyes filled with love and awe at the miracle of birth.

"So are you, Elsie love," she heard her mother-in-law say awkwardly, not normally given to saying such things, "and I reckon there are two other folk downstairs who'll be anxious to see this little mite."

"Oh, and I want to see them too!" Elsie said joyfully, with the memory of this agonising night already miraculously receding. "Please let them come up," she said to the two women attending her.

"Let's just tidy you first," the midwife said. "You want to look bonny for your husband, don't you, Mother?"

Elsie succumbed to a few more minutes' fussing, though she knew Joe would think her bonny at any time; but she wanted him here, now, to see her with a new born baby in her arms for the first time.

He had been denied that joy with Faith, but not with this little one…and she needed to see his face when he knew the sex of the baby. She needed to be sure that he wasn't too disappointed…

"Don't tell him it's a girl," she begged, as his mother left the room. "I want to be the one to do that."

It would be hard for her to contain herself, but it was Elsie's right…and minutes later Joe came into the room with Faith in his arms, and his face was worth every moment of the night behind her – Faith too, her eyes filled with wonder at the tiny child lying in the crook of her mother's arm, her other arm outstretched to draw Faith into the circle.

"My beautiful girl," Joe whispered, when he was close enough to kiss her, kneeling at her bedside and switching his gaze from mother to baby, and encompassing them both in the words.

"*Girls*, Joe," Elsie whispered back. "You have three beautiful girls now."

She watched his face anxiously, but he didn't falter. His mouth simply widened in delight as he kissed his new daughter for the first time, and then his beloved wife.

"You've got a baby sister, Faith," he told her. "A bonny little sister you can play with, just like your mummy used to play with her sisters. Isn't that wonderful?"

He couldn't have said anything more perfect, and at that moment, Elsie thought she had never loved him more.

"What's her name?" Faith said, when she had examined the tiny fingers and toes and managed to count up to five on each hand and foot.

They hadn't thought of a name. Joe's parents were superstitious in that way, and since they had all had the image of a boy in mind, it had been left until the child was born. Now that day was here, and it had to be decided.

"What do you think her name should be, Faith?" Elsie said, knowing it was too much responsibility to put on so young a child, but that it would make the baby special to her. Providing it wasn't something outrageous, of course…

Faith thought for a minute, still fingering the baby's soft, downy cheek. Then she said: "Daddy showed me the sun coming over his hill. He said it was the dawn. Can we call her Dawn?"

Elsie's face broke into a delighted smile. "I think that would be lovely, sweetheart. What do you think, Joe?"

"Perfect," Joe said, clearly too emotional to say anything more. "Now I'll take this little one away for Mother to give her some breakfast, and then I'll start telephoning people."

Elsie felt her spirits returning to a delicious normality. "And I'd like some breakfast too! Giving birth makes me feel as if I could eat an ox!"

It also made her feel wonderful, with an exhilarating sense of achievement at having done something that neither of her adored sisters had done. She was longing to see them and talk to them, and she wished, for one last nostalgic moment, that her mother could see this exquisite child in her arms; and then she was perfectly sure, as if a drift of Frances's perfume filled the room, that she did see it; that she knew; that she was so happy for this new little family.

"Elsie's had another little girl," Quentin announced on the phone to his sister Rose later that day. "They're both very well and the baby's called Dawn."

"That's lovely news, and it's just as I've always said: whenever there's bad news, there always good news somewhere to counteract it."

"I don't remember you always saying any such thing, Rose," Quentin said with amusement. "It sounds more like your vicar friend to me, but I'll let that pass for the moment. What's the bad news, anyway?"

"Immy's disappointment, of course, or had you forgotten so quickly?"

"Of course not," he said quickly, knowing that he had done just that in the thrill of hearing Joe Preston's excited voice on the phone, and then that of his little granddaughter telling him she had a baby sister to play with now, and when was he coming to see her?

"You be sure to be gentle when you tell her then," Rose warned. "Immy will be delighted to be an aunt once more, but she'll still be feeling upset because of her wedding plans being disrupted by this blessed war."

"I know. But I've got a bit more news for you too. Things have lulled down a bit here now – and I'm keeping my fingers crossed when I say that – so me and Mary have decided to take a week away to go to Yorkshire to see the new baby."

"Good for you, and be sure to give them all my love."

She kept the determined smile on her face until she put down the phone. Then her shoulders sagged in a most un-Rose-like manner. It was an inexplicable moment at a time of such optimism and pleasure in the family, but one that she could explain very well when she stopped to think about it.

She was alone in the house right now. The children had gone to school, and she had been making herself a welcome cup of tea after seeing them all off after their usual raucous morning search for shoes and satchels and yelling at one another, when the phone rang during her moment of calm.

Now it was all calm again and she was alone. There was no one to share this momentous news with. There was no Bert. There was no family of her own. No Daisy to come whirling in with some scheme of her own. No Teddy, clinging to her after his mother died. No evacuee children. Not even George, the yapping Yorkshire terrier, who had been put outside in the garden after disgracing himself on the kitchen floor during the night.

Without warning, Rose felt utterly lonely, dejected and unwanted. A sense of unreasoning panic gnawed at her stomach as she realised that when this war was over, all these borrowed children would be returning to whatever homes awaited them. Vanessa certainly wouldn't want to be stifled by a Somerset back-of-beyond, when the bright lights of London were where she belonged. Young Harry would be put up for adoption, and there would probably be plenty of folk wanting to care for children who had been orphaned during the war, especially those who had lost their own.

Teddy would naturally want to move back with his father and Mary in his old home in Vicarage Street when the danger of bombing in Bristol was over. Daisy would surely be marrying her dashing Canadian and Rose would probably never see her again – the list went on, emptying her of hope and all her usual zest for life.

"Oh, Bert," she moaned to the four walls in the empty house, "why did you have to go and die before your time by walking into that blessed lamp-post in the dark?"

The shrill ringing of the doorbell roused her, and she realised she had slumped on to Bert's armchair as a kind of comfort. Her face was damp with unexpected tears, and she dashed them away angrily. Whoever was at the door was not going to see Rose Painter any less than her usual strong-minded self.

Vicar Penfold knew her too well, however, and had admired her for too long. The fact that that admiration had turned to love long ago was something he had kept to himself for several years now; but the sight of her bedraggled hair, when she had always been turned out so immaculately, and those reddened eyes, was too much for any man to bear.

"Oh, Rose," he said simply, and held out his arms to her. "Whatever it is, let me be your friend and share it with you."

She stood back to let him inside and closed the door. Then she couldn't resist his offer of comfort a moment more, and she went into his arms and wept on his shoulder. It would have been the same no matter which of her friends had appeared at that moment, she told herself later, and the fact that it was Freddie Penfold meant nothing in particular.

"You must think I'm an awful fool," she said, when she was finally able to speak and extract herself from his warm embrace. "It's not as if I've had bad news. It's quite the contrary, in fact, which makes my behaviour all the stranger."

"Nonsense," Freddie said, not yet knowing what had caused all this emotion, but perfectly prepared to wait until she was ready to tell him. "Haven't you learned yet, Rose dear, that good news and bad can produce exactly the same rush of emotion in us? It's human nature, my dear."

She gave him a watery smile. "I suppose you have one of these daft sayings up your sleeve for every eventuality, Vicar."

"Of course I do," he said drily. "It's my stock-in-trade. But if you're going to revert to calling me Vicar again, I shall leave right away before you tell me your news and I tell you mine, and knowing you, that's something you'll never be able to resist. So why don't you go and make us a nice cup of tea while we talk, if you've no objection to my being in your kitchen?"

"None at all," Rose said, feeling better by the minute, and calling herself an idiot for letting down her guard and allowing herself to feel so pathetic. In any case, there was no need. She had plenty of friends, and this dear man was among the best of them.

Chapter Five

It was hard for Imogen to dredge up too much enthusiasm for Daisy's suggestion of a girls' weekend out in London, even though she tried, knowing her sister was doing her best to cheer her up. Of course it would be lovely to see her and Helen again, and to meet this posh friend of Daisy's that she'd heard so much about; but in the end, it was all going to be a huge anticlimax, because it would have been the weekend she and James were to have been married. She couldn't help having a horrible presentiment that she would never see him again and that it was all her fault. She knew it was completely illogical, because she had been holding out all this time, thinking it would be a good omen to wait until after the war, when dreams of peace would become a reality. Now she wondered if she had left it too late, and had condemned James...

"I'm being stupid." She spoke savagely out loud as she packed her small suitcase. "Utterly bloody stupid. Nothing's going to happen to James, or to me, or to any of my family. And if I don't stop thinking like that, I'll go completely crazy – if I haven't done so already by talking to the ceiling."

She felt her mouth curve into a faint smile. Her father always said that if you couldn't talk things out with somebody else, it was better to say it out loud, or even to shout it in the open air, and let your worries be carried away on the wind. Well, she wasn't going to go that far, thank you very much, dear Father. People around the army camp would think she was *really* mad then!

There wasn't a single thing she could do to change the situation, however, and she knew James wouldn't want her to sit around and mope. They all had to get on with things these days, and at least the good news about Elsie's baby was a joy.

"Isn't it a lovely name?" Daisy had said excitedly, being the one elected to phone and tell her the news. "I never heard it before, did you?"

"No, I didn't, but I suppose we should just be thankful she wasn't born at midnight," Immy said, forcing herself to enter into the spirit.

"What? Oh yes, very droll!" Daisy said with a chuckle. "You're all right then, are you, Immy? Daddy wondered if it might have got you down a bit, with James not coming home and all your lovely plans falling through…"

As soon as she had said it, she bit her lip, wishing she hadn't said anything at all, because she was probably just making things worse. To her relief, she heard Immy's cool reply: "I can hardly be down, as you call it, when it's such a relief to know that Elsie's come through everything safely. She and Joe must be so happy, and Faith as well."

"Oh yes, and Faith calls Dawn *her* baby, because she chose the name."

"Sweet," Immy said, suddenly having heard enough of cosy families: it wasn't helping. "I'll see you in a couple of weeks' time then, Daisy."

She rattled off the name and address of the anonymous hotel she had found. There was no way she could have gone to the one where she and James had been going to stay. She had already booked two adjoining rooms, one for her and Helen, and the other for Daisy and Naomi.

She knew how good it would be to be sharing intimate thoughts in the darkness with her best friend again, as they had often done so long ago, and the fact that Helen was James's sister might possibly help, just the tiniest bit, to bring him a little nearer.

"We'll be there," Daisy said. "And Immy – in case I haven't said it before, and I promise I won't say it again – I think you're being awfully brave about this."

She hung up before Immy could say she wasn't being brave at all, and she was bloody well furious with the army, if anyone wanted to know, and that she could cry at a minute's notice if she wasn't very careful.

However, she wasn't going to blight everyone else's weekend, when she knew they were all doing this on her account. Of course, they had been planning on a little jaunt in London too, she thought cynically – all except Naomi, who had now been roped in to make up the foursome – and she had to admit she was curious to meet this well-heeled young lady, with her chauffeur-driven car available to take her wherever she wanted when she wasn't on duty at the hospital with Daisy. There was a stately pile in the Hertfordshire countryside too, apparently.

Very nice for some, but she doubted that Naomi's home life was any more warm and wonderful than the Caldwell girls' had been in Vicarage Street.

The boys' too, she added to herself – her darling Baz, and Teddy, whose childhood they were all virtually missing out on now, because of bloody Hitler. And pretty soon she would be as much in need of a swear box as young Vanessa, she thought with a grin, but there were some situations that just demanded it.

Everyone had been optimistic when Italy had surrendered to the Allies in September, thinking this might be the beginning of the end; but the Germans were still winning the war, despite Mr Churchill's dogged morale-boosting broadcasts and the way the newspapers reported the favourable bits of the battles and kept the lists of casualties down to a minimum. Everybody knew about that by now.

Long ago, Morgan Raine had told her it was the way the reporters worked. They all longed to report a dramatic story with all the gory details, and sometimes it had to be reported, but in wartime they were all blocked by censorship, for fear of demoralising the public.

Why she should think of that rat Morgan at that moment she couldn't think, and she pushed him right out of her mind at once. Anyway, for one October weekend, the four of them were going to enjoy themselves. They had already agreed to change into civvies once they reached the hotel, and act like ordinary people, and providing Hitler didn't send over too many bombs to disrupt things, they were going to have a good time. Immy was also determined not to put a damper on the generosity of these girls in coming to cheer her up by dissolving into tears every time she remembered that this should have been the beginning of her honeymoon.

"You'll like my sister," Daisy told the tall blonde girl sitting opposite her in the railway carriage as it rattled towards London.

She had refused Naomi's offer to send for the family chauffeur, telling her it would seem too darned ostentatious to turn up in a Rolls Royce. Naomi couldn't see the logic in it, but agreed for once to travel quaintly, as she put it. So here they were, jostled together in a dire-smelling railway carriage, since most people had been caught in a sharp shower of rain. Woollen army uniforms never smelled at their best when they were damp, and some of those near them were pretty rank.

"If Immy's anything like you, I'm sure I shall like her," Naomi said. "And the other sister's quite settled for being a Yorkshire momma, has she?"

Daisy laughed. "I can't quite see Elsie in those terms, and I'm not sure she'd thank you for suggesting it. She's just – well, Elsie!"

"She won't be the same as you remember her, though, will she?" Naomi persisted. "She'll have changed by now, got a northern accent and all that, and probably run to seed as a farmer's wife."

"You do talk some rot sometimes, Naomi," Daisy told her in annoyance.

"Oh, I know," her friend said airily. "And you do see things through rose-coloured glasses, Daisy dear. You should face facts. Everybody changes, even without a blithering war to set us all back. Time changes us."

Daisy was aware that two soldiers in the carriage were grinning at them now as Naomi went on philosophising, and, just as instantly, she knew it was for their benefit. Naomi may have given up romance, as she often declared, but she wasn't above a bit of flirting now and then, especially when it was leading nowhere.

"Well, it hasn't changed your liking for the good life, has it?" she taunted, with a plum-in-the-mouth accent. "Has Daddy increased your allowance lately?"

"Not lately," Naomi said, not seeing the mockery in the question, while Daisy gave the soldiers a sly wink, and their knowing grins became wider.

One of them leaned nearer to Naomi, and the whiff of damp wool and underarms wafted towards her, causing her to flinch visibly.

"Never mind, ducks," he said, in a broad cockney voice, "if Daddy don't give yer what yer want, and yer short of a few bob, me and my mate will oblige."

"Do you mind?" Naomi said stiffly. "This is a private conversation."

"And this is a public carriage, Yer Highness, so keep yer bleedin' voice down if yer don't want us all to join in," he jeered.

"I'm sure my friend didn't mean to be rude," Daisy said hastily.

"I certainly did," Naomi told her beneath her breath with her hand held halfway across her mouth. "Did you *see* the state of his teeth?"

Oh God. For a moment Daisy thought the soldiers had heard, but by now they had lost interest, and all Daisy could think of was that Naomi really should be back with her horses, where the state of their teeth was apparently of some importance. Though she had to admit there was a definite scent of horse-breath coming their way…

It was a relief when the train steamed and snorted into London at the end of the line, and everyone got out with a feeling of needing to take great gulps of fresh air. They managed to hail a cab after an interminable wait, then fell inside it and gave the name of the hotel, and Daisy told Naomi sternly to behave herself.

"Oh rats, I was only having a bit of fun. Sometimes I think you've lost your sense of humour, Daisy. I thought this weekend was supposed to be fun, but if you and your sister are going to have gloomy faces all the time…"

"Of course we're not, and you could make a start by not being so insensitive about Imogen, and remember why we're doing this."

The taxi driver glanced back at them through the driving mirror. "You gels up fer a bit of weekend malarkey then, are yer?"

"That's right," they both said at once, and then they began laughing together, squeezing each other's hand in a mutual apology for being so scratchy.

–

Immy was clasped in Helen's arms as soon as she arrived at their hotel room. "It's so marvellous to see you," she said. "The others aren't here yet, so we can have a cosy hour on our own before they arrive from Chichester."

"How are you, darling?" Helen said, dumping her suitcase and noting the dark shadows beneath Immy's eyes. "It's such a pig that your plans fell through."

"I know, but I've accepted it now – well, more or less – and I refuse to let it spoil our time together. So don't let's be maudlin, Helen, and don't you dare start blubbing over me or I shall start as well. Promise?"

"I promise." And she meant it, she really did.

"Good. And there's happier news on the Caldwell front, anyway. You won't have heard yet, but Elsie's had her baby. Another little girl." Providing she kept on talking to get over the awkward first moments when Helen kept looking at her so anxiously, she would be all right.

"Wonderful. So let's go down to the lounge and have some tea and you can tell me all about it. I presume this quaint little hotel *does* serve afternoon tea?"

Immy laughed. "Of course. It may be small, but it's quite select."

Secretly, Helen was relieved to see her friend looking reasonably well. She had half-expected to be mopping up tears all weekend, and it truly *was* beastly that James should have been ordered back overseas on the brink of their wedding, but she should have remembered the famous Caldwell resilience.

Immy wouldn't let this get her down for long, and they could always rely on bright and bubbly Daisy to put the smile back on her face. Naomi was an unknown quantity as yet, but if Daisy liked her, she must be all right, Helen thought generously.

Of the four of them, Daisy was the only one who hadn't been to London before, and it was the dreary and familiar sight of bomb devastation that assaulted her eyes as soon as the cab took them away from the railway station and into the congested streets.

"Not been here before, gels?" the taxi driver asked her, as she gasped at some of the buildings reduced to rubble.

"No. I come from Bristol, and we've had plenty of bombing there too," she said, almost as if she needed to defend her city: *We've been bombed too, so there!* Which was so daft it almost made her laugh out loud again.

"My old woman's got people down that way, and we heard they got a pasting," he went on chattily. "So what's it to be, gels? Straight to the hotel, or do you want a tour of the ruins? I'll do yer fer a good price seeing as yer in uniform."

"Let's do it, Daisy," Naomi said at once. "Another half-hour won't make any difference, will it?"

"All right." Though she wasn't sure she wanted to see streets that had been demolished, and buildings tottering like skeletons, their glassless windows like empty, gaping eyes, the smell of dust and decay everywhere. It was like every other town and city that had suffered the pounding of German bombs, but despite her loyalty to Bristol, in a weird way this started to feel even more terrible, because it was the capital, the heartbeat of their country.

"Do yer want to see Buckingham Palace?" their driver said, after pointing out places of interest Daisy had only ever heard about, including the beautiful dome of St Paul's Cathedral, miraculously intact in the midst of so much devastation. "It's only a few streets away from yer hotel."

"That'll be it, then," she said, as the taxi meter ticked on relentlessly.

He might be giving them a good price because they were in uniform – and they only had his word for that – but they still had to pay for all this sightseeing.

She was starting to feel exhausted now. It was hardly the kind of holiday tour you wanted. Old ruins were for places abroad that had seen centuries of life and ancient cultures, not here, in this vibrant capital city of England. It brought the utter waste of it all right home where it hurt the most.

"I agree. It'll be good to get to the hotel now, Daisy," Naomi said quietly and, seeing her pale face, Daisy realised they were both feeling the same way.

It united them, brushing away the slight frisson of annoyance that had existed between them ever since the incident in the railway carriage. Life was too short for petty squabbles. If ever there was a time and place to know the truth of it, it was right here.

–

They all decided privately that making this weekend a foursome had been exactly the right thing to do. It left little time for moping, and Immy and Daisy were so glad to see one another and to exchange family news. Helen and Naomi got on surprisingly well – or perhaps not so surprisingly, since Naomi's parents were definitely upper-class; Helen's solicitor father put him a cut above the rest, and her mother was into fund-raising and Good Works, and they even discovered they had a mutual acquaintance. So the weekend was set for success.

"It's so good to be out of uniform," Daisy said lazily over dinner that evening. By hotel standards it was far more meagre than in the past, but they had all come to accept that now, and rationing was very good for the female figure, Naomi said airily, having the figure of a beanpole already.

"So what are we going to do this evening?" she asked. "I hear there's a palais not far from here. Are we all game for it?"

"*Dancing?*" Immy echoed, as if she had suggested something immoral.

Helen teased her. "Well, darling, we're not going to sit around on our behinds all weekend, are we? I'm sure James wouldn't object if you had a dance with a lonely soldier far from home."

"He might not, but perhaps I would."

Daisy sighed, uncaring whether or not she trod on her sister's toes. "Oh Immy, don't be so stuffy. You know it means nothing these days. Naomi and I only have the Forces' Clubs to go to now and then, and it would be lovely to go to a real dance hall and not be in uniform for once."

"I hadn't banked on it, but I suppose you're right," Immy said reluctantly, knowing she should have thought this through. Of course they had to get out and have a good time, or what was the point of being there at all?

She'd rather thought they would go to the park to do a bit of sightseeing in the daytime and simply sit around and talk in the evenings…as if they were in their dotage, she thought furiously. She certainly wasn't ready for that yet; nor were the others, especially Daisy, who looked as bright-eyed and eager as a young colt now, and she certainly wouldn't be worrying about her Canadian's reaction to her going dancing. Daisy was wiser than she was in that respect.

"So are we going to this palais or not?" Naomi said. "Or should we put it to the democratic vote before we decide?"

"Oh pooh, who's being stuffy now?" Immy said with laugh. "Of course we're going. We're here to enjoy ourselves, aren't we?" None of them could know what it cost her to sound as bright and gay as she did just then.

They had been in the brightly lit palais less than an hour when the air-raid siren sounded. Helen was being whisked around the floor by an enthusiastic pilot, and Immy was in the grip of an Aussie soldier called Max, whose accent sounded vaguely like the Londoners'. He was big and bluff, but he held her as if she was something very fragile and regaled her with stories about his sweetheart back home. She quite thought it was someone called Sheila, she told the others later, until he had put her right and admitted that Sheila was how they referred to all the girls, and his special lady was actually called Laura-May.

However, all conversation ended when the music stopped. They were all advised to head for the shelters,

75

and normal dancing would resume if Jerry gave them a chance. If the all-clear didn't sound within two hours, the management hoped to see them all again tomorrow evening, no charge.

"Let's go," Naomi said.

Jostled by everyone else, the four girls scrambled for the door of the palais as the lights were dimmed and then completely extinguished as the doors were opened. It was a clear, moonlit night, filled with stars. It should be a night meant for lovers, and instead it was full of scurrying feet as the air-raid wardens blew their whistles, directing everyone to get off the streets and into the nearest shelters, including the Underground station.

The drone of enemy aircraft could clearly be heard overhead, and despite the threat of imminent danger, they all felt a thrill of adrenalin circulating around their bodies. Clutching each others' hands, they were both shocked and enthralled at the searchlights criss-crossing the sky in a strangely beautiful waltz across the heavens, and at the first sight of the pattern of silver planes, caught in their beams like rats in a trap.

"Come *on*, Daisy," Helen shouted, as she stood quite still for a moment, frozen and unable to move, wondering if her beloved Glenn was up there among them, counter-attacking. She didn't allow herself to imagine it too often, but here in the middle of it, she couldn't help her vivid imagination going haywire, and she was as mesmerised as if she was held in the glare of some savage animal attack.

She sent up a silent prayer for him and all of them as the ack-ack fire began, and the air was suddenly split with the ear-bursting sound of gunfire and the shuddering explosion of bombs hitting their targets. A choking smell of smoke rose into the air as the earth shook; flames shot into

76

the sky from somewhere very near, and the wardens were yelling at these silly bitches to get down to the shelters before they were killed.

Without warning, Daisy found herself sobbing, as the others ran helter-skelter towards the opening of the Underground where they were being directed. For the moment she was completely disorientated. Surging through her mind was the voice of that mad woman Madame Fifi, telling her there was danger for someone near to her; but the danger was here and now, and *she* was in the thick of it…and Immy, and Naomi and Helen…and somewhere in the sky, Glenn would be in dire danger too, pitting his wits against some nameless German fighter pilot…and she was about to be sent underground, where the world might cave in at any second, and there would be no getting out, ever…

She felt a huge thud in her back, as if something large and heavy had fallen against her, and then someone picked her up in his arms as if she was weightless and rushed her towards the Underground shelter. She dimly recognised Max, the Aussie soldier who had been dancing with Immy and, as her sister's name entered her mind, she was suddenly screaming it out loud.

"Immy! *Immy!*"

"Don't fret, little lady, I'm not abducting you," Max's Aussie voice panted above her. "Your friends have got lost in the crush, but if you stand there in the middle of the road much longer, you'll probably get caught in the crossfire of flying shrapnel."

"But I'm a nurse – I should be helping," Daisy gasped, as some semblance of shame and reality rushed into her head.

"You can help by keeping your head down, kid, and let me get you to your friends before you batter me to death."

She hadn't realised she was beating her arms against his chest until that moment. Nor did he believe her. He didn't think she was a nurse. She must look like some flighty chit of a girl in her flowered-print dress, and not in the least like a responsible woman doing wartime work. The incongruity of it all, when she had been to Dunkirk and back, struck her with a wild urge to laugh and cry; but there was no breath left inside her as they plunged into the opening of the Underground station, and he put her on her feet, grasping her hand as they ran down the steps together, deep, deep into the jaws of hell. They trampled over bodies, apologising profusely, and trying to ignore the curses of those for whom this dreadful place was a nightly home.

"Daisy, where the dickens did you get to?" she suddenly heard Naomi scream, and then she was dragged fiercely into her friend's arms; then Helen and Immy were surrounding her and clinging to her as well, and her world turned the right way up again.

"Thank God," Immy said shakily. "You are a goose, Daisy, to get separated from us like that. Anything could have happened to you."

"I know. But what happened was Max, and he was a perfect gentleman," Daisy whispered, prepared to forgive him for the expected bruises on her back where he had belted into her as she had stood transfixed with horror.

Then the daftness of what she was saying struck them all, and, the next second, they were clinging to one another with tears of laughter and relief streaming down their faces as the bombardment continued unabated

overhead, until Naomi gasped out that everyone probably thought they must be street trollops having had too
much to drink. Which started them laughing all over
again.

–

All in all it had been a good weekend, Daisy reported to
Aunt Rose later. They hadn't had another bad raid after
that first one; they had done the sights on foot or on buses
the next day, and it was a thrill to see places she had only
ever heard of before now. Of course, it was heartbreaking
to see the enormity of the bomb damage everywhere,
and that was very sobering. But although she never said
as much, in an odd way it didn't make her feel so alone
anymore. Bristol could take it, and so could London, and
every other town and city, as Mr Churchill kept telling
them, but she was remembering his words with a new
cynicism.

What she also didn't tell Aunt Rose, and never
intended telling anyone else, ever, was about her moments
of utter panic, when she had almost wet herself, as if she
was as young and vulnerable as a child, unable to reach
the comparative safety of the Underground, unable to
move her feet, as though they were fixed in cement to
the ground.

She had faced death before – dealt with pain and
suffering and death before. She had been to Dunkirk, for
pity's sake, yet that first night in London had been one of
the worst in her life. How quickly the flirtatious gaiety of
the dance hall had turned to sheer, demoralising panic.
She was ashamed of it, but she would never forget it,
because it proved that you were never invincible, however

much you thought you were. In the end, it was also utterly humbling, and she vowed never to let herself feel so vulnerable again.

Chapter Six

Quentin and Mary decided to delay their trip to Yorkshire until a few weeks before Christmas, to give Elsie and Joe time to get adjusted to the new baby. They intended being back home for the festivities at Rose's Weston home, of course, because they would never be forgiven if they were away at such a time; but seeing Elsie and the babies so near to the date was almost as good as being all together for Christmas, and her in-laws had decided to make the visit a sort of pre-Christmas celebration. Nothing could compare, though, with the delight of seeing baby Dawn for the first time, or renewing acquaintance with Faith, who was growing into a real little beauty now: even at two years old she knew just how to twist a man around her little finger, with those large brown eyes and that glorious red hair.

"'Tis a sign of temper, some say," observed the other grandmother fondly, "but we think 'tis just high spirits, don't we, Father?" she asked her husband.

Thomas Preston chuckled. "Oh aye, Mother, that we do, 'cept when she wants summat and can't have it. I'd say 'tis temper then all right."

"Come on now, Dad," Joe put in with an uneasy laugh, in case Quentin thought his father was being critical of their mutual granddaughter. "Don't go making out she's fretful all the time, when mostly she's a little angel."

Quentin chaffed him. "You don't need to bother on my behalf, Joe. I've had three daughters of my own, remember – and sons too – and I know what a handful they can all be at times. But we wouldn't change them, would we?"

"That we wouldn't," said Hetty. "Not for all the tea in China, and that's a fair amount, so I'm told."

She looked across at Mary, who so far hadn't had the pleasure of holding baby Dawn in her arms and was hanging back until the invitation came. Elsie saw the wistful look at the same moment and took the baby straight to her.

"Your turn to say how it feels to be a grandmother, Mary," she said softly, and with that one sweet gesture, she drew her right into the family circle.

"I think it's wonderful," Mary told her, and Elsie knew at once just why her father loved this woman who had taken her mother's place in so many ways. But never in the way that mattered to Frances's daughters.

"Are you going to visit the folks in York?" Joe asked.

Quentin shrugged. "I suppose I should call and see Owen, if only to say I've made up my mind that if he ever rebuilds his shop in Bristol, I shan't be interested in taking over again. I never thought I'd say my days as a shopkeeper are over, but the firefighting keeps me busy these days."

"It won't last for ever, Daddy," Elsie said. "Once the war is over—"

"Ah yes, my love, but the fire service will still be needed, even in peacetime, so I may well decide to stay on. But there's plenty of time to think about that."

"You think the war will go on a lot longer yet then, do you?" Joe's father asked, and without warning, the atmosphere in the warm and cosy farmhouse had become more sombre.

"I pray to God it won't," Quentin said heavily. "I don't see any end to it yet, though, and two of my girls are still involved in it, and their young men too."

He was aware of a sudden tension in the room as Mary put her hand on his arm. He noticed Joe's darkening face and remembered the trauma he'd come through when his own war had ended in injury.

"Good Lord, Joe, you know I didn't mean to imply anything. You served your country well for as long as you were able, and all credit to you."

"I'm sure Joe didn't take it personally, Daddy," Elsie said quickly. "But we all do our bit in different ways, and we do it here on the farm, supplying local shops with whatever produce we can, as far as the Ministry will let us."

"Bloody red tape," Joe muttered.

"Language, Joe," his mother said automatically.

"Buddy red tape," Faith said joyously. "Buddy red tape!"

It was so artless that they all burst out laughing, though Hetty Preston couldn't resist muttering that Joe should be more careful in front of the child.

"She's such a bright little girl," Mary said, tactfully turning a potentially awkward moment into an asset. "She'll be a quick learner when she goes to school, and she'll be able to teach this little one a thing or two as well. They'll be such lovely company for one another, just like your girls, Quentin."

The sleeping Dawn opened her eyes at that moment and blinked at Mary, who flushed with pleasure as the baby caught at her finger and held it tight.

Inevitably, the women were less interested in war talk, and they left the men to put the war to rights between them, while they indulged themselves in baby talk and petting the two delightful little girls.

"Are Daisy and Immy coming home for Christmas?" Elsie asked Mary.

"I don't think so. Daisy's not certain, as she may well be on duty at the hospital, and I'm not sure about Immy either. I have the feeling that if a duty is offered to her, she'll take it."

"That doesn't sound like Immy at all," Elsie said in dismay. "We never wanted to be anywhere else but at home for Christmas. I know I won't be in Weston, but I'll be with Joe, and that's home now – if you know what I mean."

"That's right," Mary said as she floundered. "We always want to be with the people we love at such times. But Immy's still feeling badly about James being sent abroad, and we have the feeling that she'd rather keep busy than spend Christmas without him, especially as she expected to be married by now."

"Poor Immy," Elsie said, safe in the security of her own marriage.

As if to end the small feeling of gloom that had descended on them all, Faith began tickling Dawn's feet and woke her properly with a protesting squeal.

"Dawn wants dinner," she announced.

"What you mean is, *you* want dinner, you little minx," Hetty told her. "It's not time yet but come with Grandma and I'll find you a biscuit."

-

They all pronounced the visit a great success, even though the Bristol folk were both conscious they were guests in the Prestons' home, and that these other grandparents would always have the priority with the little granddaughters, simply because they were with them all the time.

When it was time to leave, Elsie had clung to her father tightly. "I love you, Daddy, and I do miss you all, even though I love Joe so much, and I truly love it here too. But I still miss you."

"Of course you do, darling, and I wouldn't expect anything else. But life's made up of goodbyes, and at least we get the chance to see each other now and again, don't we? So be happy, my love, and take care of these precious girls."

She realised he was also thinking of all those they would never see again, and she gave him a last hug before letting him go.

Mary tried to boost his flagging spirits on the train going south again. At least it would be an overcoat warmer there, she thought with a shiver.

"Did you mean what you told Owen Preston – about not being a shopkeeper ever again, Quentin? I really thought it was in your blood."

"It was. It is. And I don't really know what I meant. I just didn't want to be beholden to the man again, and it seemed a good way of making my point."

"But if a shop came your way after the war?"

"Who knows what any of us will be doing after the war?"

"Well, not sitting around bleating about our lot, I hope, when there are others far worse off than we are," she said smartly.

"Is that what I'm doing?"

"Aren't you?"

He realised that this argument was in danger of becoming a quarrel, and he didn't want to quarrel with Mary. He reached over and squeezed her hand. "Why don't we just wait and see what fate's got in store for us, darling? It's all any of us can do these days."

Even as the words left his mouth, he prayed they weren't prophetic. He had always been a man who believed in making his own destiny, but you could never count on that anymore – not while larger elements than himself had a hand in it and he wasn't just thinking about Adolf Hitler.

–

Christmas 1943 promised to be a frugal affair. Food and fuel were scarce, and so were new toys. Everything was going towards the war effort now, and to help the local children, Vicar Penfold had advertised a special occasion three weeks beforehand. Any household having toys in good condition was invited to donate them for children's Christmas presents. There would be tea and biscuits in the church hall on the donation day, staffed by lady volunteers.

"And guess who's making some of the biscuits!" Rose Painter remarked.

Vanessa snorted. "He takes advantage of you, that's what he does."

Rose paused in her flour-and-margarine kneading and glared at the girl. "You're an uncharitable miss, aren't you? Would you want the local children deprived of everything this Christmas? We're fortunate that Mrs Luckwell is giving us a chicken, and my brother will be bringing some of his rations to make the day as happy as possible.

And remember how it would be for you without a family around you!"

Nessa flushed darkly. "I know that. And I'm not uncharitable, or ungrateful. I'm just – oh, you wouldn't understand!"

She rushed out of the kitchen, leaving Rose staring after her, wondering if they were actually tears she'd glimpsed on the girl's face. Vanessa was such a little toughie, and tears were quite out of character, but Rose should have remembered that girls of her age could be as unpredictable as the weather.

She wiped her hands on a cloth. The biscuit-making could wait. She followed Nessa upstairs and found her lying on her bed, hands clasped behind her head, staring at nothing at all. Seeing her stretched out like that, Rose was forcibly reminded that she was growing into a young woman now and wouldn't take too kindly to the younger boys' ragging anymore, nor to being treated as one of them.

"What's wrong, my dear?" she said quietly.

"*Nothing.*"

"And that's the daftest answer to a perfectly sensible question. When I was your age—"

"Oh yes! And I suppose you were the perfect little angel, weren't you!" Nessa said rudely.

"Not at all. I was madly in love with my best friend's brother, and he didn't even know I was alive. I wrote his name a hundred times all over my school book until my mother caught me doing it, gave me a whack across my bottom for my trouble and told me I was a wicked girl for harbouring bad thoughts."

Vanessa looked at her in total astonishment. Rose laughed and sat down on the edge of the bed beside her.

"Nessa dear, I wasn't born old!" And she wasn't old now, she told herself smartly – only in the eyes of this chit and the younger ones. Freddie Penfold certainly didn't think so…

"I know, but I thought you and Uncle Bert – well, you always looked so happy together – when you weren't arguing, that is," she added for good measure.

"We were happy, and he was the best," Rose said steadily. "And our arguments didn't mean a thing, except to make us more sure than ever that we'd each found the person we wanted to spend the rest of our lives with."

She swallowed, because the pain of knowing that they weren't going to spend any more of their lives together could still catch her unawares; but if a little intimate talking was going to help Nessa to see her way through the minefield of adolescence, then she had to do it. It was what parents were supposed to do, anyway, even pseudo-parents such as herself.

"What about this other boy then?" Nessa said.

"What other boy?"

"The best friend's brother that you were madly in love with. Did you ever…kiss him – or write him love-notes – or anything?"

It was all so transparent now. Nessa had written a love-note to a boy and had no reply. If she had been a betting woman, Rose would have bet money on it.

"Well, no. I was only eight years old at the time, and he was twenty-one. I was still a baby in his eyes, and it wouldn't have been appropriate, would it? But if I had been sixteen, and he'd been a boy of about the same age, it might have been different. And I'm sure my mother would have been more understanding then."

She knew she could hardly go any farther without embarrassing the girl completely. It was up to her now whether she wanted to confide in her or not. Rose was acutely aware of how badly she did want that confidence: to feel like a real mother for a brief moment in time, with a daughter who thought her the best friend a girl ever had.

"His name's Charlie," Vanessa said abruptly. "He's in the sixth form at the boys' grammar, and he plays football. I didn't write him a note. It was a poem, I never dared to give it to him, and now you'll think I'm really bleedin' soppy, won't you?"

"Of course I won't. I think a poem's really special," Rose said, her heart aching for the sheer misery in Nessa's eyes. First love could be so very painful, and Nessa was clearly suffering the pangs of it now.

"Do you want to see it?"

"Only if you want to show it to me, and I would think it an honour and a privilege if you did."

"Really?"

"Really."

And if she didn't hurry up, the tension in the room would have them both wailing over one another, and Rose knew of old that Nessa would never forgive her for witnessing her weakness. She was such a mixture of the vulnerable and the brash, and she was nearly sixteen, when every small drama could be a tragedy.

Nessa brought out the crumpled bit of paper from her satchel. The poem was short, but it was full of sentiments ranging from innocent adoration to admiration of Charlie's prowess on the football field.

"I think it's lovely," Rose said at last, handing it back to her.

"I shan't give it to him," Nessa said, taking a deep breath. "In fact, I'm not even sure I feel the same way as I did when I wrote it. All the girls in my class are mad about Charlie, anyway, so I might not bother."

Oh yes, Rose thought. That was fickle adolescence all right.

"Well, why don't you give yourself time to think about it? And while you're doing that, come and help me make these wretched biscuits for the church's toy afternoon before the mixture ends up like cement."

She turned away, thinking she wasn't going to get any response, but then Nessa sat up slowly and caught at her hand.

"Thanks, Aunt Rose," she said clumsily. "You're much better to talk to than any of them bleedin' welfare workers. They'd probably have said I was a tart in the makin'! It's a pity you ain't got kids of your own."

Rose forced a laugh. "Why would I need them, when I've got you, love!"

–

She wouldn't have said it was a turning point in their relationship, but she realised Nessa was behaving as if they had a secret between them now. She would no doubt have regarded it as thwarted love, sadly wringing the withers, as they used to say in all the penny dreadfuls, Rose thought with a wry smile; but presumably the unknown Charlie quickly went the way of all youthful football heroes. Nessa decided that the toy afternoon was something to do and threw herself into the preparations as a kind of peace offering for her moods.

"That girl of yours isn't turning out too badly after all," Freddie Penfold remarked to Rose, when he discovered

Nessa had been badgering her friends at school to contribute their unwanted toys for the local children's Christmas fund.

"Amazing, isn't it?" Rose said with a grin, more pleased than she would ever have believed at hearing Nessa described as "her girl".

Only for the duration, Rose, her brother had often warned her. But where was she going to go back to after the duration, anyway? To London, where she had no living relatives? To fend for herself in whatever way she could? What were any of them to do when this war finally ended – all the little evacuees who had left their homes, frightened and bewildered. They were growing into different children from the ones who had arrived in the country, and hardly remembered their real homes, their real parents, if they had any left.

"Rose. Rose, where have you gone?" she heard Freddie say, and she realised she had been staring into space for the last few minutes.

"Nowhere in particular. Just dreaming."

He put his hand on hers as she began sorting out the box of soft toys that had arrived at the church hall that morning. He was more perceptive than she thought. Or maybe not, because that was part of his job too.

"Rose, my dear, you've been more than a mother to Vanessa, and to all the children you've looked after in the past few years. But even if – when – they all have to return home, there will always be people who need and love you."

"I know that," she said quickly, not wanting him to say anything too personal when she was already feeling less than her normal efficient self, and she wasn't ready for this yet – if ever. "I'll always have my brother's family to fuss over, and I've got good friends in the town."

"You have indeed," Freddie agreed, letting go of her hand, knowing it wasn't yet the right moment to say what was in his heart. Rose wasn't the only one needing love, and if he had to wait a lifetime he would wait until she was ready. He only hoped and prayed he wouldn't have to wait that long.

–

"Daisy's coming home for Christmas after all," Quentin told his sister on the telephone a few days before the great day, by which time the toys had been wrapped and labelled and distributed to various homes and schools in the town. "You'll have room for one more, won't you, Rose?"

"I should just say we will," she said in delight. "But what about Immy?"

"I'm afraid not," Quentin said. "She's not saying much about her movements, but I have a nasty feeling she may not be too near to home."

He was cautious, not wanting to say any more. He didn't *know* any more, damn it, but from Immy's cagey words, he had to assume that she might be going to France; and he didn't want any of his girls to go there – not now, not in wartime. He wanted them all at home, safely cocooned in the family where no harm could come to them. It was a futile hope, and he knew that Daisy, too, would go like a shot if she was called upon to serve abroad; but never had a father felt more impotent to safeguard his children.

"Well, it can't be helped," he heard his sister say calmly. "But she'll know we're thinking of her, and I daresay it'll be some comfort to know she and James are in the same part of the world."

"Good God, I hope not," Quentin said at once, imagining his beloved Imogen somewhere in the eastern desert where James Church was almost certainly with his tank regiment now.

"I didn't mean that literally – just that they'll both be proud to be doing a good job for their country and helping to end this miserable war. Anyway, we'll drink a toast to them both on Christmas Day, and we'll look forward to seeing you and Mary and Daisy very soon," she added, before she made matters worse.

"Is Daisy coming for Christmas?" Teddy said, hovering at her heels, jumping up and down like a yo-yo and exciting George even more than usual. "Will she bring a present for me?"

"Is that all you can think about?" said Nessa, passing by and giving him a playful cuff about the ears. "I thought you were going to be Joseph in your school nativity play. We're all coming to see it, mind."

Teddy scowled, all thoughts of presents forgotten for the moment. He didn't have any stage ambitions like his mother and Daisy had once had, but he had a natural ability that wasn't going to be ignored by his teachers.

"We've got to have a *doll* for the baby Jesus," he scowled again. "And I'm not holding it, so there. I'll look like a sissy! And I'm not kissing Amy Ford either, she's a soppy *girl*."

Nessa went off, laughing. Poor Teddy, not yet old enough to enjoy the prospect, but old enough to be red with rage at the thought of everyone watching him in his school nativity play. She, for one, wouldn't miss it for anything!

Christmas came and went, and with another new year came the fervent hope that perhaps the end was in sight at last. Then, after what had seemed like a minor lull in it all, Germany began to launch the heaviest series of raids on London for three years. People were calling it the "little blitz", just as if the toll of casualties and destruction was any less tragic than what had gone before.

As the months went on, and nothing seemed to be achieved, hopelessness began to sap everyone's natural resilience. News bulletins pronounced that the Germans were in retreat from many areas of fighting, but it all meant little compared with the fact that there was still no sign of total surrender, and the casualty lists were heavy from forces on land, sea and air.

The dreaded telegrams continued to arrive. Families grieved for loved ones they would never see again, or spent agonising hours trying not to imagine what being prisoners of war meant for their sons and daughters. Inevitably, there was a growing sense of bitterness in many hearts. What was it all for? When would it be over? And how would the world be changed at the end of it all?

"When all's said and done," the pub pundits declared, "no matter what the government says or does, it's the little people who are suffering. It's us who are going without, with not enough food to put in our kids' bellies, and God knows what our brave boys at the Front are facing now."

"And He ain't telling," one and another agreed.

Church services were constantly full, in the hope that the Almighty would see an end to all this suffering, but very often ministers were hard put to it to deliver sermons that spoke of hope and trust in the Lord, when half of every congregation had seen family bereavements.

Some steadfasts, like Rose Painter, though, had every faith that God would see them through, and supported Vicar Penfold in all that he was trying to do to bolster up his flock.

"She's really got the God–bug now," Vanessa Caldwell-Brown confided to Hilary Dobbs, her best friend.

Hilary gasped. "You shouldn't say such awful things, Vanessa."

"What? That she's got the God-bug? Why not, if it's true?"

"Perhaps it is, but calling it that isn't right," Hilary said uneasily.

Vanessa hooted. "Why not? Do you think I'll go to hell or something just for saying it? If it's the truth, why would God care, anyway?"

She wouldn't go so far as to add "if He exists", because that would be too much like tempting fate. Besides, she didn't really want to get into any more arguments with Hilary about religion. Since Hilary's mother was a slight acquaintance of Aunt Rose's, it might all be reported back to her, and then Nessa would be in real trouble.

Even more importantly, Charlie White was coming towards them out of the boys' main school entrance, and her heart skipped a beat. She hadn't *quite* got over her pash for him yet, whatever she might have told Aunt Rose. There were some things you didn't tell your mother, or your pretend auntie.

"What are you two looking so sneaky about?" her hero said irritably, when they virtually barred his way.

It wasn't exactly forbidden to talk to the boys outside school hours, but it wasn't encouraged either, which made it all the more exciting when the opportunity arose. Not that he had even looked at her yet, Nessa admitted.

"Nothing," Hilary mumbled, red-faced as usual. "We were just going, weren't we, Nessa?"

"The name's Vanessa, *actually*," she heard herself say, and then wished the ground would open up and swallow her as Charlie White grinned down at her from his lofty height.

"Are you the one who got into trouble for throwing some of the younger kids' hats about last week?"

Vanessa groaned. Now he'd think she was a bully as well as a twerp for standing around gaping at him.

"It wasn't her fault," Hilary retorted quickly in her defence. "They were teasing her for being an evacuee."

"Shut up, dummy," Nessa hissed. She thought she had refined enough of her accent now, but it always came out at the worst of times. Like now, when Charlie White was looking her over in a way that got her tingling. He'd surely want nothing to do with her now, if he ever had...

"Want to come to the flicks on Saturday morning?" he said.

–

"I just don't know what happened," she reported to Aunt Rose in a dazed voice. "One minute I thought he was going to laugh at me, or insult me, and the next he was asking me out. Well, actually, he went on to say that he had to look after his kid sister, and that if I was there too, he wouldn't look such a sissy. He still asked me, though, and I said yes. It was all right, wasn't it?"

"I expect it is, especially if you take Teddy and Harry along too."

Vanessa howled with rage. "Oh, that's not fair!"

"Yes, it is. If this Charlie thinks anything of you at all, he'll be pleased to see you're willing to take charge of your cousins as well."

"They're not my..." but she could see by Rose's clamped lips that she was going to get nowhere, so she was forced to agree to it. Anyway, as long as Charlie was there as well, who cared how many of the little brats they had to take along? Her spirits began soaring again. Let Jerry do his worst, you couldn't change the call of "yooman nature", which was her current expression for it.

Chapter Seven

"Well, here's a turn-up: Vanessa's got a young man," Elsie reported to Joe, reading her aunt's latest letter. "At least, that's what she's calling him, but Aunt Rose says she thinks he's only tolerating her to play babysitter for his little sister. She's probably heading for a fall."

"She'll get over it," Joe said lazily, far more interested in his own little family than in the Caldwell goings-on down south.

"And Daisy's worried about her Canadian. She hasn't heard from him for some time, and she's not even sure where he's stationed now. Oh, Joe," she said, catching her breath as she folded up the letter, "I'm so glad you're out of it, and we're so lucky to have our little Faith and Dawn." When he didn't reply immediately, she glanced at him sharply. "You *are* glad too, aren't you?"

He gave a shrug. "Of course I'm glad that we've got our little babbies. But glad to be out of the war? You wouldn't ask me that if you were a man."

"What do you mean?"

He threw aside the newspaper he had been reading. "A man is meant to be the hunter, Elsie, to go out and fend for his womenfolk, not sit on his backside watching the world go by; and reading about other men's exploits makes him feel less of a man."

Her heart leapt uneasily. He sounded so bitter, almost as he had when he had first come home, war-wounded and frustrated because he was no longer part of the action; she thought he had got over all that long ago.

"How can you say you're sitting on your backside, as you so eloquently put it, when you're doing a fine job on the farm? People always need food, Joe."

"Oh aye, I know all that. It don't make me feel any better to know that even your Daisy's doing her bit. That slip of a lass couldn't make up her mind about anything at one time and look at her now! Been to Dunkirk and back, and still nursing and seeing sights you wouldn't wish on your worst enemy."

"You went to Dunkirk and back too, Joe."

"So I did and came back half a man. Or as good as," he said, which they both knew was a gross exaggeration.

"There's two bonny little girls to prove that's not true! And besides…" She bit her lip, trying not to show how upset she was becoming.

"Besides what?"

"How do you think I feel, when you're comparing me with Daisy – and Immy too, of course – for being so involved in war work, when I can only take care of babies. How inadequate do you think that makes *me* feel, Joe?"

He was genuinely shocked, but still feeling too aggrieved on his own account to think before he spoke. "Don't be so daft. I wasn't comparing you with anybody! There's no shame in rearing babbies, either. It's what women were made for."

"And that remark just about puts women's values back a hundred years," she said furiously, gathering up Dawn from the rag rug in front of the fire, grabbing Faith's hand and stalking out of the room.

He apologised after a suitable interval, of course, and the making-up was as sweet and tender as ever, but it made Elsie realise that once a man had been through the ordeals in wartime that Joe had, he was changed in many respects. She had known that from the day he'd come home, and it had been so hard to find the tenderness in him that she had always known. He had been harder, ruthless and bitter. She had thought all that had passed; but now she knew that it festered and rankled that other men were still doing the things he could no longer do.

She knew, too, that homemaking and bringing up babies was a worthwhile job, but there had always been a sense of envy in her that she couldn't do what her sisters were doing. Not nursing – she would have balked at that – and she couldn't drive a car, nor be as clever and comfortable in the company of other ranks as Imogen apparently was. But there must be something she could do, even tied to the house as she was with the two little girls.

Remembering the exquisite clothes she had made in preparation for the girls' births, her old craftwork came to mind. She was an expert needlewoman and knitter, and if she could put those skills to some use, she wouldn't feel so left behind.

"How would you feel about us starting a knitting circle for servicemen's comforts in the farmhouse?" she asked Joe's mother. "My Aunt Rose belongs to one in Weston, and I don't see why we couldn't do it here, if you would agree to having some of the neighbours in once a week or so. I'm sure we wouldn't be a bother, but if you don't like the idea, I'll understand," she added cautiously, mindful that it was her mother-in-law's house.

"It's a grand idea, lass, and we should have thought of it long ago. The folks around here will be glad to do all they can for our brave lads. We'll put a notice up about it in the church hall."

What would they all do without their church halls helping to bring communities together, thought Elsie, unconsciously echoing her Aunt Rose's continuing thoughts.

–

Like everyone else in the country, Daisy knew there was something in the wind. It began to feel as if they were all waiting for a time-bomb to explode, anticipating the day when the powers-that-be decided the time had come for the Allies to invade France and rout the Germans once and for all, one magical day when it would all be over, and they could all sleep easily in their beds again.

"It won't happen like that," Naomi told her in one of their hospital breaks. "It won't be the end. It'll just be the beginning."

"You sound like Mr Churchill now," Daisy said crossly. "Since when did you become such a know-all about Army Intelligence?"

"Since I was talking to my father about it on my last leave. He says we're all burying our heads in the sand if we think the invasion is going to mark the end of the Nazis. They're still in Italy, aren't they, despite the fact that Italy surrendered months ago? Our chaps haven't even captured Rome yet."

"Italy doesn't just mean Rome…"

"It does if you've been there, darling," Naomi the world-traveller said coolly. "It's the heart of the country, just like London is here."

"Well, you'd know about that, wouldn't you? The farthest I've been abroad is to Dunkirk," she said pointedly, "and that wasn't at my daddy's expense."

Naomi looked at her with genuine hurt. "You do get touchy sometimes, don't you, Daisy? We can't help where we're born, nor whether we're rich or poor. But sometimes I think the richer people are, the more generous they are to other folk. And I don't just mean by giving them hand-outs, either."

"What do you mean then?" Daisy said, not prepared to weaken yet.

"Generosity of spirit, darling, that's what I mean. You have it in abundance when you're dealing with the poor sods on the wards, but sometimes I think you've got a real grudge about people better off than you, and it doesn't suit you."

"That's nonsense—" she started indignantly, and then they were called back to their duties and the chance to argue was gone.

There was probably some truth in it, anyway, Daisy admitted – at least where Naomi was concerned. Compared with most nurses at the hospital, Naomi had it all. No wonder people sometimes called her "Your Highness", and not always kindly. She certainly acted like royalty at times, but the fact that her accent was normal and unforced never bothered her.

She also had all the generosity of spirit she spoke about, and Daisy was growing increasingly fond of her. She knew very well that her own scratchiness lately was due to not having had any real news of Glenn for ages now.

There was a scrappy phone call now and then, but since he had been promoted to flight lieutenant, she had no idea where he was or what he was doing, and the fear that he might be tiring of her was always present in her mind. She couldn't have borne it if he didn't want her anymore, when she loved him so much. It wasn't fair to take it out on Naomi, though, and the next time they were off duty she resolved to make it up to her.

They were firm friends again by the time the news came in mid-February that the RAF had launched a very large-scale night attack on Berlin, causing great exhilaration that their planes had penetrated right into the heart of Germany, because if Rome and London were to be the yardsticks by which Naomi measured the importance of a country, then Berlin was surely Germany's heart.

For those who wanted to know statistics, it was said that over a thousand aircraft had been involved in the attack, and that two thousand tons of bombs had been dropped, at an average of eighty tons per minute.

"It's great news!" people said, congratulating themselves as if each and every one them had been personally responsible for dropping the bombs.

"It's frightening," Daisy muttered, thinking of Glenn and how reticent he had been to tell her anything of his plans lately. Was this the reason? Had information been officially blocked? Or was he just thinking of her reaction when she knew he might have been involved? The fact that the attack had been reported so prominently signified its importance. Remembering that night in London when she had been frozen to the spot before Aussie Max had scooped her up and rushed her into the Underground station for shelter, she could only imagine what those

German people in Berlin must have been feeling when the British bombs rained down on them.

"Good God, Daisy, you can't afford to think like that," Naomi snapped. "It's dog eat dog in wartime."

"Well, I'm only displaying the generosity of spirit you seem to set such store by," she snapped back. "Though you seem to have forgotten all about it now!"

"No, I haven't. I'm only saying that you of all people – a nurse – can't afford to get soppy over what's happening. War is war, darling, and we all have to accept that people will get hurt."

"Do you think I don't know that? It's because I'm a nurse that I know the effect of bombing. I've seen it in Bristol at first hand, so don't tell me I don't know what it means." She swallowed painfully, having to say what was in her heart. "I also know it stands to reason that not all of those thousand planes came back safely, even if the Air Ministry keeps pretty quiet about that."

"But you don't even know if Glenn was involved in it."

"I don't know that he wasn't, either."

Three days later there was a phone call for her. She didn't know the voice, and every nerve in her body seemed to be tied up in knots as she heard the message.

"I'm calling on behalf of Flight Lieutenant Glenn Fraser, Miss Caldwell. Your name was given as a main contact."

Her heart surged sickeningly: why couldn't Glenn call her himself? The questions swirled around her head – wanting answers, not wanting answers.

The man went on apologetically: "I'm an orderly at a military hospital near Dover. Flight Lieutenant Fraser's plane was shot down and he was brought here last night. Right now he's undergoing an operation on his back, so there won't be any further news for some hours," he said cautiously, "but I thought you would want to know, and if you want to call later, I can give you a contact number…"

Of course she bloody well wanted to call later, Daisy thought savagely. She was in turmoil at the news, but she knew that the orderly was just a voice on the phone, and probably wouldn't know the extent of Glenn's injuries, or how serious they were…he didn't even sound more than a boy…Oh God! Spinal injuries conjured up visions of paralysis, and she knew Glenn would rather die than be beholden to strangers, or loved ones, for the rest of his life…

This was one of those times when nursing was the worst of professions to be in, because you knew what might be entailed. It was far better to be ignorant of procedures and prognoses…She realised someone was shaking her and turned her wild eyes to see Naomi by her side.

"What's happened?" she said quietly.

"It's Glenn," she stuttered. "He's been wounded – a spinal injury…"

"Oh, Daisy, I'm so sorry. Are you sure?"

Naomi's face seemed to float in front of her like a ghostly apparition, and she pulled herself together quickly. A fat lot of use a nurse would be if she went to pieces at every bit of bad news. It wouldn't go down too well on her record with the staff here, either. Especially with her secret ambition to be in on the invasion, if and when the call came for nurses, as it surely would. It was something she hadn't told anyone yet, but right now it seemed of far less importance than finding out for sure how badly Glenn was wounded.

"I'm sure he's been shot down and wounded," she said shakily. "But I don't know how bad it is. Glenn asked an orderly to let me know – unless he wasn't in any position to ask him at all. It could just have been that they found my name in his pocket, and decided to inform me, just in case…well, in case."

"Stop it, Daisy," Naomi snapped. "You're not doing any good by thinking the worst. At least you know he's alive, or you wouldn't have got such a message at all, would you? And if you were told it was a back injury, at least he's not blinded or disfigured…"

"We don't *know* that, do we? Anyway, I'm going to see if I can get a few days' leave and see for myself," she said feverishly. Nothing was going to stop her. She might not be Glenn's mother or sister or wife, but she was the next best thing.

As it happened, she encountered no problem in getting leave. She, like all of them, had frequently not bothered to take any leave that was due when casualties came in thick and fast, and so the end of that week saw her on a train to Dover. She longed to see Glenn again, but she couldn't deny that a huge part of herself was scared to death at how she would find him.

–

"That young idiot should never have called you," Glenn said, his voice muffled from so-called painkilling drugs and the effort to talk at all for the stinging pains in his back. The second operation in two days had taken all his strength and waking up to see a cloud of red hair surrounding the face of an angel leaning over him had made him think for a few seconds that he must be in heaven.

Then he recognised Daisy and knew that he was – or at least as much in heaven on earth as he could cope with through the pain.

"I thought you must have asked him to," Daisy said, choking. "He said I was your main contact here, so you would want me to know what had happened."

"I was in no state to ask anybody to do anything when they brought me in," he muttered. "I was better off than most of the guys, though – those that bought it, and those who had half their faces burnt away. At least I got the best of the deal."

Saying so much was exhausting him, but he knew she would want him to talk. She had come all this way, practically flown here, and if he hadn't felt so bitter about everything and at such a bloody low ebb, he'd have swept her into his arms and told her how much he loved her. But he wasn't capable of sweeping anything right now, with drips and tubes sticking out all over him like a pincushion, and the bloody awful stabbing pains in his back that wouldn't go away no matter how many drugs they pumped into him.

"This is really encouraging news, Flight Lieutenant Fraser," one of the doctors had told him the previous night. "The fact that you're able to feel the pain is proof that none of your vital organs nor your spinal cord was damaged. You've been very lucky."

"Why don't you give me something stronger to stop the bloody pain then?" he growled.

The doctor looked briefly sympathetic, then shook his head. "It's important that we register the level of pain you can tolerate. The drugs will help you considerably, but to be sure there's no further setback, there's a limit to how much we can give you."

Why had he got the feeling that at any moment he was going to hear the smug bastard tell him to be a big strong boy and it would all be better in the morning? But he didn't, and it wasn't.

"Is it very bad, Glenn?" Daisy whispered. "Nobody will tell me anything."

As she leaned towards him, he breathed in a drift of her perfume, and a semblance of normality flashed through his mind for a moment. She was his darling, the most adorable thing to have come into his life, and he couldn't bear for her to see him like this.

"It's not so bad," he said, with a great effort. "At least it's nothing that won't mend. I'll be up and about before you know it."

"Thank God. I was so afraid it might have been a spinal injury."

He didn't say anything for a second, and when he did, his speech was slow and laboured. "Would it have made a difference, Daisy?"

"What do you mean?"

He gave a harsh, hollow laugh that didn't sound like a laugh at all. "Hell, who am I kidding? Of course it would have made a difference. What girl in her right mind would want to push a cripple around in a wheelchair for the rest of his life?"

Daisy gasped. "Do you think so little of me that I wouldn't have done so if it had been necessary?"

"And do you think me so small a man that I would have let you? I nearly said spineless, and that would *really* have been a laugh, wouldn't it?"

She felt angry tears fill her eyes. She had heard this kind of talk so many times before, this self-hate and sense of hopelessness when the drugs and the terrible wounds almost turned the minds of the patients. She knew it would pass – it almost always did – but she didn't want to hear it from Glenn, and it certainly didn't make him less of a man in her eyes.

"You could never be a small man, Glenn, nor a spineless one. You'll always be a hero to me, so less of the self-pity, if you don't mind!" She didn't know if he would hate her or not for chivvying him like this. It was the way she had treated patients in the past, and would do so again, but never with the same sense of heartbreak she was trying so desperately to hide, because none of them had ever been so dear to her as this man – so strong, and yet so helpless now.

"You're a bit of a tyrant on the quiet, aren't you, Nurse Caldwell?" he said at last, but with the faintest hint of a smile in his voice now.

She leaned forward and kissed his lips, so dry from the drugs. It wasn't done for nurses to kiss their patients, but she wasn't his nurse and he wasn't her patient. It wasn't done for a young lady to come storming into an unknown hospital and demand to see her near-fiancé, either, but she had done just that, and didn't regret it for a moment as she saw a spark of pleasure in his tired eyes.

"I'll leave you to sleep now and try to find out just what they're doing with you," she said more efficiently, knowing that, if she didn't, she'd probably burst into tears and that wouldn't help him at all. "I'll be back in a little while, Glenn."

"Is that a promise?"

"Oh yes, I'm not going anywhere."

She managed to call Naomi that evening before she checked into the small boarding house where she intended to stay for these precious few days.

"It's not as bad as I feared, and I suspect that young orderly will get reprimanded for scaring me like that. I'm glad he did, though, or Glenn would probably have tried to keep it from me, and I'd have been even more worried at not hearing from him."

"So what do they say?"

"He caught quite a lot of shrapnel in his back, but thankfully it missed the spinal cord and, even more thankfully, the crew managed to get their plane back to England before it finally went down. There's still some internal bleeding, so he's got to be kept perfectly still for a week or so until they can be sure it's stopped. He looks pretty ghastly, of course," she said, pausing to swallow the lump in her throat, "but I think he was glad to see me all the same."

"I'll bet he was. And Daisy, I'm so glad. I know how much he means to you. Are you going to let his family know?"

"He wants me to write to them, but, by the time they get the letter, he'll be long out of the hospital."

"And flying again?"

"I hope not. But I doubt if he sees it that way. They never do, do they?"

She hung up the phone and made two other calls to her father and to Immy. Immy was the one who would understand her feelings most of all – and Elsie, of course: Elsie knew all about having Joe wounded, and then being discharged – but it was to Immy that she poured out her heart.

"I just couldn't bear to see him lying there so still," she sobbed. "I just wanted to hold him in my arms and tell him everything would be all right, but I couldn't do that because he was held in some kind of a clamp thing to stop him moving, and anyway, I daren't seem *too* concerned, of course, or he'd think he was worse than he is. And he *will* recover, Immy, so we're lucky really, aren't we? And I'm sorry to sound such a wet ninny…"

"You don't sound like that at all, darling, and you're being perfectly brave about it. Anyway, I'm so thankful for you that he's not any worse."

It wasn't the time to convey her own fears about James; thankfully, Daisy was too preoccupied with Glenn's news, and what she was going to write to his parents when they didn't even know her, to ask about James.

"They're not going to let him out of hospital for some time," Daisy went on, not willing to let it go while she had a captive audience. "And then it'll be convalescence. I know what Glenn's thinking. He hasn't said as much, but I know he's afraid he'll be grounded, and it will be awful for him if that happens, because he loves flying so much. Am I being cowardly, Immy, if I say I'll be *relieved* if that happens? I wouldn't let on to him, of course."

Immy managed to stop the flow. "Of course you're not being cowardly; it's what every woman feels. But I thought you said his injuries weren't that serious?"

"The shrapnel went very deep and was so very near to his spine that it could have meant total paralysis," she said, shivering violently as she said the words. "They think there may still be tiny bits lodged somewhere inside him, but they can't get at them, so he'll probably be living with it for the rest of his life – or until medical science turns up some new and wonderful method of dealing with it. I'm not sure he realises yet just how lucky he was."

Knowing Glenn, she was sure he wouldn't see it that way at all; but if flying meant endangering his own life and those of his air crew, she knew he would never be allowed to do it again.

"Well, you've got to hold that thought in mind, and keep smiling, Daisy," Immy was saying now. "You won't do him any favours if you go and see him with worry written all over your face."

"You don't need to tell me that. I'm a nurse, remember!"

"I remember," her sister said softly. "And a damn good one too."

When she hung up, however, her face was smudged with tears of her own. James Church's unit was lost somewhere in the desert and there had been no trace of them for some weeks now. She hadn't burdened any of her family with the news. It had come from his parents as next of kin and, being the stalwarts that they were, they had told Immy she wasn't to think the worst, because mistaken news happened all the time in the confusion of war, and then their boys turned up safe and sound. Of course, Helen was being brave about it, and so must she be.

She tried, she really did, even though it felt as if her world was falling apart; but it would be too cruel to tell Daisy now and add to her misery, or Elsie, cocooned in her own happy world. Her father would grieve for James as he had grieved for Baz in the weeks of not knowing his fate, and she couldn't put him through that again. Nor could she bear to hear all their words of comfort and false hope, either, Immy thought fiercely. Anyway, speaking the words out loud would just make it seem real, and right now it *wasn't* real, it wasn't definite.

So she kept the news inside herself, except for the one evening when she simply couldn't help blurting it all out to Captain Beckett, and felt his fatherly arms wrap around her as she sobbed her heart out.

Chapter Eight

Elsie was jubilant. Compared with what her sisters were doing for the war effort, she still felt it had been a pretty pathetic effort on her part to suggest holding a weekly knitting circle in the farmhouse, but the neighbours had caught on to the idea with great enthusiasm. It was also a chance for a good old gossip, and to enjoy Elsie Preston's delightful little girls for a couple of hours.

She soon discovered that the Yorkshire women were quick and expert knitters – all those long hours minding the sheep, she told Aunt Rose glibly – but they hadn't thought of getting organised in this way until Elsie's suggestion. She had even written to the Ministry to obtain addresses of where to send their finished articles and got a grateful reply.

Rose was enthusiastic when Elsie told her what she was doing. "Tell your ladies to put a little note in each pair of socks, or whatever they're making, to cheer up the serviceman who receives them," she advised. "That will make it far more personal. Anyone who felt they wanted to give their address as well might even get a reply."

Elsie wasn't so sure about that. Most of the knitters were buxom farmers' wives, whose husbands might not relish their wives receiving letters from young men at the Front. She knew Joe wouldn't! But it was up to them to decide. For now, she was just happy to be doing something for the war effort, for however long it still remained necessary. As the early months of the year gave way to a hesitant spring burgeoning in the dales, there was less talk of this projected invasion of occupied France that the newspapers talked about with such great hopes.

–

By now, it was very different in the south of the country. It was becoming increasingly obvious to everyone, especially in the south-eastern corner, that something was in the wind. Camps were springing up all along the coast, beaches were swarming with men in battledress and full kit, and it was clear that they were in training for the big assault that was as yet still an unknown quantity. Tanks and vehicles of all kinds began heading south in huge convoys from their training grounds in the north to prepare for carrying assault troops. Barrage balloons were much in evidence along the coastal defences.

It all caused great excitement among adults and children as the troops passed through towns and villages, causing crowds to pour out into the streets, waving flags and cheering them on. It was good for morale, and it was almost like a victory celebration already, Daisy Caldwell told her friend Naomi, when the off-duty nurses at the military hospital had done their share of flag-waving too.

"I wouldn't say that, but at least it makes everyone feel more optimistic," Naomi agreed. She glanced at Daisy. "How about your Glenn? How was he the last time you saw him?"

She hardly liked to mention him too often, since it always cast such a shadow over her friend's face. He was out of convalescence now, and his own worst fears had been confirmed.

"I think he's slowly coming to terms with the fact that he's grounded," Daisy said. "He's not an invalid, but he's not suited to desk work, either; and when I tried pointing out that he'd hardly have been flying planes when he returned home, he nearly bit my head off, so I leave well alone. To be honest, I think he's missing Canada more than ever now. At least the great outdoors and wide-open spaces would be some compensation, I suppose."

Naomi hardly knew how to deal with this subdued Daisy, so unlike her normal bubbling self.

"What will he do when he goes home after the war?"

"I don't know, and I don't ask, but he's got a pretty resilient nature, so I just hope he'll find satisfaction in his new role. Oh, let's leave it for now, shall we? What's the progress on you and the new young doctor in Casualty?"

Naomi laughed. "He's asked me to the monthly dance, and I've said I'll think about it. It never pays to seem too keen, does it?"

Daisy laughed back. "One of these days you'll go too far with your teasing, and you'll find yourself left on the shelf with the rest of the jars of jam."

"What jam?" Naomi said, pulling a wry face.

Rations were becoming scarcer, and the queues on every shop corner got longer and longer when anyone got a whiff of a suspicion that a small delivery of fruit had arrived. Children were growing up hardly knowing what an orange or a banana looked like, and Ministry of Food health and nutrition notices appeared everywhere, urging mothers to make sure they took their cod liver oil and vitamins.

Many people were becoming impatient now, wondering when it would ever end. They were tired of tightening their belts and being told to make do and mend, to save every scrap of metal to go to make planes, when most suspected that it was all just a government ploy to make them feel they were doing something for the war effort. Gardens and parks had been dug up to grow vegetables for years now, and still the war dragged on as digging for victory seemed no more than a mockery. No wonder the thought that another spring might make the hoped-for invasion into France a certainty was in everyone's heart.

Imogen's month-long worry for James Church was over, and she, at least, was determined to see it as a good omen that a turning point was surely coming in the fight for freedom. There was a phone call for her in the early hours one morning; she answered it with hands that shook, hardly able to believe that it might be good news, and still fearful that it could be the very worst of all.

"Imogen," the voice said, and she nearly dropped the telephone.

"James, is that you?" she gasped. "Oh, I was so worried, so afraid..."

She was crying into the phone, and she knew it was no way to speak to a conquering hero, or whatever he might call himself. To her, he would always be a knight on a white charger.

"Calm down, sweetheart. I know this must have been a terrible time for you and the family but as I can only make one call, Immy, I want you to let my parents know I'm all right. Will you do that?"

"Of course I will – but why can you only make one call? James – oh dear God, you're not – you're not a POW, are you?"

The hideous thought that he might have been taken prisoner and incarcerated in one of those terrible Nazi prisons was literally a fate worse than death, according to the more lurid reports but if they were so barbaric, the logical thought struggled into her mind, he surely wouldn't have been allowed to telephone anyone at all…

She heard his soothing laugh. "No, darling, I'm not a POW, but I don't have much time, and everyone's queuing up to use the phone, so I'll have to be quick. This line's bloody awful too…"

She knew that from the way his voice kept fading; but the fact that he was alive and speaking to her swamped every other thought in her mind.

"So where are you?" she stuttered. "What happened to you?"

"You know I can't say where I am right now, but I can tell you what happened. Our unit got stuck in a violent sandstorm in the desert, and it was some experience, I can tell you."

The sudden note of awe in his voice enraged her. He might have been in great danger at the time, but some part of him had *enjoyed* the danger, as they all did. It was a *man* thing, and one that she couldn't share.

"Some of us really thought we were going to meet our Maker," she heard him say more quietly. "We all did our share of praying, but there was nothing we could do but sit and wait and think of our loved ones and pray the sand wouldn't choke us to death until we could dig ourselves out. By then, we were in a different world, surrounded by newly formed dunes, with no sense of direction at all.

It wasn't the best of times, Immy, and it puts a different perspective on going to the seaside."

For a single second she felt the fear in him then, and instantly forgave him his sense of adventure.

"Thank God you came out of it safely," she said softly.

"Amen to that, but I'll have to go now, darling. Tell the folks, won't you?"

"Of course. And I love you, James."

He didn't answer, and she put the phone down slowly, wondering if he was still too caught up in the terrible ordeal it must have been. Or, more prosaically, if the men waiting to call their families had inhibited him. He was their leader, after all, and must be seen to be a man of steel.

She phoned his parents at once and calmed his normally stoical mother before she took control of herself again and promised to let Helen know he was safe. Then Immy went back to her quarters, lay on her bed, and wept.

The relief that James was safe was overwhelming, but for those few brief moments she had really felt he had gone somewhere very distant from her to a world she couldn't reach – not only in space, but in experience. Whatever happened as this war progressed, they would all be changed, simply because of the experiences they had endured. They would all need to adjust to living in a free world with no fears of being blown to bits by an enemy bomb at any time of the day or night, or of their country being overrun by an evil foreign force. It was a strangely disturbing thought, even while they all yearned for peace.

Her thoughts ran on haphazardly. James would always be an army captain. The army was his life, and she would eventually become an army wife. That was something she hadn't really quantified, either. In peacetime the living would be good, but since there were always areas in the world where there was fighting, and where British troops were called on to keep the peace, there would always be periods of anxiety.

Immy was overtaken by an attack of nerves that was harsh and unexpected. Her whole body was shaking so much that the miserable army bunk they called a bed creaked and groaned beneath her slight weight. She heard it and despised herself for her weakness, and without warning she was remembering James's own words: *We all did our share of praying, but there was nothing we could do but sit and wait and think of our loved ones* and *pray the sand wouldn't choke us to death until we could dig ourselves out.*

A swift sense of shame overcame her own fears then. What kind of an army wife was she going to be, if she could fall apart at the second major disaster that had befallen them? The first had been their failed wedding plans, of course…but even as she thought it, she felt a glimmer of her old optimism.

Maybe all this had proved her innate belief in omens and talismans. She had always wanted to wait until after the war to be married properly, wearing a white dress and veil in a church at home, with all her family around her. She had truly believed that it would be the right thing to do, and that it was a hope for the future. She had always thought, however foolish it might seem to outsiders, that her deepest beliefs were going to keep James safe. Maybe this had proved it. Maybe, if this terrible sandstorm had occurred after they had been married, the outcome wouldn't have been so wonderful. It was such a slender thread to cling on to, but it was all she had, and one that she was never going to let go.

"It's wonderful news about James," Quentin Caldwell said, happening to meet James's mother in the town a week or so later.

"It is, isn't it?" she said graciously. "We never had any real doubts, of course. James has always come through any situation, but then, we didn't actually know what this one entailed. It can't have been very pleasant, and I daresay even if we knew all the details now, we wouldn't be feeling quite so reassured."

Quentin agreed, hiding a secret smile. Ladies like her never revealed their real feelings. The phrase "stiff upper lip" must have been invented for them.

"You probably never will know all the details until after the war's over, especially from James himself. They rarely want to talk about their ordeals until much later, in my experience."

"You'd have been involved in the last one, I presume?"

"Oh yes, I was in France, up to my eyes in mud and bullets, as they said," Quentin assured her, not wanting this rather superior woman to think he didn't know what it was like to go to war. She was pleasant enough, but he always had the feeling she considered herself a cut above the rest of them.

He immediately amended his thoughts when she put her hand on his arm and gave it a small squeeze.

"We must all pray for our sons and daughters, Mr Caldwell, and for the day when they come home safely. I understand that Imogen and James have now decided to wait until after the war to be married, so our families will have a wedding to look forward to as well, which will be a very happy occasion for us all. I'll say good day to you now."

He watched her pick her way through the rubble of the street on her way to take charge of a second-hand-clothes-sorting afternoon. She was a little starchy, her speech a little pedantic, but her heart was in the right place, he decided.

"You could have knocked me down with a feather when I glimpsed a tear in her eyes when she spoke of our Immy and James's wedding," he told Mary later that evening. "I always thought she had a ramrod for a back-bone, and she probably does, but there's a good heart in there somewhere as well."

Mary laughed. "Oh, honestly, my dear, any woman who does as much as she does for the servicemen's comforts can't be all bad!"

"You know all that, do you?" he said in surprise.

"I've met her once or twice with my ladies' group. She's a successful fund-raiser for the widows and orphans too – practically a saint in the making."

"Good God," Quentin said. "If that's the case, give me a deliciously well-rounded flesh-and-blood woman any time!"

"Get on with you," Mary chuckled as he put his arms around her waist and playfully patted her backside. But she couldn't deny her pleasure in the fact that this wonderful man had fallen in love with her, especially after his whole world had collapsed when his beloved Frances had fallen to her death in the Avon Gorge. She hadn't known him then, but she knew how much he and his close-knit family had grieved for her, believing that life could never be the same for any of them again. But just as a seed can grow and survive in the ashes of a forest fire, the seed of love had sparked for them both, and Mary had never been so happy as she was now.

"Why are you gazing at me with that soppy look in your eyes?" Quentin teased, his arms still firmly around her.

"I was just thinking how much I love you," she said shyly.

"No more than I love you, Mary," Quentin said, thanking God he had found such a love for the second time in his life.

–

Spasmodic bombing raids continued, and it never paid to be complacent about Hitler leaving certain areas alone. As long as the war continued, you could never feel completely safe. Just as townspeople took a deep collective breath, the wail of the sirens would wail again, sending everyone scurrying for the shelters.

Bristol had had a relative lull, and Quentin considered himself very lucky so far. The entire row of shops where he had once been king was no more, but Vicarage Street had escaped completely, even though the street immediately behind it had been demolished, and some were wary about the effect on the foundations in nearby streets. Complaints had been made to the council, who promised to give them every attention, but these days their attention was so often taken up with other, more pressing things. Thankfully, the whole street still stood, solid and defiant, as he often told Mary, just as they were.

However, now things had started again, and he was anxious to get home one early morning in May, bone-weary from his nightly firefighting shift. There had been pockets of fire springing up all over the place from indiscriminate incendiary attacks and the effects of gas being ignited. He was exhausted, longing for some food in his rumbling stomach, and a good strong cup of tea, and he was worried after hearing rumours of bombs dropping on the area near his home.

In the dawn light, the city always took on an eerie appearance, often disorientating when the eyes had been strained to the utmost in searching the skies for enemy planes, or launching a desperate attack on burning buildings with hoses that always seemed too short, and water supplies that always seemed hopelessly inadequate.

Once the all-clear sounded and the shift was finally over, and he began the walk home, he was never less than touched by the sight of the gaunt, skeletal ruins of what had once been fine civic buildings rearing up into the skyline. A great number of the city's churches hadn't escaped the onslaught, for all that God might have kept them safe, according to some cynics; and streets that had once resounded to the sounds of family life and children's laughter were simply mountainous stretches of rubble and decay.

As he turned into his own street, he was thinking gladly of the hot tea Mary would have left in a flask for him, and then tumbling into bed beside her for a couple of hours before she got up to begin the day, when he stopped abruptly. For one horrific moment, he couldn't even begin to take in what his eyes were telling him was true. Bizarrely, all he could hear through the sick pounding in his head was the voice of the vicar intoning the last words over Frances's open grave as the coffin was lowered into the ground...

In the midst of life we are in death...

"No!"

The single word was wrenched out of him as he saw the ruins of his house and those of the immediately neighbouring ones. There was no evidence of fire, simply a huge, choking pall of smoke above the piles of stone and broken glass. There was the usual fug over the city, and the wind was taking the smoke from Vicarage Street down towards the river, so that he had been totally unaware of the carnage until he had turned the corner of the street. Then his legs seemed to turn to water. He couldn't run, couldn't think.

His only thought was for Mary, and the one thing screaming through his head right now was that it couldn't be happening again. God couldn't be so cruel.

Then his feet began to move, and he was running, desperately shouting her name as he reached the remains of his house. He was on his knees, clawing among the rubble, in what he knew in his heart must be an impossible task. His knuckles quickly became torn and bleeding, his fingernails almost ripped off, but he felt none of it.

He had no sense of time, and harsh sobs had risen from somewhere deep inside him as other hands began to grab hold of him to get him away. He swore at them savagely, too engrossed to notice or care what anyone was yelling at him. If Mary had perished, he would want to perish too, however dangerous the area was now…

"Mr Caldwell, come away, please! There's nothing you can do here…"

"For God's sake, man, listen to us…"

The voices went on, screaming, begging. Then came a familiar one: "Quentin! Quentin! I'm here. I'm safe!"

Mary's near-hysterical voice penetrated his senses. He was almost prone across the rubble by then, as if his very presence would restore her to him. He had been working all night; lack of sleep and food made his senses swim, and he thought he must be seeing a vision as his head twisted around and he saw her moving towards him, her arms outstretched.

She wore a dressing gown over her nightgown, and the belt was coming loose, so that it flapped around her. Her hair was in less than its normal neat and tidy state, but right then, to him she had never looked more beautiful, and she was neither angel nor spectre, but a real, live woman, his wife.

"Mary," he croaked. "Thank God. Oh, thank God. I thought...I thought..."

It wasn't manly to weep, but he knew he would have needed to be made of marble to do anything else as he clasped her tightly in his arms and rocked her to his chest. His tears mingled with hers as they clung together word-lessly for a few moments, before friends and neighbours gathered around them and helped them to their feet.

"What the hell happened here?" he managed to say in a voice so hoarse, yet so filled with emotion it was quite unlike his own.

"We thought at first it was just as the authorities said, Caldwell," one of the garrulous neighbours said import-antly. "We knew the foundations of these houses were undermined from the bombing in the next street, and they should have evacuated us long ago. But it wasn't that after all. Your house got a direct hit, man, and t'others alongside it caught it as well. There was no way to get hold of you, Caldwell, but, in any case, it seems that you and your wife were the lucky ones. You were out on duty, and she had gone along to number 21 during the night, when old Mrs Bailey took ill," he said, finally gasping for breath.

Thank God for Mrs Bailey, thought Quentin weakly, as he rambled on. On such slender coincidences were lives saved; but the families who lived on either side of them, their neighbours all these years, had obviously not been so lucky. He held Mary more tightly for a moment.

"Let's go home," he muttered without thinking, and then stopped, realising that there was no home to go to anymore. Everything they had was reduced to a pile of smoking rubble. The house where his five children had been born and had such happy childhoods, was flattened. It was the last link with Frances.

He heard a small sob come from somewhere very close to him and realised that Mary was suffering with him. He felt a swift compassion, because she had lost her home too, and now they had nothing anymore…only each other.

"The Robinsons have invited us into their home until we can sort ourselves out," she mumbled. She was still shaking, but fractionally calmer than he was, since she had had more time to come to terms with what had happened. "Mrs Robinson will lend me some clothes, and then we can decide what to do."

What could they do? It was something that had happened to so many people, but now that it had happened to Quentin, he could only feel a complete numbness, of being unable to cope with even the simplest things in life anymore. It was taking away not only his sense of control, but his very manliness.

Mary was still talking, using the kind of therapy Daisy always said the doctors and nurses employed to steady the nerves of shell-shocked patients. Someone had produced a steaming cup of tea and thrust it at him, and he drank it without noticing how it scalded his mouth.

"I have some old friends in Devon who would probably take us in until we get ourselves sorted out, Quentin,"
he heard Mary say now.

"No," he said sharply. "That won't be necessary. My
sister has plenty of room in Weston, and I know it's
what she will want, rather than having us move in with
strangers."

She managed to resist saying that her old friends could
hardly be called strangers, but she was thankful enough
to feel a spark of the old pride returning to him, and she
didn't argue, although she felt a touch of normality in
the midst of this nightmare, at the thought of sharing a
house with Rose Painter. Much as Mary liked her, two
women sharing a kitchen was never good news, especially
when rations made it near-impossible to agree on feeding
a family, but now wasn't the time to argue about it.

"Now then, you two," they heard Mrs Robinson from
number twenty-seven say busily. "There's enough time for
all that canoodling later, but first of all, I daresay you could
both do with a fresh pot of tea and some nice hot porridge
for your breakfast, couldn't you?"

They looked at one another mutely, and Quentin felt
a weird desire to laugh out loud at the incongruity of
the words. They had just lost everything, but feeding the
inner man – and woman – was still the panacea for all
emergencies. No matter what, life went on.

Chapter Nine

Daisy was on the telephone to Imogen the minute she heard the news.

"But are you sure they're both all right?" Immy said frantically, unable to grasp anything else for the moment.

"I'm quite sure. Aunt Rose has just called me and asked me to get on to you as soon as I could. The house—" she swallowed hard for a moment as visions of the past crowded in on her – "the house doesn't exist anymore, of course, but Daddy and Mary are perfectly all right, apart from the shock of it all. He was out firewatching, and the angels must have been looking after Mary, because she was taking care of old Mrs Bailey down the street. It must have been ghastly for him, though, because he came home to find the house had had a direct hit, and naturally he thought Mary had been in it, knowing she would never go to the shelter except under protest."

"Thank God for that. So what are they doing now?" Immy said, still unable to really believe what she was hearing as Daisy babbled on.

"They're going to move in with Aunt Rose, temporarily at least. I don't know how they'll all get along together for any length of time. I know all regular leave is cancelled, but I've wangled a compassionate forty-eight. I'm going down there next weekend to see for myself."

"Good for you," Immy said, feeling unreasonably jealous that her scatty sister had known all the facts before her, and now seemed to have got everything worked out, even down to getting some leave, when she and Captain Beckett seemed to be at everyone's command lately, with the prospects of the invasion looming ever more largely in military circles.

"Will you try to get down, Immy?" Daisy asked, after a short pause.

"I shan't be able to," her sister said crisply. "It's bedlam here, and you probably know why."

Daisy's thoughts shifted at once. "Of course I do – or at least, I can guess – and if there's any chance I can be in on it, I shall."

"Oh Daisy, don't—" Immy stopped quickly: how could she say that they had already had fatalities in the family when Baz had drowned off the coast of France, and then again when Uncle Bert had died so tragically after an accident in the blackout?

Her father and Mary had had a lucky escape, Daisy's airman was safe – though her first one had been killed, she remembered – and James hadn't perished in the desert; but their luck couldn't hold for ever.

"Don't what? Don't apply to go to you-know-where?" Daisy said, as cagey as they all were. Careless talk, and all that rot…

"What do you take me for – a coward?" she went on.

"Never that, darling. I just want you safe, that's all. I want all of us to be safe, and home again."

"Well, that's something we can't be, isn't it? Since we don't have a home to go back to anymore. And I have to *go* now, Immy, because I'm being called for, and I've got work to do."

She slammed down the phone before she burst into tears. Until now, she had been so brave at hearing the news about Vicarage Street. Somehow – and God knew how – she had managed to keep all her innermost feelings in check. Even telling her friends at the hospital about it all had given it a sort of distant drama, almost as if she was talking about a scene in a play that had nothing to do with her at all. But talking to Immy had made it all so vividly real. There *was* no home to go back to now. They were like thousands of other people, bombed out and homeless. They all had to accept the reality of it. Her father and Mary had had to face the physical results of it in that terrible dawn, but whether or not Daisy could ever go back to Bristol to see for herself was something she refused to even think about as yet. Maybe she would *need* to…

When Naomi found her, she was hunched up against the wall near the communal telephone, a million memories rushing through her mind. Her friend put her arms around her. There was no need to ask questions.

"Cheer up, old girl. You know you can always come and bunk up with me at my place for as long as you like," she said.

Daisy managed a weak smile. 'Bunking up' at Naomi's near-stately pile was quite an understatement, but she was totally sincere, and Daisy loved her for it.

"This war is changing all of us, isn't it?" she said bleakly. "All the people we knew and loved who aren't there anymore. All the places we thought were so solid and dependable. It's breaking up homes. Breaking up people's lives. It's not fair. It's just not *fair*, Naomi."

"I know, darling," Naomi said soothingly, "but it can't go on for ever. We've just got to look for the silver lining, like the song says. And at least you've got Glenn safely on the ground now, haven't you?"

"Oh yes, for now. But soon as he's fully fit, I know darned well he'll apply for flying duties again."

"Well, if it makes him happy, sweetie," Naomi said guardedly, not too sure how to handle this brittle Daisy, whose moods seemed to swing between high and low these days. This latest blow was a terrible one for her whole family.

—

A week later, Daisy wished she didn't even have to get out of the train at Bristol Temple Meads station. There were so many times when she had gloried in the wonderfully graceful edifice from Isambard Kingdom Brunel's vision, especially that breathless time as a small child when her parents had taken her on a train to Weston for the very first time.

Now, she didn't want to look anywhere but at the small suitcase at her feet as she waited for the local train that was to take her down to Weston, and Aunt Rose's. Her father and stepmother were already there, apparently more relieved to be alive and well than mourning the loss of an old pile of stones. Or so Vanessa had told her excitedly on the telephone when Daisy told her the time she expected to arrive.

"Don't be so stupid, though that's just the sort of reaction I'd have expected from someone like you, without a brain in her head," Daisy snapped.

"I've been bombed out too, remember," Vanessa snapped back.

"Oh yes? Well, from what I've heard, it was a miserable little place and your father was always getting drunk – if you even knew who he was – and your mother had a string of boyfriends, so it didn't matter anyway."

Unable to stop herself, Daisy heard herself saying the very things she would have despised in anyone else. She would have to apologise eventually, but right now her stomach was too tied up in knots by all that had happened, and then by this little madam's insensitive remarks, for her to think sensibly. She heard Vanessa gasp.

"If Aunt Rose knew what you were saying to me, she'd box yer bleedin' ears," she yelled. "Anyway, yer no better'n than the rest of us vaccies now, are yer? You ain't got nowhere else to go *neither*, so there."

Daisy banged down the phone. At this rate, there'd be nothing left of it, she thought wildly. The girl was as impossible as she had always been…but Daisy had just done the unforgivable thing, and been absolutely beastly to her about her past, which she had sworn never to do.

She was still smarting over that conversation when the local train pulled up at Weston station at last. Once, you'd never have known it was Weston unless you were familiar with it, because the signs had been taken down for security reasons; but now they were back – as if the Jerries had a map of every little village and town in England, anyway, she thought scathingly. Then she revised that thought, because they probably did.

She stepped outside the station, immediately breathing in the freshness of a seaside town where the wind was notorious for blowing straight up the Bristol Channel and whipping up the sand in your face, and where the tide went out so far you almost felt as if you could walk right across to Wales – if anybody wanted to.

You couldn't feel the sand from the railway station, nor could you smell the salt air, unless your imagination was working overtime, but at that moment Daisy had such a stinging in her eyes, she might as well have done.

Then she heard someone shout her name, and the next moment she was clasped in someone's arms.

"It's so good to see you, darling," she heard her father say.

"And you, Daddy," she gasped, even though she could hardly see him at all, because her eyes were awash with tears now.

Knowing their old home had been flattened by a single German bomb had been one of the most traumatic moments of her life, and she had done her duties at the hospital like an automaton, holding in her emotions for far too long. But the comfort of his arms around her finished all that, and, before she knew it, she was blubbering like a baby against his chest.

"Come on now," he chivvied her. "This is no way to greet your old dad!"

"I know, and I'm sorry," she gulped. "It's just…just that you look so *normal*."

He gave a soft laugh as he picked up her suitcase and walked her towards the familiar old family car with his arm still held tightly around her waist. "Well, how did you expect me to look?"

"I don't know. Upset, I suppose, and well, devastated, really. You know – about the house – our home…"

She was in danger of starting all over again; she gave an enormous swallow and tried to pull herself together. This was doing no good at all, and it was hardly the way a nurse was expected to behave but she was a daughter before she was a nurse. Even so…

"We've all got to adjust, Daisy, my love," Quentin was saying quietly. "And the quicker we do it, the better.

There was nothing to be saved of the house at all, but you know the old saying: "When one door closes, another opens," in this case, it was your Aunt Rose's, bless her heart."

"And you and Mary are adjusting to that all right, are you?" she said, with the ghost of a smile.

"Adequately, if not perfectly," he said ambiguously, which made her smile all the wider. Aunt Rose could be a bit of a tartar even though her heart was in the right place, and Mary was a sweetie, but she had her own ideas about homemaking, and the two of them together...

"Oh!" Daisy said, as her father opened the car door for her, and she looked into the rear seats. "I thought you'd be meeting me on your own."

Vanessa glared at her, while Teddy jumped up and down excitedly.

"I wanted to meet you, our Daisy, and so did Harry, but he's got the runs as usual, the little twerp, so Aunt Rose said he had to stay home."

"Lovely," she muttered. Nothing had changed there, then.

Then she made a huge effort. She was the older one here, for goodness' sake, and if she wasn't mistaken, Vanessa's face looked pinched with misery.

"So how goes it, Nessa? Still plaguing the life out of the grammar-school boys on the playing field?"

"A bit," she replied haughtily, and then scowled as Teddy hooted.

"Nessa's got a boyfriend, and she takes me and Harry to the flicks on Sat'day mornings just so she can see him."

Her face went crimson, and Daisy knew it was crisis time. Her father was too busy cranking up the car engine now to notice what was going on, and wouldn't have known how to deal with it, anyway. But Daisy did.

"Bad luck, Nessa, having to be landed with those two little squirts, but just be thankful they don't allow animals into the cinema, or you'd be dog-sitting George as well. I suppose he *is* still ruling the roost?"

She was rewarded by diverting Teddy's attention to his latest tale of how wonderful George was, and how Mary was cross with him for eating one of her brand-new slippers the first night she and Quentin had moved in.

"I'm not surprised she was cross," Daisy said in sympathy. "I don't suppose she had many clothes to bring with her."

"Aunt Rose helped her out," Nessa put in, still a bit sullen. "And then we went to the vicar's afternoon church sort-out to find a few more things."

"Good for you," Daisy said, breathing more easily.

There was no point in being at loggerheads with the girl, and she knew she had been as much to blame as Nessa for their previous upset, if not more.

It was also time she put things in perspective. For the past week or so she had been burning up with emotion at what had happened to her old home. She was quite sure Immy and Elsie would have been feeling the same way, simply because being so far away made them all feel so impotent and helpless. While the rest of them here, even those most closely involved – her father and stepmother – had simply got on with things and made the best of it. It filled her with momentary shame that she had taken out all her frustration on Nessa.

"So what are you going to do now, Daddy?" she asked, as the old car wheezed its way up the hills to Aunt Rose's home.

It had also been *her* home for a long while now, she reminded herself, since she had chosen to come and live here after her mother died. If she looked at it sensibly, she realised with a little shock that she had left Vicarage Street a long time ago.

"I've already got a temporary job with the local fire service. There's no shortage of jobs in that department these days, love."

"Dad's got a uniform now," Teddy boasted. "It's not like one of them Yanks, but it's a uniform, all the same."

"Lovely," Daisy said, grinning at Vanessa, who finally managed to smile back after a heart-stopping moment. Daisy wondered suspiciously just who had insisted that it would be a good idea for her to come in the car to meet Daisy. She was sure it wouldn't have been her own. Aunt Rose's methods could sometimes be devious, but they generally worked.

However, she forgot all about such cares when they finally arrived at the house, and the welcoming committee came spilling out to greet them.

George yapped as loudly as he could, practically turning somersaults in his excitement while Mary tried in vain to restrain him. Harry forgot all about his nervous attack of the runs and bellowed at Teddy that he had missed seeing George chew another slipper. Rose almost danced down the front garden to take Daisy in her arms for a rare moment, and then told her she was looking peaky and that her hospital obviously wasn't feeding her enough, so it was high time she got some of Rose's spam-and-potato pie down her.

"Oh honestly, Aunt Rose, give me time to catch my breath," Daisy said, laughing all the same, with the thought flashing through her head that it was so wonderful, so simply bloody wonderful to be home.

—

"All this time," she told Alice Godfrey, when the family had done all their talking, and she had finally got an hour to herself to catch up with her old friend's latest news, "all this time, I was raging at what the Germans had done to our house, and the minute I got here, I knew I was home. And even more than that, I knew I'd been so rotten to Vanessa when she'd just called it a pile of old stones. But at that very minute, I knew she was right. It was far more important to know that Daddy and Mary were safe."

"I hope you told Vanessa that," Alice said, as they strolled along the sands on that gloriously warm May afternoon. If you ignored the sight of the barrage balloons overhead, and the many signs of a town prepared for battle, you could almost have imagined this was any seaside summer afternoon.

"I did," Daisy said solemnly. "I well and truly made my peace with her, and we're bosom buddies now."

"Good Lord, you didn't need to go that far, did you?" Alice grinned.

"I think she's got something on her mind, actually. I get the feeling she thinks of me as her older sister, though she'd never deign to say so, of course."

"Well, what took you so long to realise that! Why else would she want to be called Vanessa Caldwell-Brown if she didn't long to be a part of your family?"

"*Any* family, you mean."

"No, I don't, Daisy, I mean *your* family. Sometimes I think you underestimate just how wonderful they all are, and how resilient too. Anyone would be glad to be a part of them, and I'm not saying any more, or you'll think I'm going all soppy in my old age."

"And talking of soppy," Daisy said, going bright pink at such unexpected praise, "how's the great romance? Have you fixed a date for the wedding yet?"

"Not yet. We're taking a leaf out of your Imogen's book, and waiting until after the war. Which won't be long once the invasion gets under way, will it?"

"So they say." She was cautious, but Alice caught on at once.

"You know something, don't you?"

"How would I know anything? I'm just an army nurse, not a clairvoyant."

She hadn't meant to say the word, but it reminded her at once of Madame Fifi, who had said that something bad was going to happen to her, or to someone of hers – or something like that. She couldn't remember exactly, because she had deliberately shut the woman's words out of her mind, but just sometimes, the gist of them flared up inside her again. Something bad had already happened to Glenn, so if that was the extent of it all, she could forget it.

"Come on, Daisy, you've got that closed-in look on your face now," Alice was saying urgently. "You do know something, don't you?"

She shrugged. "You'd have to be deaf, dumb and blind not to know there was something up. The whole of the south coast is like one vast military exercise area. It's pretty exciting, Alice, preparing for the invasion at such close quarters."

"And you want to be in on it when the action starts," Alice said shrewdly.

"Why not?"

"*Why not!* Because it will be bloody dangerous, that's why not, and you're just a kid, Daisy."

"Well, thank you for that vote of confidence! I am nearly twenty-two years old, and I *have* seen action before, you know. I did go to Dunkirk."

"Oh Daisy, I know all that, and please don't get huffy with me. But you know I care about you, and the thought of any nurses having to go to France and get involved in what's bound to be a terrible time just scares me to death. I don't understand why it doesn't scare you too, especially after what happened to your brother." She paused. "Or is that it? Do you have some crazy idea of vindicating his death by going over there and killing Germans?"

"Hardly. I'm a nurse. Our job is to save lives, in case you've forgotten, not to finish them off."

They were standing quite still on the sands now, the afternoon tide rippling in along the sunlit shore as they glared at one another. They were oblivious to it all until they heard a slow handclap behind them, and they jerked their heads around to see Vanessa puffing up behind them.

"Blimey, I'm not the only one she has a go at, then," she greeted them cheerfully. "So you're aiming to go to France, are you, Daisy? Aunt Rose won't like that."

"It's so unlikely to happen I wish I'd never mentioned it. In fact, I *didn't* mention it. It's just Alice putting two and two together and making five as usual." But she didn't look at her friend when she said it, because of course she wanted to go. It sounded like a wonderful adventure, even though she wasn't daft enough not to know that it would be dangerous too. To be in on the end of it, when their troops marched triumphantly through the streets of Paris and all the other places she'd only ever heard of…seeing the Germans fleeing or holding up their hands in surrender, and knowing the Allies were the victors at last…How could she confess that the thrill of it all far outweighed any thought of danger?

"What are you doing here, anyway?" she asked Nessa crossly.

This was her precious time with her friend, and she didn't want this little snoop interfering. Though not so little now, of course. Nessa had always been tall for her age and had always looked older. In her summer frock now, her hair loose, she could easily pass for eighteen, and Daisy hoped uneasily that she wasn't going to cause Aunt Rose any trouble.

"Your dad wants you to meet him in the High Street. He's got something to show you. Something about a shop. Anyway, I only came to give you a message, and now I've done it."

She flounced off as well as she could on the soft sand, heading towards the far end of the beach where a small group of her classmates laughed and chatted among the dunes. The older girls watched her go, automatically linking arms again.

"I see trouble there," Alice said at last, echoing Daisy's thoughts.

"Me too, but if we don't want to sound like two old battle axe matrons, let's forget her. I don't want to spend my time here worrying over Nessa Brown."

Anyway, she had to meet her father in the High Street. Something to do with a shop. Ironically, Daisy felt less than pleased. Her father should be moping at Aunt Rose's, not gallivanting about looking for something to buy for

Mary. Unless it was clothes, of course, and he wanted his daughter's advice.

She couldn't see him at first. There were plenty of people about on this fine May afternoon, but when she did, she saw that Mary was with him. It began to feel a bit like a deputation. Quentin greeted her at once.

"Daisy, do you remember your aunt's American friend, Gloria something-or-other, who owned a little dress shop? She went back to America soon after the war began, following government advice."

"Well, vaguely," Daisy said, a bit slow-witted right then to click on to where all this was leading. "What about her? Is she coming back to Weston now the danger here is all over?"

She crossed her fingers as she spoke, and then bit her lip as she saw Mary squeeze Quentin's arm, because the danger hadn't been all over for these two, had it? And they were coping with it far better than she was.

"Her shop's been in the hands of the estate agents all this time, until she decided what she wanted to do about it. Rose mentioned it to me quite casually, and Mary and I have been to see the agent to find out more."

"And?" Daisy said.

"Gloria's not coming back to England and she's willing to lease the shop. What do you think of your old dad becoming a shopkeeper again?"

There was no denying the sudden light in his eyes. He was a shopkeeper at heart, and it had been a bitter blow for him when debts overcame his ability to continue owning the Bristol haberdashery shop that had been his pride and joy. He had had to swallow his pride when Preston's Emporium had bought out the entire row of shops, including Caldwell's Supplies, but it had also been a turning point, because he had eventually been made manager of the new shop, and young Joe Preston had come there to work and fallen in love with his daughter, Elsie. Fate had a strange way of dealing with people sometimes.

"I think it's wonderful — if it's what you want, Daddy, and I don't need to ask twice about that, do I? But what about your firewatching?"

"I'm a new boy in town, darling, and I've hardly got my feet wet yet. I can still be attached as a volunteer to do my bit whenever I'm needed and, in any case, nothing's going to happen immediately. The shop has been neglected, and it will need a lot of work, but Mary and I are prepared to get our hands dirty and do it all ourselves. We'll have to, since we can't afford to pay outsiders to do any of it."

"Well, you seem to have it all worked out," Daisy said, glad for them, and a little jealous of their closeness too. But overall, there was a growing gladness inside her that their world was gradually turning the right way up again.

"So let's go and take a look at the place," Quentin said, with the old lift back in his voice. "Caldwell's Supplies is about to enjoy a resurrection!"

"It was such a strange leave," Daisy told Naomi when she returned to the hospital. "Over before it had begun, really. But I was expecting tears and depression, and instead, my father was acting like a child with a new toy."

"It's the best thing that could have happened," Naomi agreed, having no idea of what being a small shopkeeper entailed. It all seemed like such a lot of work, but if the news made her friend happy, then it made her happy too.

"The weekend dance is still on," she added. "Are you coming, or are you going to sit and write to Glenn yet again?"

"Well, I do want to tell him everything about my leave, and about Daddy's news. His own father had a general store in Canada, so I know he'll be interested, and I do my best to cheer him up. He's officially well now, but he's still down in the dumps about pushing a pen all day."

"Don't let it get you down, Daisy. Let's have a couple of hours at the dance and you can write to him later," she urged. "I really need your company, and you know how I hate going there on my own."

"All right." She gave in, even though everyone knew Naomi had the confidence of an elephant. The atmosphere at the dances now was becoming more hectic than ever as the excitement grew, anticipating the beginning of what was being called the Second Front. The club was open to all servicemen in the area, which meant that GIs as well as local troops were much in evidence, making a hit among the nurses and other personnel.

They had been there about an hour, when Daisy heard a transatlantic voice ask her to dance. She turned quickly, to stare in disbelief into Glenn's smiling eyes. Then she was in his arms, held close to his heart, and seeing Naomi's triumphant face over his shoulder, she knew this had all been set up beforehand.

Chapter Ten

"You look so well," Daisy gasped against his chest as they danced to a slow waltz as a respite among the frenzied jitterbugging of the Yanks.

"I am well, sweetheart. Well enough, anyway."

She looked up at him sharply. At that moment, there was the same glint in his eyes as she had seen in her father's so recently. "Oh, Glenn…"

"Now don't go all teary on me, honey. It all happened pretty quickly. The medics said I'm fit enough to resume flying duties, and that's good enough for me. They're not going to refuse any guy who's willing and able to fly these days, so I'm back with my old unit near here. I was going to contact you at home, but then decided against it, and Naomi and I cooked up this little surprise instead."

She didn't need telling why they would be glad of every competent airman they could get. Losses among aircrews had always been heavy, no matter how the government tried to play them down. Didn't she know that personally? She had already lost Cal. She held on to Glenn more fiercely. She couldn't bear to lose him too, but she couldn't quench that spark in him, either.

"Just come back safe," she whispered, making an enormous effort.

"You bet, when I've got you to come back to," he said, just as they all did.

It made her all the keener to apply to go to France as well, if nurses were needed, as they surely would be, but to her fury and disappointment there was no question of it. Nurses would be needed here for the expected casualties, and since their hospital was in a vitally accessible part of the country, they were holding on to every single member of staff.

So Daisy couldn't go. But Imogen would.

She opened the sealed orders Captain Beckett handed her, informing her that as his official driver they would leave for France once the first wave of Operation Overlord troops had made a successful landing. With a minimal staff, they would establish a field HQ in a small village near Bayeux, where they would transmit information back to the War Office. Their own departure date was uncon-firmed as yet, and depended on the date of the invasion, but the beginning of June was a definite likelihood.

The relief of knowing it was all going to happen at last was immense, but Immy couldn't help a feeling of shock, because she had never expected to be involved herself.

"Are you nervous, Imogen?" Captain Beckett asked, while she was studying the various orders and instructions.

"I'd be lying if I said no."

"Good. I'm nervous too. It's a healthy reaction, and it's what makes a good team, Corporal Caldwell, because we trust each other, and we've learned to rely on each other. If I'd wanted a devil-may-care young woman working with me, I'd have chosen someone else."

"Thank you, sir," she said solemnly.

"So now we wait. And one more thing: as always, we tell no one of our mission. Once the field HQ is up and running, we will be able to get messages back to our families, but until then, we observe strict security. Is that understood?"

"Completely, sir."

Over the next couple of weeks, however, she felt in a weird state of limbo. The war was still continuing. Towns and cities were being bombed on both sides; the war against Japan, brought about by the bombing of Pearl Harbour, was a major focus of the Americans' attacks while being staunch supporters of and participants in the Allied cause in Europe. Italy was being liberated, and there was much talk of the French Resistance movement, which was going to play a major part in contacting them and aiding in setting up their own field HQ near Bayeux.

Yet to Imogen it still seemed so unreal, as if the world was still waiting for something to happen, holding its breath, just like with Dunkirk; and the worst of it was that she was unable to tell anyone of her own part in it. Whenever James managed to call her on the phone, he too had become cautious in what he said. Their conversation became stilted, and something of their old loving banter had disappeared, all because of the intrusion of this bloody, bloody war.

She knew she should be thankful enough to know that he was back in England and based "somewhere on the south coast", but even that minimal amount of information was enough for her to know that his own orders were concerned with the Second Front. It was frustrating and nerve-racking.

At the end of May came the shocking news that forty-seven British and Allied airmen prisoners of war had been shot by the Gestapo after escaping from their prison camp. Nearly a hundred had got out from the so-called escape-proof Stalag Luft III in Silesia, and fourteen were still on the run. The Germans claimed that those who had been shot were resisting arrest, but whatever the truth of it, it didn't make comfortable reading in the newspapers.

"Nazi bastards," Quentin Caldwell said savagely, throwing down the newspaper in disgust. "Who knows what happens to those poor devils in the prison camps? I doubt they know the meaning of common humanity."

"You don't know that, Quentin," his sister said, with a warning glance towards the two small boys playing with the dog on the hearthrug.

"I know enough to guess," he went on. "And I can guess how our Daisy will be feeling too, wondering what kind of fate is in store for her young man."

"Doesn't Daisy want Glenn to be an airman again then?" Teddy asked him, his face puckering.

"Of course she does, my dear," Rose said quickly, glaring at her brother, and knowing that the boys only saw the glamour attached to the Brylcreem boys, and none of the danger, and she saw no reason to disillusion them at their tender age. At least neither of these two children would ever be involved in the war, because no one could foresee it going on for years and years, but she mentally crossed her fingers at the thought as Quentin glared back at her.

Unfortunately, her brother's euphoria over leasing Gloria's old shop had dwindled when he had seen how much work was involved in restoring it. His depression and shock over losing the Vicarage Street house had finally emerged, just as Rose had known it would. You couldn't keep such trauma locked inside you for ever, and she and Mary were doing their best to cope with the black moods into which he frequently descended – doing their best with surprising equanimity, too, she acknowledged.

"I'm not going to be an airman," Harry declared. "I'm going to be a sailor."

Too late, Teddy kicked him on the shin, making him howl with outrage. Harry didn't know much about Baz, and Teddy couldn't really remember what his brother looked like, but he knew a bad sign when he saw it, and the way his father went stumping out into the garden now was one of them.

"What did you do that for?" Harry yelled.

"You dope. What did you go and say you wanted to be a sailor for in front of my dad? He'll be in a bad mood all day now."

Vanessa came downstairs from experimenting with a stub of lipstick a girl at school had given her, hoping Rose wouldn't notice her suspiciously red mouth, and was in time to get the gist of what was going on.

"I want to talk to him, anyway," she said, turning on her heel before Rose's eyes could narrow. To everyone's surprise Vanessa and Quentin had struck up an unlikely friendship, particularly since she continually chaffed him in a cheeky way that none of his children had ever done. Maybe that was the reason for it.

She stood and watched him now, her arms folded, as he stabbed at the garden path with a broom to clear away the leaves the strong winds had blown down overnight.

"You'll do yerself a bloomin' injury going at it like a bull at a gate, Daddy Quent," she said, with her own name for him.

He didn't answer, just went on sweeping with his back to her.

"All right, ignore me then. I'm used to it," she went on. "I was only going to ask yer something important, that's all, but if you're too busy it don't matter."

"It *doesn't* matter," Quentin corrected automatically.

"That's what I said. It don't matter."

Caught out, he gave a sigh and turned round, leaning on the broom, to find her laughing at him. She knew her grammar all right, when it suited her. "So what do you want to ask me that's so important?"

Her manner changed at once and he could see how tense she was.

"I've got to do these bleedin' — these stupid school certificate exams soon, and it's a waste of blee— a waste of time, innit? I want to leave school now."

"And what would you do if you did? Even if it was allowed?"

"Come and work with you, of course. In the shop. That's what I want to do."

Quentin gave a brittle laugh. "My dear girl, it will be months before the shop is anything like ready. There's so much to be done, painting and renovating…"

"I can do all that stuff. I'm good at painting. The teachers say it's all I *am* good at. I can make you a shop sign as well. You ask Aunt Rose. She'll tell you."

"What's behind all this, Vanessa? Has something happened at school? You're not being bullied or anything, are you?"

He nearly said because of her accent, but he knew she could smarten it up when she chose. In any case, he guessed she'd be big enough and brash enough to deal with any bullies.

"No, 'course not," she said. "It's something else. But it don't matter."

"Yes it does, and you'd better tell me now you've got this far."

She took a deep breath and then spoke quickly, because, if she didn't, she'd never be able to say it at all. "There's this girl in the sixth form, see? She's been expelled and now we're all getting lectures rammed down our throats because of her, and we haven't done anything!"

"Have you talked to Aunt Rose about this?"

"No."

"Well, why not? And why was the girl expelled? It must have been something pretty serious."

"I ain't told Aunt Rose, because she'd lecture me too, and the kids would start telling tales on me for liking one of the boys at school. She was expelled because she's having a baby."

"Good God."

Hearing her shocked and jerky voice, so unexpected from her usual confident manner, Quentin was out of his depth. He wasn't sure why Vanessa had chosen to tell him, except that it was obvious she'd had to tell someone, and if Daisy had been home for any length of time, it would probably have been her.

"You have to do your exams, Nessa," he said, more gently, when she still stood there, arms hugging her chest, waiting for answers he didn't know how to give.

"Why do I? I hate that school now."

"Did you know this girl?"

"Not really. But now you know why I don't want to stay there, and why I'd much rather come and work with you in the shop. You could talk Aunt Rose round, couldn't you?"

He didn't see the logic in it at all, but he could see that it was desperately important to her.

"I'll make a bargain with you. I'll discuss it with Aunt Rose and suggest that you must stay until the end of this term and take those exams, and no matter what results you get, if you still want to leave, you can work with me in the shop. Unless you change your mind."

She threw her arms around him. "Thank you, Daddy Quent. And I won't change my mind, honest I won't. And I'll be really good around the house too."

"Well, for a start you could wipe some of that red muck off your mouth. Mary will think I've been attacked by a scarlet woman," he said with a grin.

She left him, laughing uncertainly, but the news about the girl at school was going to break soon, and when it did, there would be an awful stink about it. There were already rumours that the girl had been out with a Yank, but nobody knew the truth of it, and her family had whisked her away from the town very soon afterwards.

Whatever Quentin said to his sister, Rose didn't go on and on at her as Nessa had expected but told her casually one evening that it would probably be a very good idea for her to work in the shop when it eventually opened. Quentin could keep an eye on her, and her maths had better improve when she had to give people the correct change, or she'd be for it.

Surprisingly, the scandal about the girl who was expelled died a quick death. She was no longer to be seen in the town, and the pupils were forbidden to discuss her. Besides, the Caldwell family, the town, and the whole country had more important things to think about than one disgraced schoolgirl.

Elsie had taken the news of her old home being bombed very badly. She was torn between the need to rush down to Weston to comfort her father and the knowledge that it would do no good at all.

"You can't do anything, Elsie," Joe told her patiently. "Just remember how lucky your father and stepmother were. If they'd been home at the time, it would have been a tragedy, but I'm sure they're settled enough at your aunt's place now. And what about the babbies? You wouldn't take them on that long journey, and I know you wouldn't want to leave them behind."

She chewed her lips until they hurt. His logic made her angry. Didn't he see that she needed to feel the closeness of her family again, to feel that not everything was lost? Didn't he see that she felt so isolated here, so very far away from everyone she loved? She bit her lips even harder because of course she wasn't far away from everyone she loved. She loved Joe and Faith and baby Dawn, and the Yorkshire in-laws were good folk who made her feel she really belonged...but it wasn't the same. It wasn't the same.

Nobody seemed aware of how distressed she was feeling at what was happening in Somerset. Everyone's thoughts were on the expected imminent Allied invasion of France, and every wireless bulletin was listened to avidly. The newspapers were full of expectation, and only a fool would have known it wasn't about to happen. If there were any German spies around, they would surely know all about it by now, and have reported everything back to Adolf Hitler.

For Elsie, except for the reminder of Joe's war wound, the war had still not really touched her until now, when it had hit at the heart of her family, and she could hardly bear not to be among them. She hadn't felt this low since before Dawn was born, when her insides had all been in turmoil, preparing for the birth of a new baby. She felt a sudden jolt in her nerves. Surely it couldn't be that. Not so soon. Not when Dawn was still barely eight months old. It would seem so reckless of them…and so unwanted. The very thought of it upset her intensely.

Almost as soon as the possibility was in her head, Elsie knew she didn't want another child. Well, maybe one day, but definitely not yet – not until it could be brought into a brave new world without the threat of bombings and destruction hanging over everyone.

Joe's father found her in one of the outhouses, slumped on a bale of straw, with tears streaming down her face.

"Why, whatever's wrong with thee, lass?" he said in astonishment, clumsiness making him revert to his old country speech. "If 'tis summat our Joe's done, I'll have his guts for garters…"

"No, of course it's nothing that Joe's done."

Oh Lord, I hope not, Elsie thought, with a glimmer of humour. Anyway, it took more than one to make a baby, didn't it?

"What is it then?" Thomas Preston asked gently, taking her hand in his weathered one. "You know, if there's summat troubling thee, then it troubles all of we too. Is it one of the babbies, mebbe?"

She shook her head, fighting back the tears.

"Then it's your pa. But you shouldn't fret so badly, Elsie love. From what I saw of him, he's a good, strong man. He'll not let things get him down, and, if I were you, I'd go indoors right now and write him a cheerful letter and send him them photos Joe took of the babbies, so he'll know we've not forgotten him. I'll wager you haven't done that yet."

No, she hadn't. It hadn't seemed the right time to brag by showing off the photos of the two happy little girls, laughing in their mother's arms, at a time when her father must be well down in the dumps and still in a state of shock, but now she knew that it was exactly the right time.

If she started counting back to her recent monthly visitor, she knew very well that she wasn't expecting another child, and that it was simply a bad case of the baby blues that new mothers often got. Mother Hetty had been talking about it lately in that obscure way of hers when she wanted to get a point across about a delicate matter.

Elsie realised now that she should have seen that it was directed at herself. The baby blues might have been a bit late coming, but if the news about Vicarage Street had undoubtedly triggered them off, it just proved that Mother Hetty was a bit of an amateur psychologist in her own way.

"I'll go and find those photos right now," she said, taking a deep breath and smiling weakly at Joe's father. "And you're a love to have reminded me."

"You're a love too," he said, his face red at saying such praise out loud.

She ran back into the cosy farmhouse, to where Joe's mother was cuddling baby Dawn as she dropped off to sleep. Faith was playing on the rug with a brightly painted cotton-reel train that Joe had made for her. It was a picture of such perfect domestic harmony that the soft tears sprang to Elsie's eyes again, but this time they were tears of thankfulness to know how much she was blessed. At least she could share that happiness with her own family by sending them the photos of her children.

—

Vanessa studied them carefully when they arrived, by which time they had been passed around the whole family except for Teddy and Harry, who came last in the pecking order because of their ages.

"Do all babies have such big heads?" she said at last.

Rose snorted with outrage, on the defensive at once. "What a thing to say, Vanessa! Dawn is a beautiful little girl."

"I didn't say she wasn't. I just wondered if all babies were born with big heads compared with the rest of their bodies, that's all."

Mary Caldwell looked at her shrewdly. She and Rose had managed to sort out the domestic duties between them now, after a bit of a flurry at first over who did what, and she had taken charge of the bedrooms, while Rose was still queen of her downstairs domain. Mary had seen all the biology books Vanessa had scattered about in her room and, remembering the young girl who had been expelled from school, she could guess why the question had been asked.

"It does seem that way, doesn't it?" she put in before Rose could open her mouth to start probing as to why this unusual interest. "But I agree with Rose: Elsie has two beautiful children, and you must all be proud of them."

"Let me see," Teddy said. "Elsie's not *your* sister, Nessa!"

"Mind your manners, Teddy – and just be careful to keep them well away from George," Rose said shortly, still not too pleased at Nessa's implied slight. "Your father will want to put them in an album, or perhaps even frame them so we can all see them."

Harry couldn't have cared less about the family photos. At seven years old, babies bored him, but he supposed he should take a look.

"The big one's got hair that looks like carrots," he said at once, "and the little un's nearly bald."

"Thank you, Harry," Rose said pleasantly, taking the photos neatly out of his grasp. "Lots of babies are born nearly bald, and the hair grows later. Dawn is only eight months old, so there's plenty of time for her to have curls like Faith, and it does not look like carrots. It's called auburn."

Nessa sniggered. "I pity her when she goes to school, then. There's a girl in my class with hair like that, and we all call her Carrots."

"Ah yes," Quentin said, deciding it was time he took charge before mutiny happened between her and his sister, "but nicknames are usually terms of affection, so I'm sure she doesn't mind."

"Nessa, come and help me with the bedding, will you?" Mary said quickly, sensing arguments, and took the next half-hour putting her to rights over the size of a baby's head in proportion to the rest of its body in a calmer way than the teacher in charge of a class of goggle-eyed schoolgirls ever could.

–

"It beats me how she could make it seem so un-scary, though, when she hasn't had any kids herself," Nessa told her friend Hilary.

"Some people can just tell it properly," Hilary said, having had the details explained to her in a graphic way by Nessa now. "But I'm still not having any. I don't fancy any kid biting my tweets for its dinner."

"Your *tweets*?" Nessa hooted. "What the bleedin' hell are your tweets?"

"Oh shut up. I wish I'd never asked you about it now. You seem to have gone all gooey over this Mary person, anyway. I reckon you've got a crush on her."

"Don't be daft! She's married to my Uncle Quent, so I've got to get on with her now they've moved in with us, haven't I?"

"How long are they staying?"

"Dunno. For good, for all I know."

"Or until your Auntie Rose marries the vicar," Hilary said with a snigger, ducking out of the way as Vanessa hit her with her school hat and chased her screaming along the road.

That was something else she intended asking Mary about, and the opportunity arose when Rose had gone to her church meeting, Quentin was doing a voluntary firewatching shift, and the boys were in bed.

"Mary," she began, having discarded the idea of calling her auntie, "do you think it's a good idea for people to get married again after their first husband dies?"

"What a question," Mary said, looking up from the newspaper she was reading. "You'd hardly expect me to disagree with it, would you?"

Nessa went bright red. "Oh Lord, I was forgetting. I didn't mean you, of course I didn't. You didn't have a husband who died, did you? At least, not recently, not for years and years, so I suppose that doesn't count…well, no, that's not what I mean, either…"

Mary put down the newspaper. "What a tactless girl you can be sometimes, Vanessa, but I'll overlook it since I'm well aware of your natural curiosity. I had a very happy and loving marriage, and my husband was killed in the First World War. I never even thought of marrying again, and then I met Quentin, and he was looking for paying guests. A friend and I answered the advertisement. But we certainly didn't think about getting married for years later."

"Oh Gawd, I really didn't mean to pry," Nessa said uneasily. "Anyway, it wasn't about you. I was just wondering how long it was proper to wait, that's all."

"Well, if we're not talking about me, who are we talking about?"

"Nobody."

As Aunt Rose's grandfather clock began to chime the hour, Nessa flinched, as if it was censuring her. And Mary saw.

"You think Aunt Rose is going to run off and marry the vicar, do you?" she said with a laugh, and then the laugh faded as she saw the girl glare at her. "Nessa, there's no proper length of time to grieve," she said more gently. "It's what is right for each person, and I don't think anyone would begrudge the partner who is left finding happiness again, do you? I think it's the mark of having once had a happy marriage, that you can consider doing it again."

"Well, *is* she then?" Nessa said rudely. "And if she does, what's going to happen to me?"

Sheer misery shone in her eyes then, and Mary's soft heart melted for her. "Whatever happens, you'll always have a home with her, Nessa, and with us. We're all one big family now. Does that answer your silly little worry?"

"I s'pose so," Nessa said thickly, and rushed upstairs before she disgraced herself by blubbing all over Mary's accommodating shoulder.

Chapter Eleven

The family were never exactly sure what it was that Imogen did in the ATS. Driving an officer around all day hardly seemed like a proper job, and the fact that it was something to do with Intelligence was not to be freely bandied about. Even with Imogen herself, it had only slowly dawned that Captain Beckett was not all that he seemed to be but by now she had been drawn into his confidence – or as much confidence as he thought it prudent to divulge.

She was sure now that they were going to be very much involved in Operation Overlord – or would be, once the landings had been successfully achieved. The most exciting news was of the daring plan to float a harbour right across the Channel under the noses of the Germans, so that the ships could dock safely and discharge their men and vehicles.

There would be thousands of parachutists landing on French soil as well, and all the services were to be involved in what was being called one of the great invasions of the century. Whatever plans Hitler might have had of invading Britain, they could never have been more daring than this.

"He'll expect us to bombard Calais, being the nearest point from Dover," Captain Beckett informed Imogen as the date grew nearer. "In fact, that's what all our Intelligence boys have let slip, so his troops will be concentrating

on that area. Instead of which…" He paused with a satisfied smile.

"Instead of which," Immy finished for him, "they will
be landing on the Normandy beaches."

"Correct. Thousands and thousands of them, British,
Americans and Canadians among them, and God willing,
it will be a resounding success."

Immy shivered. It had to be a success. The whole of
Britain, and undoubtedly the whole of France too, would
be praying for it. It would be a triumphant achievement if
it succeeded, and a total disaster if it failed; but you didn't
dare think of failure. This invasion, on which so much
depended, marked the beginning of the end of the war
at last, and once it was over, people could resume their
ordinary lives again.

She shivered again, thankful that Captain Beckett was
leaving the room, as uneasy doubts crept into her mind.
For how could any of them ever hope to resume what
they had once had? Everything had been changed for ever
when Hitler had marched into Poland on that fateful day
in 1939, and here they were, nearly five years later, still
fighting a war that nobody wanted, losing lives, losing
hope…

She was angry to find herself slipping into a depression
when things were looking so good now – or so everybody
said. It would all be over by Christmas: how many times
had they said *those* words, in this war and the last? But
maybe this year it would come true. If only she and James
hadn't seemed to be moving inexorably apart, not only
because of distance, but because of this wretched need to
keep their movements secret from each other.

It wasn't *fair*, she thought, as belligerent and childish as
her sister Daisy had ever been at that moment.

Daisy and Naomi had a rare few hours off, and spent it at the coast, watching the comings and goings of the masses of men and machinery arriving hourly.

"If Hitler doesn't know something's in the wind by now, he's a real dummy," Naomi observed. "We all know there are spies everywhere. Otherwise why are we always being told that careless talk costs lives?"

"I know, and he can hardly be unaware of all this going on! But wouldn't you think that would make them sitting targets?" Daisy said uneasily.

"Of course not," Naomi told her crisply, seeing the way her thoughts were going. "Jerry's far too busy bombing our cities to bother about what's going on along a strip of coastline."

Even if that strip extends most of the way along the south coast of England...

"I just wish I knew what Glenn was up to. It's as if a blanket of secrecy has come down over everyone lately," Daisy said, unconsciously echoing Immy's thoughts.

"He'll probably be involved in dropping some of the parachutists over France and turn out to be a real hero."

"I don't want him to be a hero. I just want him safe," Daisy snapped.

The more she thought about it, the more she knew it was true. Heroes were for story books and legends; but they were all heroes, anyway, she thought perversely, every one of them who took to the skies, or the sea, or who fought on the land. Bloody heroes, every one...

"Let's go back before I get really maudlin," she said now. She stood up from the breakwater where they had been sitting watching proceedings from as near a vantage point as they were allowed. "It's getting chilly."

It wasn't, but she couldn't help the feeling of foreboding that chilled her blood every time she thought of Glenn and the days to come. Everyone thought optimistically that this invasion was going to be the end of it all, but it wasn't. It was going to be just the beginning.

The weirdest thing of all was the sudden disappearance of all that activity along the south coast. On the 6th of June, the invasion began before dawn, and what had once been a throbbing mass of men and machines covering every inch of coastline, suddenly vanished, as if some ghostly hand had come and spirited them away. In fact, it had been something far more prosaic: merely the orders from High Command to send in the troops and the parachutists now that the weather had cleared a little. Until that day, it had been too bad to consider anything on such a grand scale.

Now it was all being set in motion, and every hospital was on high alert for the expected casualties. It stood to reason that you couldn't expect everything to go smoothly, however highly trained the services were. Nor could they rehearse exactly what was going to happen – and who knew whether or not Hitler was going to be completely fooled into thinking that the invasion was going to happen at Calais?

Not that any place names had been given out in advance, but anyone with a basic knowledge of geography and a bit of gumption assumed that it would be farther down the French coast, and that meant Normandy. On duty that evening, Naomi and Daisy had time to reflect during one of their quiet spells over a cup of tea in the hospital canteen.

"I'm thankful we're not on any of those hospital ships," Naomi said to her friend, when the news trickled through

166

that the first successful landings had been made. "I don't know how you coped with it at Dunkirk, Daisy, but I know I would have been a shivering wreck."

"No, you wouldn't," Daisy assured her. "Think how far you've come already. There was a time when you couldn't face the thought of seeing blood – you were nearly as bad as Vanessa – but now you come on the wards and take your turn in looking after the patients. I'm proud of you, Naomi."

"Good Lord, are you really?" she said, going bright pink. "I never thought I'd hear anyone say that to me!"

"Why not? Let's face it, you weren't born to do menial work, and the fact that you've really got stuck in is something to be admired."

"For goodness' sake, stop it. You'll make me think I was either little more than a social butterfly in my past life, or I'm a blessed saint now!"

"That just about sums it up, doesn't it? Our past lives, I mean. We've all changed, haven't we? You know what it's like to live in the real world now, and I – well, my views have completely changed from what they were before the war."

"You really wanted to be an entertainer like your mother, didn't you, Daisy?" Naomi said, ignoring the slight that she hadn't known how other people lived, until now. She could ignore it, though, because she knew it was true.

Daisy shrugged. "It was a pipe dream, really. I only saw the glamour of it all, but I never had an ounce of her talent. It would have been nice, but I have to satisfy myself by doing a turn now and then for the patients. They seem to like it."

"You're much better than just doing a turn for the patients."

"Yes, well, just as long as you don't offer to do a duet with me, I'll get along just fine," Daisy said more tartly as the air-raid siren began to wail out.

Naomi laughed, linking arms with her as they went back to the ward once more. Neither of them could forget the time when they had decided to team up, and Naomi had spoiled the entire performance by developing one of her allergies and giving a few honking sneezes right in the middle of the song. The audience had thought they were a comedy act, to Daisy's chagrin, just when she had been hoping to impress a professional singer who happened to be in the audience on that particular evening. She grinned, remembering. It had been so awful at the time but was so hilarious in retrospect.

"Jerry's coming over again tonight," she said, hearing the dull whine of enemy bombers heading for the English coast. "I thought they might have been otherwise occupied, fighting off our boys."

She said it deliberately, knowing Glenn would have been in the midst of it all, but determined not to let herself think the worst. He was a survivor. He had said so often enough himself, and she had to believe it.

The news broke the next day of the biggest land and sea invasion in recent times. According to General Eisenhower, the Supreme Allied Commander, the landings had been a complete success, and throughout the night RAF bombers had pounded the German batteries along the French coast. Despite high seas still causing problems for landing craft, the operation was all going according to plan, and the strongest German defences were still concentrating on the Pas de Calais, where a huge armoured force was still in readiness.

By nightfall, Prime Minister Churchill reported that the Allied forces had already penetrated several miles inland. It would seem to be only a matter of days before they pushed the Germans back and liberated Paris, and hopes were high that such an event would truly signal the end of the war.

Along with the rest of his family, Quentin Caldwell listened to the wireless reports and read the carefully worded newspaper reports with mixed emotions. The end of the war would bring back his beloved daughters to a more normal way of life, but not his son.

Nothing could bring Baz home, and, in a way, he grieved for Baz more now than when they had first had the news of his death. It was an irrational feeling, but it was the thought of the world being at peace once more that would really pinpoint all those who would never come home again. There would be thousands and thousands of them, no matter how the government tried to hush up the actual figures. You couldn't have a war without casualties on both sides, and his own wife Mary had known widowhood at a very young age.

She watched the changing emotions on his face now, as he listened to the latest broadcast, the disembodied voice intoning the latest victory, and how our brave boys were making such inroads into the German defences. She could read his feelings so well, even if his sister Rose, still busy with her endless knitting, seemed quite unaware of it. She reached out and squeezed his hand.

"It's the best of news, my dear," she said softly. "It had to come, and it's been a long time coming, but we must just put our trust in God that it will all be over soon now."

"Amen to that," Rose put in, as always attuned to the conversation, even while appearing to be oblivious to it.

"Oh well, you would say that, wouldn't you, Rose?" Quentin said abruptly. "You and that vicar of yours make a good pair, but no amount of praying's done anything to stop this war so far, has it? Anyway, I've heard enough for one night, and it's my turn for the hot water tonight, so I'm going to have a bath if none of you object."

He stomped off upstairs, leaving the women looking after him in astonishment. Normally, he listened avidly to every bit of news, and then gave his own opinionated version of it.

"Well," said Rose, affronted. "There was no call to bring Freddie into this."

"He's worried," Mary said. "Everyone's getting so elated about the invasion, but he thinks of Immy and Daisy all the time, and their young men too. And I'm sure he didn't mean to be unkind about your vicar, Rose."

"Why do you both keep calling him *my* vicar? He's not my vicar. He's everybody's vicar!"

Mary decided it was time to speak up, even if she risked Rose's waspish reaction. "That's as may be, but anyone can see he has a very soft spot for you, Rose, and you can't tell me that after all this time, you don't feel a fondness for him too."

"A fondness, perhaps, but that's all it is."

"Why does that have to be all it is? Tell me to mind my own business if you like, but haven't you ever thought about getting married again, Rose?"

"Certainly not," Rose said shortly. "And I don't want to discuss it."

She couldn't forget it, however. It wasn't the first time Mary had hinted at the fondness between herself and

Freddie Penfold, and even that little minx Vanessa had teased her about it from time to time. She was perfectly willing to admit that it existed. Freddie was her very good friend, but as for anything more…as for the intimacies of marriage…those belonged to her and Bert, and nobody else.

Freddie, of course, didn't see it that way. He was a patient man, and his patience would probably last for ever, if need be, but he wasn't sure that Rose Painter was the type of woman who would be satisfied with a patient man. He already knew that her relationship with her late husband had been a volatile one, and he knew that she wasn't a docile woman. That was what he liked about her. No, liking was far too insipid a word. It was what he loved about her. He knew too, that she cared fiercely for her brood of substitute children. If he had to, he would be more than willing to take on the entire bunch of them, even the precocious Vanessa. But still he held back from asking the question that burned brightly in his parochial brain. He wanted her to marry him, but he could be as proud as she was stubborn, and he only intended to ask her once. If her answer wasn't the one he wanted, he wasn't sure he could go through the ritual again.

Mary sought out her husband once he was out of his bath and in their bedroom, having swilled down the regulatory five inches of bath water, and smelling faintly of Wright's coal tar soap.

"What's wrong, Quentin?" she asked quietly.

"What's wrong is that in all this excitement over the D-Day landings, which I don't deny, of course," he admitted as she opened her mouth indignantly, "is that everyone seems to have forgotten the threat of this new weapon Hitler's been developing for months now. And I've been talking—" He stopped abruptly, as if he had already said too much but it was too late.

"Talking to somebody who knows something?" Mary said at once. "Well, whatever it is, I doubt that any new enemy weapon will get this far, will it?"

"Why not? Distance didn't stop him bombing Bristol nearly out of creation, did it, woman? And this new thing…"

Mary sat down on the end of the bed as he brushed his hair. Still thick, despite the silvery threads running through it, she thought approvingly. Then, seeing the frown between his eyes, she returned to the apparent seriousness of this conversation.

"Whatever this new thing, as you call it, is supposed to be, you can either tell me something about it, or forget it and stop worrying me, Quentin."

"I'm sorry, my dear," he said, instantly contrite. "I didn't mean to alarm you, but you must have seen for yourself that all the barrage balloons have been removed from the coast recently. And everywhere else along the Somerset coastline too," he added.

"Well, that's good news, isn't it? It means the author-ities consider we're no longer in danger in this part of the world. Jerry will be too busy fighting off our victorious troops in France!"

"No, it's not good news, Mary. The barrage balloons have all been sent to the south coast to try to ward off this new missile that's been developed. It's a pilotless thing, by all accounts, and it's simply directed towards its target and explodes. Unless it's intercepted, there's not a bloody thing that can be done to stop it."

He didn't often use expletives, which told Mary that he was taking this new threat very seriously indeed, but she still couldn't quite believe in the power of a pilotless missile that could be directed towards a target and then explode. There had been rumours of such things in the past, but few people had given it credence. The fact that Quentin was doing so now made her suddenly afraid.

"So where do you think they'll be sending these things?"

"Where else? London, of course, and the south-coast ports. But I'd rather you didn't say any of this to the others. There'll be time enough to alarm them when it happens."

"Don't you mean *if* it happens?"

"No, love. I mean when," he said, with a heavy sigh.

—

James Church would have given much to have told Imogen he was going to be in the thick of the D-Day operations, but she would have guessed it anyway – he was certain of that. Even if her Captain Beckett hadn't given her pretty heavy hints, she was intelligent enough to know that his recent silence could mean only one thing.

Before dawn on the 6th of June, his tank rumbled off the carrier into the shallows of the Normandy beachhead amid heavy fire from the German defences. His gunner shouted to him that it was a bloody amazing sight to see the sky filled with parachutists being dropped from planes overhead, although some of the poor buggers never made it, and were shot down and left hanging from their 'chutes like puppets as they plunged to the ground or straight into the sea. But you didn't have time to spare to ponder on their fate. You had to keep moving and pray to the Almighty that you weren't going to be the next target for an enemy shell.

There were other poor devils, the commandos who were first ashore, wading neck-deep with their weapons held above their heads, and who risked being picked off one by one by the crossfire from German pillboxes. The bombardment was deafening. Inside the tank it was always hellishly noisy, stifling and claustrophobic, but none of them had time to think about that on this day of days. The objective was to get ashore and establish themselves, and despite being met by intense opposition, the ruse that had gone before them held.

Hitler had been expecting the invasion to occur much farther north, and the bulk of his troops were waiting there. The enemy was taken completely by surprise, and although they attempted to demolish certain key bridges before the Allies could seize them, their efforts were foiled by the sheer volume of Allied forces. Squadrons of RAF bombers continued to protect the naval operations and land forces, as well as attacking gun emplacements and road communications. Enemy torpedo boats were driven off, one of them being sunk and another one severely damaged.

James, along with his fellow tank crew and every other serving man who wasn't temporarily deafened by the battering of those momentous days, raised a cheer when they heard that the Germans were falling back from Rome. Italy and France were slowly and surely being won over by the Allies.

–

"It'll soon be over now, you'll see," Naomi told her friend Daisy a few days later.

By then, casualties were being received at many of the hospitals along the south coast, and theirs was no exception. Daisy was filled with apprehension every time a new intake was brought in by ambulance, with horrific tales to tell of the blasting the invasion army had received.

"I know it's being hailed as a victory, but it sounds more like going into hell to me," she said, white-faced, as one young infantry soldier who'd taken a direct hit in the stomach was graphically relating his own story.

"You don't think like that when you're in the thick of it, nursie," he said in a laboured voice, speaking louder than he realised, being still partially deafened. "It's what you join up for, see – to see the world, and do your bit for king and country. It's the adventure as much as anything."

"Oh yes, and was this all part of the adventure?" she said, indicating the gaping wound that she was attempting to staunch, but no amount of pressure or antiseptic dressing seemed able to stop it, and it was starting to alarm her.

"It's a trophy, see?" he said proudly. "My old man got something like this in the last lot, so now I'll have something to show him too, won't I?"

"I think I'd better get the doctor to take a look at you, Tom," she said quickly as the wound suddenly gushed. It went very deep. Daisy knew that frothing, bright-red blood indicated a burst artery, and she wasn't equipped to deal with it.

"Don't leave me, nursie," he said with an attempt at his normal cheek.

"I'll just be a minute," Daisy gasped, and almost flew across the ward floor to where the duty doctor was attending someone else.

"Doctor, can you come to see Private Slater? He's losing a great deal of blood, and it's urgent—"

"They're all urgent, nurse. Keep up the pressure on that wound, and I'll be there as soon as I can."

Daisy turned back without a word, feeling an innate rage at his apparent lack of caring, even though she knew in her heart that it wasn't that. It was just that there was so much work, so many patients – an endless procession of broken young men who had all gone to war for king and country, many of whom were never going to see their homes and families again.

Tom Slater was one of them. By the time she reached his bed again, she could see the life draining out of him. The wound continued to bubble, and the bedding was covered with a red stain now. There was nothing she could do to stop it. His face was as white as the sheets had once been, his lips blue, his eyes vacant and almost sightless now.

"Looks like my number's up then, don't it, nursie?" he managed to wheeze as she continued to press the heavy dressing against his wound, knowing it was hopeless, and trying desperately to resist the urge to sob.

"Never say die, soldier," she mumbled.

He gave her the ghost of a smile. "Not until the last breath, eh?" he whispered, and the next moment his head lolled to one side and he was gone.

Daisy caught her breath in one huge, gasping sob. She had nursed him for more than twenty-four hours now, been with him almost day and night, and known him as intimately as she had ever known anyone, because that's what happened when you nursed someone, listening to all their secrets, helping with their private moments, their naked fears. It was like losing a little part of herself every time one of them died, knowing she hadn't been able to help. She had been as impotent as that poor useless thing between his legs that had needed help even to pass water because of all the drugs that had been pumped into him to stop the pain.

"Nurse!" she heard a sharp voice say. "You're wanted elsewhere."

She became aware of the ward sister dealing with Private Slater now, and two orderlies were rushing to his side at her command, to wheel him out on the bed and take it to the morgue, tidying him and preparing him for the ritual of laying-out, plugging all the orifices, as they called it, including that ghastly shell wound, and making him sweet for whoever might come to claim him.

Then the bed would be scrubbed with disinfectant, and clean sheets and bedding would be put on it, before it was wheeled back into the ward for the next poor devil to take Tom Slater's place.

"I've been told to fetch you and give you a cup of tea, Daisy," she heard Naomi's anxious voice say beside her as she stood transfixed.

"I have to continue with my shift," she gasped.

"No, you don't. Sister said you're to take half an hour off, so do as you're told, or you'll end up in one of the beds yourself."

She let herself be guided by Naomi, feeling as if her head was floating somewhere above her. This wasn't what she had gone into nursing for, she thought furiously, as if she was in some kind of Greek melodrama. This wasn't the gentle kind of nursing that went on in a country hospital, with old ladies coming in with varicose veins, or grand-fathers with a touch of angina, or children with sprained ankles that could be put right with a tight bandage and an aspirin. This was raw, savage brutality, and she didn't know how to bear it.

"Stick your head down between your knees," Naomi told her, pushing her into a chair, and putting the words into action as she shoved Daisy's head down low. "I don't want you throwing up all over me or passing out on me. What kind of a nurse are you, for God's sake?"

Daisy recognised the bullying note in her voice for what it was and gave the weakest smile. "A pretty feeble one right now, if you must know."

"That will pass, and by the way, Private Slater thought you were an angel."

"Don't be daft. And anyway, he's with the real ones now, isn't he?"

With that, she burst into searing, agonising tears, and Naomi simply sat and held her until the storm passed.

Chapter Twelve

Vanessa Caldwell-Brown wasn't too concerned about what was happening in France. She was fed up with listening to the news broadcasts. It seemed as if that was all anybody talked about these days, and the whole bleedin' country was getting worked up over it. Besides, she was up to her eyes in these perishing school certificate exams now, and it was all a waste of time. She was good at a couple of subjects but rubbish at the rest, and if you didn't get enough passes, you failed the whole lot.

Bleedin' waste of time, in her opinion, especially as she'd now wheedled round the whole lot of them to let her work with Daddy Quent in his new shop. Weekends, she was already helping him strip the walls of the old wallpaper and getting handy with a paintbrush.

She went home on her bicycle on that sunny June afternoon, leaving him and Mary still admiring their handiwork, and then frowned as she saw the old car belonging to one of the town-hall busybodies outside the house. She knew it well enough. Every time there had been something to do with one or other of the evacuees, the rusting old Morris had come puffing up the hill, on its last legs – just like the old biddies inside it, she added privately to herself.

The boys were nowhere to be seen, and she remembered they had gone over to the Luckwell farm to play with the Luckwell vaccies. There was only Aunt Rose inside with one of the town-hall ladies, and both were looking po-faced. Nessa sighed, wondering what she had done now. She racked her brains, but there was nothing that she could think of, unless one of the little brats had been telling tales about her chatting to the Yanks. Most of them had gone now, anyway.

"Come and sit down, Vanessa," Rose said at once. "You remember Mrs Harker, don't you? She's got some bad news for you, I'm afraid."

"She ain't sending me back, is she?" Nessa said in alarm, feeling her heart jump sickly. "You know I want to stay here with you now!"

She wouldn't go so far as to say they were all the family she'd got now – and the best family she'd ever had, if the truth were known. She couldn't be so soppy as to say such things out loud, especially with that hawk-eyed Mrs Harker looking down her thin nose at her.

"It's nothing like that, dear," the woman said, clearing her throat. "But actually, I do think you'll want to go back to London for a brief visit when you hear what I have to tell you."

She didn't *actually* ever want to go back there again, Nessa thought, mimicking her voice in her head. The thought took her by surprise, but it was true. She was happy here now, and she wanted to stay for ever.

"What is it then?"

Mrs Harker shuffled some papers in her lap. "We've had some correspondence sent to us regarding your grand-mother."

"My *what*? I ain't got no grandmother. She died years ago."

"Well, not according to this report, dear. She's died in a London hospital, and your name was the only one she mentioned in her ramblings. She was quite senile, and never made much sense, which is why it's taken the authorities a while to trace you. She left a few bits and pieces, and they all belong to you now, but you have to sign for them, and to assure them that you are the legal granddaughter of Mrs Flossie Gibbons. That was your grandmother's name, I take it?"

"I s'pose so," Nessa muttered, suddenly white-faced. "I only ever knew her as Gran, though some of her mates called her Flossie, so I s'pose it's her. But I ain't seen her for years, and she always hated me anyway. She was always mean to me mum, saying she was no better than she should be, and that I'd prob'ly go the same way. She always seemed ancient then, and she prob'ly lost her marbles years ago, so why would she want to leave me anything?"

Mrs Harker cleared her throat. "It's just that the hospital need to dispose of her belongings and they've now handed them over to the almoner..."

"What you mean is, she didn't leave anything to me at all. They just want to clear things up, all nice and tidy!"

Rose intervened. "I'm sure everyone means it for the best, Nessa."

"Well, I don't want nothing from her, and I ain't going to London to collect it, anyway! They can burn it, for all I care."

She flounced out of the room, her eyes suddenly stinging, her lovely day spoiled. She flung herself down on her bed, but flashes of memory kept intruding. Her mother, dressed like a tart – but, to a six-year-old, looking like a princess – out for an evening's drinking with whatever bloke took her fancy; and Flossie, Gran Flossie, tut–tutting, and saying she'd take the kid home with her for the night, which she often did, tucking her up on a put-you-up bed that stank of cigarette smoke in her miserable one-up, one-down mews place behind the Dog and Whistle pub, reeking of ale, with drunken sailors in and out of the place half the night. Nessa shuddered. No wonder she had thought Aunt Rose's house was a palace, even if she'd never appreciated it at first. Gran had been a good enough soul, in her rough-and-tumble way, though never one to show affection, and Nessa had been more likely to get a cuff around the ears than a kind word.

She was still smouldering over the memories she hadn't wanted to remember, but couldn't quite forget, when Rose came into her bedroom.

"Are we going to talk about this?" she said mildly.

"Nothing to talk about," Nessa said, her voice muffled as she lay face down on her bed.

"Of course there is. We have to think about sending you to London to collect the things that belonged to your grandmother."

She sat up jerkily, her eyes filled with fright. "I told you, I ain't going. She don't mean anything to me!" she shouted. "I don't want to go back there ever again, and you can't make me!"

"You didn't feel like that when you ran away from here, some years ago, as I remember," Rose said, still determined to stay calm, but not unaware of the misery in the girl's eyes.

"I didn't know you prop'ly then, did I? I didn't know which side of me bread was buttered – or margarined," she added with an attempt at humour. Her throat filled. "Don't make me go, Aunt Rose," she muttered.

Rose came to the bed and sat down beside her. "I won't make you go, my love, but I think you owe it to your grandmother to do this. There may be little mementoes she would have wanted you to have."

"There won't be. She never had nothing. None of us did."

She looked down at her hands, ashamed of what she was saying, ashamed of what she remembered about those times, and knowing that it was only since being here, with this family, that the comparison had become so acute. The Caldwells and the Painters were ordinary people, but her own had been so much farther down the social scale that she didn't even want to acknowledge it, and that made her feel bad too. There was the awful feeling inside her that if she once went back, she would be drawn back to that life.

They would make her stay, because that was where she belonged. She'd be common Nessa Brown again, living off her wits like the rest of the gutter-rats, not the grandly self-styled Vanessa Caldwell-Brown that she had become.

"You don't think I was suggesting you went to London alone, do you?" Rose said calmly. "Naturally, as your guardian, I would go with you."

After a startled moment, Nessa's eyes glittered, and she flung her arms around Rose, stammering out words of gratitude, before Rose managed to extricate herself.

"My goodness, you'll have me crying in a minute, and that would ruin my image for ever, wouldn't it?" she said with a crooked smile, more affected than she had believed possible by the girl's reaction. She had never really thought of Vanessa as a daughter, but right now she knew she would defend her rights as fiercely as if she was. "Let's take another look at the papers Mrs Harker left behind, and, when my brother gets home, we'll ask him to see about making arrangements for us."

"And we'll definitely be coming home again?" Nessa persisted.

"Of course we will. Where else would we go?"

–

Two days later they stepped off the train at Paddington, Vanessa nervous and highly strung, and Rose trying to hide her own apprehension at never having been to the city before. She and Bert had made a few trips to Cornwall with the family when her brother's children were all young. It all seemed so ludicrous and provincial, seeing how far the girls had travelled now: Immy driving her Captain Beckett all over the country; Elsie living in Yorkshire in what Rose always considered a pretty barren and alien part of the world, but one that Elsie assured her was just rugged and beautiful; and Daisy, going Lord knows where and doing Lord knows what, even to being part of the Dunkirk evacuation. And Baz, sweet young Baz, wanting so badly to be a sailor and paying for it with his life.

"Come on, Aunt Rose, we can't just stand here like ninnies. Should we get a cab to the hospital, do you think?" she heard Nessa say now.

Worldly Vanessa, who had been up and down the country a number of times herself, but who looked less than sure of herself right now.

"A cab, yes, I suppose we had better," she said vaguely. It would most likely be an extravagance, but since neither of them had any idea about buses or trams either, it seemed the only sensible thing to do.

They went to the top of the incline to the main road, where the traffic was congested and very loud, and she had never felt such a country hick as she did right then, with Vanessa standing out in the road and waving her arms like windmills for one of the black taxicabs to stop.

"Where to, ducks?" the driver said as it slewed to a halt.

Rose gave him the name of the hospital, and they fell inside the cab with their small overnight bags. They weren't intending to stay any longer than necessary, and as the taxi took them through the bombed-out streets, they both became silent, seeing the devastation all around them.

"First time in London, gels?" the driver said, eyeing them through his rear-view mirror.

"Nah, I used to live here," Nessa said importantly, "but my auntie's never been 'ere before."

"That so? Bit of a shocker to come visiting in wartime, ain't it?"

"We had it bad in Bristol too," Rose said, as if she had to defend herself, and wishing he'd keep his eyes on the road.

"I thought that was a West Country accent. My old lady sent my two girls to Devon for the duration. They ain't coming back until it's all over, which won't be long now by all accounts, will it?"

"So they say," Rose said.

She realised Nessa wasn't saying much now, shrinking back in her seat and taking note of the destruction in the streets they were passing through. She always said she'd lived south of the river, wherever that was, but London was London, and it had once meant a lot to her.

The hospital wasn't too far from the railway station, and once they had paid their fare, they walked silently through the gates and into the reception area, asking for the almoner. They were asked to sit and wait, and the antiseptic smells of the hospital began to permeate their senses and overwhelm them.

"I don't like it here," Nessa hissed. "Gawd only knows how Daisy can work in these places, among sick people and all the blood and stuff."

"She does it because she likes helping people," Rose told her. "And you're either born to be a nurse or you're not. We're not all made the same way, love."

"Thank Gawd. How long are they going to keep us waiting, anyway? I need a pee, and I knew we should have gone to the boarding house first."

She knew Rose disapproved of such words, but her nerves were so jerky and so on edge that she couldn't be bothered to tidy up her speech. Who cared, anyway? Who really bleedin' well cared anything about her?

She felt Rose's hand close over hers as they fidgeted in her lap.

"I'm sure it won't be long now, Nessa, and then we'll find the boarding house and ask the landlady to make us a nice cup of tea."

"Then we can go home tomorrow," Nessa stated, daring her to say otherwise.

A woman in a smart suit came towards them before Rose could say anything, a sheaf of papers in her hands.

"Are you Miss Vanessa Brown?" she asked, at which Nessa nodded dumbly. "I was told on the telephone that you would be accompanied by your guardian."

"Mrs Rose Painter, that's right," Rose said evenly.

"Follow me, please," the almoner said, and led them to a small office away from the business part of the hospital, where Nessa breathed a tiny sigh of relief.

They sat down on the other side of the desk from the almoner and waited.

"Your grandmother, Mrs Flossie Gibbons, had very few possessions, Miss Brown," she said. "I'm sorry we had to bring you all the way from Somerset, but although she didn't leave a will, she did indicate that whatever goods and chattels she had were to be passed on to you, and hospital protocol requires that you sign for it personally to keep our records straight."

At her so-correct words, half of which she didn't understand anyway, Nessa felt a wild urge to laugh. Bleedin' stuff and nonsense. All this fuss over a few bits and bobs that would probably amount to nothing.

The almoner handed her a cardboard box tied with string, no bigger than a box containing a gas mask.

"Please inspect the contents briefly, Miss Brown, though you will probably prefer to mull over them in private. We usually find that's the case with objects left by a dear relative."

Nessa felt Rose's foot kick hers, just as if she expected a hoot of laughter from her at the thought that bleedin' Gran Flossie had been a dear relative, instead of an old hag who smoked too much and drank too much and had only taken her in out of a sense of duty, not love. But she was forced to glance inside the box. Since she had no idea of anything her gran had once possessed and had no intention of telling this stiff-necked woman so, she merely nodded her assent.

"It looks all right to me, so let's get on wiv it," she muttered.

"Then if you would sign the necessary papers to say you have claimed the goods and chattels of Mrs Flossie

Gibbons, that concludes our business," the almoner said, retying the box swiftly.

Once out of the hospital, Nessa took huge gulps of air. London was never the best of places for breathing clean air, but right now anything was better than that awful place where people got ill and died and left behind their rubbish.

"So that's that," Rose said briskly. "Let's find another cab and give the driver the address of the boarding house, and then we can relax for a while."

She could see that the girl was obviously unsettled by the whole affair, and she couldn't blame her. Finding an ancient relative still alive – or one who had been until recently – and having to come here for this miserable box of junk, was something she wouldn't have wanted, either.

By the time they reached the boarding house, Nessa wasn't saying anything at all, and sat hunched up in the corner of the taxicab. The small box was on her lap like a reproach, and Rose guessed the last thing she wanted to do was to open it again. So the sooner she did so, the better.

They were given a room with two narrow beds in it, the windows heavily criss-crossed with tape, and a prominent notice telling the residents to pull the blackout curtains before putting on any lights. The landlady promised them a pot of tea in half an hour when they had settled in. So now there was nothing left to do but to untie the string around the cardboard box and take a proper look inside.

"Do you want me to open it for you, Nessa?"

"I feel more like dumping it."

"You can't do that. Have you realised that this is all that's left of your family? You owe it to your grandmother to see what she's left you" – though Rose was as sure as Nessa that it would be only a few pathetic bits and pieces.

"You do it then," the girl said rudely. "I told you before: I've got to find the lavvy before I pee myself."

Rose knew she was trying to provoke a response, but as she started to untie the string on the box without comment, Vanessa fled down the passage to find the communal bathroom.

When she came back, the contents of the box were laid out on her bed.

"Gawd Almighty," she whispered.

She had only taken a token look inside it at the hospital, not really seeing anything. There were two small photographs in battered frames. One was of a smiling woman dressed rather flashily, with a baby in her arms. The other was of a small girl of about six years old, sitting on an older woman's lap.

"Is it you?" Rose asked.

Vanessa nodded, and her voice was choked. "It's me mum in that one, and I s'pose the baby's me, and that's me and Gran. I don't remember it. I never thought we had money for taking pictures."

She looked at the rest of the items. There was a filigree brooch with a cheap red stone in the centre, and a pair of matching earrings.

"These were me mum's," she muttered. "Gran always said she looked like a tart in them, but me mum looked lovely in red."

She dropped them again and picked up the tattered story book that had her name on the flyleaf. It was written in childish handwriting that was obviously Vanessa's. It said: "Vanessa Brown, aged six. Her reading book."

Apart from that, there were a couple of scarves and a pair of fingerless grey woollen mittens. Seeing them, Nessa caught her breath.

"I think Gran used to wear these when she worked on a stall down the market, so she could handle the pennies prop'ly. I'd forgotten she did that." She looked at Rose with tears flooding her eyes now. "Isn't that awful? I'd forgotten her, but I s'pose she must have thought about me a bit to have kept all this stuff."

Rose put her arms around her, feeling the tension in her slender body, and sensing the need to grieve that hadn't yet come. "I think she thought about you more than you knew, my love. A family never forgets, really, and perhaps she just wanted to remind you that she loved you, even if she could never find a way to show it. Some people can't, Nessa."

"I know," she said in a brittle voice. "But I don't want to think about it now. I'd rather have me cup of tea, so I'm stuffing this lot back in the box for now."

But in the darkness of night, Rose was well aware of the muffled sobbing from the other bed in the stark little room and knew that they were healing sobs. You had to grieve before you could move on. Eventually it was something everybody came to realise. Freddie always made a point of telling it to his parishioners whenever they had suffered a bereavement, and it was both a comfort and a necessary rite of passage.

In the early hours of the morning they were woken abruptly by the sounds of air-raid sirens and of aircraft overhead. They weren't the sounds they were used to – certainly not RAF planes – and for a moment Rose's blood froze. Moments later the sounds had stopped, and then there was an almighty explosion somewhere close, rocking the house, and making Vanessa scream with fright.

Next minute they heard a rapid knocking on their door and on every other door in the house as the landlady's husband shouted to their guests to get down to the shelter at the end of the street right away. Rose and Vanessa threw on their coats over their nightgowns and rushed out of the room to join the rest of the boarding-house guests assembling below.

"Come on, you women, down the street to the shelter," someone yelled at them, pushing them unceremoniously out of the house.

Moments later they were bundled inside the shelter, along with several dozen others, all shivering in the cold of early morning. Some were praying loudly, and Vanessa groaned, hoping Rose wouldn't do the same. It was all right praying inside your head, and she was quite prepared to do a bit of that, since God would hear it just the same as if you were doing it out loud.

"What's happening?" she heard Rose say shakily as another droning aircraft suddenly seemed to stop in mid-air, followed by another ear-splitting explosion.

"You been living on another planet, missus?" one of the women said. "Don't you know the sound of doodle-bugs when you hear 'em?"

"We live in Somerset," Nessa said, trying to sound important. "What the bleedin' 'ell are doodlebugs when they're at 'ome?"

The woman scowled. "All softies down there, ain't they? Well, for your edification, my duck, doodlebugs is what we calls them new weapons of Adolf's, though some call 'em buzz-bombs too, because of the noise they make. The papers are calling 'em VI bombs, but it's all the same in the long run. The planes ain't even got a pilot in 'em, so only Gawd or the devil knows how the bleedin' 'ell they can fly, but they'll still kill you if they've got your number on 'em. As long as you can still hear 'em, though, you're safe, see? It's when they stop that you know they're coming down, and you never know who's going to get it next."

"That's what Daddy Quent was talking about," Vanessa stuttered to Rose. "He wasn't so daft then, was he?"

"He never is," Rose said through equally dry lips.

She had to admit that she was more scared than she had been in her life before, but she was determined not to let Nessa know it. The truth was, she had never been in a situation like this before. She had never had bombs falling all around her, the way the family had in Bristol. She hadn't known what it was like to have your eardrums feeling as if they were about to burst, nor to have to run through the street to the safety of the shelter with the scream of fire engines rushing past them, and the sight of flames rising high in a nearby street.

"Don't worry, Aunt Rose," she heard Vanessa whisper, her small hand clutching hers. "I'll protect yer. We're a fam'ly, ain't we?"

"Of course we are," Rose said, squeezing her hand hard, and thinking it quite the most surprising thing she had expected to hear.

How long they were all huddled in the evil-smelling shelter she couldn't have said. The knowledgeable ones guessed how far away each bomb blast was coming from, while the rest stayed silent, or kept up their interminable praying. The time passed, interspersed with the drone of the doodlebugs, and then that unnerving silence until the shelter shook so hard it was a wonder it didn't come crashing down on them but evidently it wasn't their number that was up just yet.

"Don't worry, missus," one and another of the Londoners would say. "You'll soon get used to it when you've been here a while."

Oh no, she wouldn't! She didn't intend to get used to it, Rose thought fervently, with a burst of her old spirit. The minute they could get out of here, she and Vanessa were getting on a train for Bristol.

No wonder the parents up here had rushed to send their little kids to the country for safety the minute war broke out, if this was a daily dose of what they'd had to live with all these years. She felt more compassion for them now than she had ever done.

The onslaught went on for several hours before the all-clear finally sounded, and they emerged into a grey dawn, the pearly morning light clouded by a choking pall over everything. Buildings still smoked and occasionally burst into flames as gas pipes ignited. The whole area was teeming with people now: Civil Defence workers, firemen, ordinary people trying desperately to clear the rubble in search of relatives.

"We were lucky," Rose heard the landlady bawl in her ear above the din. "The house is still standing, so if yer want to come back indoors, I'll get started wiv a fry-up now that Jerry's done wiv us."

"Thank you," Rose said jerkily. "And then we'll settle our bill and see about finding a train back to Bristol."

"You ain't staying wiv us for another night of fun then?" the woman said with a mocking grin.

"No, thank you," Rose said grimly. "We've done what we came for and we just need to get home."

That wasn't as easy as it sounded, and they had to wait several hours at Paddington before there was a train to take them back. When it finally drew into Temple Meads station at Bristol, there was another frustrating wait for a local train to take them home to Weston. Rose had managed to telephone Quentin from Temple Meads and he was waiting for them when they arrived, so they could fall into the old family car, totally exhausted.

"How did it go?" Quentin asked cautiously, seeing Nessa's white face.

"Well enough, but we'll tell you all about that later," Rose said, with a warning look. "As soon as we get home, we both need a bath and a hot drink and then bed."

"We were in the middle of a doodlebug raid, Daddy Quent," Nessa said suddenly. "That'll be something to tell the girls at school, won't it?"

"It certainly will," he said, seeing how swiftly she was seeing it all as an adventure, even if that hadn't been the object of the trip to London.

That night, when Rose checked on her before going to bed herself, she saw that the two battered photographs had pride of place on Vanessa's dressing table. One of her gran's old scarves was around her neck.

Chapter Thirteen

Vanessa's fright over the doodlebugs soon subsided, and the trip to London soon emerged as a huge adventure, to be told with ghoulish relish to Teddy and Harry.

"There were dead bodies flying about everywhere," she told the boys as they listened, goggle-eyed, to her tales of aircraft without pilots shooting out of the sky in broad daylight, aimed directly at people's houses, with no chance of anybody getting out of the way, and being blown into thousands of pieces.

"How did they know which houses to bomb?" Teddy asked practically.

"They didn't, you dope. They just aimed anywhere, knowing they'd be sure to hit somebody. It might even happen here," she added.

"I don't want to see dead bodies flying through the air," Harry began to wail. "That's what happened to my mum and dad."

"Oh, stop whining, I was only joking. Of course it won't happen here!" Nessa said, realising she had gone too far, and that they could be in danger of a wet bed tonight if she didn't tone it down a bit. "And I didn't really see any dead bodies flying about. It was only a lot of old dumps that were blown up. Old Jerry can't even aim straight. Everybody knows that."

"Why'd you say it then?" Teddy asked, prepared to argue after enjoying the thought of seeing dead bodies flying through the air, and planning his own tales for his equally ghoulish school friends.

"I expect I've been seeing too many news flicks lately," she told him. "Let's forget it, and I'll have a game of snap with you both." If she didn't shut them up soon, there'd be hell to pay when Aunt Rose came home from seeing her vicar.

By now, Nessa was thinking of her gran in a mellower light. She had deliberately shut her out of her mind for years now, but she had to admit that there had been times when she was glad to go and sleep in her miserable hovel, in preference to hanging around for her mum to come home from the pub with some new chap she didn't like. It was why she had decided to keep the two photographs, if only to remind her of how much better off she was now.

She accepted that too. Aunt Rose was a brick, and if only she would marry her vicar, maybe they could all go and live in the vicarage, which was plenty big enough for three, and she didn't mind the vicar so much now. Daddy Quent and Aunt Mary could carry on living here with the boys, and Daisy could come back whenever she wanted to. It was all neatly worked out in Nessa's scheming little mind – if only Aunt Rose would stop keeping the vicar hanging about.

–

Daisy was thinking less and less about coming home, and more about the endless numbers of wounded being sent home from France – those that were capable of being sent anywhere. Some were in French hospitals, and some would never come home again. It was the legacy of war. She'd had a brief phone call from Immy, telling her that she was about to go overseas, but to say nothing to the rest of the family until she could give them a bit more information.

"She didn't say where she was going," Daisy told Naomi, "but it's obvious it's France, isn't it? And I wish she wasn't. I wish none of us was involved in this blasted war at all."

"It's a bit late to say that, isn't it?" Naomi said mildly. "You're an army nurse, and I'd half-expected you to be clamouring to go there yourself. Whatever happened to your Dunkirk spirit, anyway?"

"It disappeared, along with every other ambition I ever had."

"Good God, Daisy, stop talking like a geriatric. You're doing what you wanted to do, aren't you? Nursing, I mean. It's your vocation, isn't it?"

Daisy looked at her irritably. "You never knew me before I was a nurse, did you? – When I was just the youngest of the three Caldwell girls, the one least likely to make up her mind to anything! Everyone called me a scatterbrain then, because I changed my mind so often. One minute I was going to go on the stage like my mother, the next minute I was going to be a nurse. I chopped and changed from day to day until they all got fed up with me, and nobody took me seriously."

She paused for breath, and Naomi laughed, not quite sure how to take this sudden intense mood. Daisy used to be such *fun*.

"Well, nobody could say that about you now, darling. You're a born nurse."

"That's just it," Daisy snapped. "I don't think I am, and it's a pretty daft thing to say about anybody, anyway. Nobody's a *born* nurse. Nobody knows what they're going to be good at when they're no more than a squalling infant."

"Talking about squalling infants—" Naomi tried to change the conversation before it developed into a full-scale argument that neither of them could win – "how are those two lovely nieces of yours? The ones in Yorkshire, I mean. Have you heard from your sister lately?"

"Oh, Elsie's all right. She did the right thing, marrying her chap at the very beginning of the war and then getting pregnant straightaway. Even Joe did it right, getting wounded so he had to be discharged, and they could live cosily ever after in that draughty old farmhouse! Not that he meant to get wounded, of course."

Naomi looked at her in alarm now. It was so un-Daisy-like to criticise either of her sisters, whom she obviously adored.

"You don't mean any of that," she said flatly.

After a moment, Daisy's face crumpled. "Oh, of course I don't, and it was beastly of me to say any of it. I think Elsie was very brave to marry Joe the way she did, and he's a hero, and the babies are lovely, and I'm a pig."

She caught the look in Naomi's eyes and started to smile; within seconds the mood had vanished, and they were both laughing and hugging one another. But it was an indication of how brittle Daisy was feeling lately, and they both knew it was all because of anxiety over Glenn.

Some of the new patients were airmen who had been involved in D-Day and afterwards, and many of them had suffered horrific burns to their faces as well as every other part of their bodies. The hospital had opened a special burns unit to deal with these cases, and the nurses all had to take their turn. They were the worst times for Daisy, knowing that any of those young men might have been Glenn.

She couldn't rid herself of the fear that she was never going to see him again. Her vivid imagination took her to places she never wanted to go, anticipating the moments when she would hear the worst news of all – anticipating how she was going to deal with it. Naomi kept telling her it was due to the extra hours they were all having to work, but Daisy knew in her heart that it was more than that. It was a sixth sense that was stronger than anything she had ever known.

So when there was a phone call for her late one evening, she went to answer it with a sick dread, trying to prepare herself for bad news, and then stared dumbly at the wall in front of her as she heard the voice at the other end.

"Are you still there, honey? It's me, turning up like the bad penny at last."

She still couldn't speak. Her throat felt as if it had closed up, and then she heard the soft, sexy laugh she knew so well.

"Come on, Daisy, say something, for pity's sake! This isn't some heavy breather, you know. It really is me!"

"*Glenn!*" She burst out at last. "Oh God, I thought…I've been thinking…" She smothered a sob, and then rage took over.

How dared he not get in touch with her before this! D-Day was two weeks ago now, and surely there could have been some message!

"Where the hell have you been all this time?" she yelled into the phone. "Do you know how worried I've been, not hearing a word from you?"

"Hey, slow down, honey," he broke in with a laugh. "I'm sorry, but it couldn't be helped. There was nothing I could do. As soon as one sortie ended, we were off again. It's been pure hell. But marvellous too," he couldn't resist, adding.

"*Marvellous!*" she spluttered. "Is that what you call it?"

"Well, you do if you're a pilot, darling, but hey, I didn't mean to get you all steamed up like this. I wanted to tell you I've got a few hours off tomorrow, and if you can manage it, we can meet. I can get over to the hospital about two o'clock and we can go for a drive somewhere. What do you say?"

Her animosity vanished as quickly as it had come. "I'll manage it if I have to twist the ward sister's arm," she said shakily. "Oh Glenn, I'm sorry for being so nasty just now…"

"Hey, no need for apologies, Daisy. We're all pretty strung-up these days, but let's forget it and enjoy the time we've got, okay?"

"Okay," he said, choked, trying to ignore the ominous sound of those words. He didn't mean it that way, but it was hard for her to see anything but gloom and doom these days. But not tomorrow. Tomorrow, she was going to see her beloved again, and her heart leapt with joy at the thought of it.

"I'll see you tomorrow then, Daisy," Glenn said softly.

"Yes, tomorrow," she breathed into the phone, and put the instrument back on its cradle as gently as if she caressed a lover.

She almost danced back to her room. Naomi was reading, but she looked up anxiously as Daisy came back to the room they shared.

"Well, I can see by the look on your face that something's cheered you up," she said thankfully. "Who was that on the phone then?"

"It was Glenn, and I'm seeing him tomorrow afternoon if I can get the time off. Correction. I *will* get the time off!"

"Of course you will. You've been doing so many extra hours lately, Sister wouldn't dare to refuse you, darling. So can we go to sleep now?"

"We can try," Daisy said with a laugh.

Sister was only too glad to relieve Daisy for the afternoon. Naomi hadn't been the only one to notice the dark shadows beneath her eyes lately, and seeing her young man again was the best tonic anyone could have. Daisy certainly thought so when she saw Glenn arrive in a borrowed car that afternoon.

It wasn't the done thing to fling herself into his arms, especially when she was pretty sure there would be interested eyes watching them. So she contented herself with squeezing his hand and sliding into the front seat of the car beside him, until he turned and looked at her, with all the love she had ever dreamed of in his eyes. He touched her cheek with one finger in lieu of a kiss.

"I'd almost forgotten how wonderful you look," he said softly. "I want to hug you here and now, but perhaps it would be better to wait until we're out of range of your hospital spies!"

Daisy laughed, feeling on top of the world at last. "What a thing to call them! But you're right. There will be plenty of people very curious and very keen to see my handsome Canadian, since I've talked of little else!"

"So let's forget them and get out of here where we can be alone."

Without waiting any longer he drove the car out of the hospital grounds, and within twenty minutes they had reached a quiet stretch of grassland bordered by trees. Once they were safely parked, Glenn took out a rug from the back seat of the car and they lay down on it on the warm grass in the shade of a small copse, with the sunlight dappling through the branches of the trees on that perfect June afternoon and all thoughts of war were a million miles away. He put his arms around Daisy and drew her close.

"Do you know how often I've dreamed of doing this, sweetheart?" he murmured against her cheek.

"Probably about as many times as I have," she whispered back. "And how many nights when I've dreaded that it might never happen again."

She wished she had never said the words, but she couldn't stop them. He eased back a little, looking deep into her eyes.

"You know I'll always come back. I did today, didn't I? Like the bad penny that always turns up, remember?"

"There's nothing bad about you, Glenn. You're just…just…" She was suddenly shy of saying all that was in her heart and, seeing it, he teased her, easing the tension out of the moment.

"Come on then. Out with it, woman. What am I? Mr Perfect? A knight in shining armour? Sir Galahad?"

"All of that. But most of all, just my Glenn."

His arms held her tight, and she could feel the erratic beat of his heart against her own. She wore a soft summer frock in her favourite powder blue today, and the filmy fabric hid nothing of his desire for her. She felt her own heart begin to throb more fiercely, knowing that this day could mean far more than one more outing together. If she wanted it. If she let it.

"I want you to belong to me more than anything in this world, Daisy," Glenn said, just as if he could read every passionate thought in her mind at that moment. "And I believe you feel the same. But not like this. Not on one stolen afternoon when we might both live to regret it."

She started to speak, to deny the very idea that she would ever regret anything that happened between them, but he put his fingers against her mouth.

"I mean what I say, my darling. I love you too much to risk what we have between us now. When this war's over and we can begin a new life together, that will be the time. I want everything to be done properly, and for the world to know that I respect you as well as love you with all my heart. Do you understand?"

"I do," she said slowly, and as solemnly as if it was a vow. She understood, but it wasn't what she wanted. Right now, she wanted him to sweep her into his arms and forget all about conventions and propriety. Right now, she wanted him to make love to her so desperately it was a physical ache inside her.

But after all, the conventions were too ingrained in her to beg, and she knew in her heart that he was right. He was so wonderfully right. Even if the words were never said, he wanted her to face her family and know that she had never given herself to a lover before they were married, however strong those feelings had been. And she had no doubt that they were just as deep for Glenn. It was just that he was so much stronger than she was. Oh yes, he *was* her knight in shining armour. He was everything she had ever wanted. Could there ever have been two lovers as much in love...?

"I have something for you, Daisy," he was saying now, as the charged moments imperceptibly passed. "The minute I saw it, I knew it was meant for you."

He sat up, and she followed suit as he took a small box from his pocket and handed it to her. She opened it carefully and then gasped.

"Oh, it's lovely, Glenn. It's just perfect!"

"So are you, sweetheart," he said.

She took the necklace out of the box and draped it over her fingers, loving the way the sunlight sparkled on the slender silver chain and especially loving the letter D that dangled from it.

"I've never seen anything like this before," she went on. "It's really special, as if it was made just for me. Put it on for me, will you?"

She lifted up the weight of her hair for him to fasten the chain around her neck, and when he had done so, she felt his lips kiss her nape. It sent shivers of delight running through her, and she twisted round in his arms to hold him tight and kiss him full on the mouth.

"For God's sake, Daisy, you'll have me forgetting all my good resolutions in a minute," he said in something like desperation.

She wriggled away from him at once, knowing he had meant what he said, and even though she desired him more than she had ever desired anything in her life at that moment, she wouldn't make him break his resolve. She already knew about the schoolgirl at the Grammar

School who had been put in the family way and sent away in disgrace, and she would never want such a thing to happen in her family. Nor would she burden Glenn with such an event.

There would be time enough for that when the war was over and they were married and living a blissfully happy life with no threat of an enemy trying to take it all away from them. She caught his hand and pressed it to her lips.

"You know how much I love you, don't you, Glenn?" she said tremulously. "And I'll wear my necklace always to remind me of this lovely day."

"A day that has to end pretty soon, I'm afraid, honey," he said regretfully, glancing at his watch. "I wish we could stay here for ever, but it's not to be."

She didn't need to ask if it meant he would be on duty again that night. So would she, anyway. The war didn't stop for lovers, but just for these few hours it had stopped long enough for them to renew their feelings for one another.

"So how did it go, or shouldn't I ask?" Naomi greeted her when she and Glenn had finally parted, and she was trying hard to stem her tears.

"No, you shouldn't ask," Daisy retorted, "but he gave me this. And it wasn't even my birthday," she added as a joke, as she showed her friend the necklace.

"It's beautiful, Daisy," Naomi said, admiringly. "But you'll either have to keep it for special occasions, or keep it tucked down the front of your uniform, or Sister will be after you. She doesn't approve of wearing jewellery while on duty."

"I'm not taking it off, that's for sure. As long as I'm wearing it next to my skin, I'll know Glenn is safe."

She spoke bravely, knowing there was no such guarantee, and that plenty of others must have thought the same. The feel of the silver D against her skin was a comfort all the same, and a sweet, poignant memory of that lovely day when they had so nearly given in to their desire but managed to resist it.

For Glenn Fraser, daredevil flying was his life, at least while the war lasted. It was wrong to think of it as an opportunity he would never have had otherwise, but he knew he wasn't the only one to think that way. Besides, when it was all over, he'd be perfectly happy to settle down to a more orderly way of life back home in Canada, as long as he could have Daisy with him.

He often wondered about that statement, though. Not about having Daisy with him, of course – that was never in doubt after she'd agreed to marry him – but settling down to a more orderly existence…It sounded so tame and going back to the old routine in a lawyer's office no longer held the charm that it once had done. He always knew it had fulfilled his father's dreams for him more than his own, he admitted, and he had more far-reaching ambitions now.

Perhaps he could use his flying skills in some other way – maybe as a mail carrier, or even in some kind of stunt capacity, though he wasn't sure how Daisy would take to that, and she would be his first consideration.

He was feeling exhilarated, both from the thought that he had found the love of his life, and from the wild excitement he felt from flying into danger. There was nothing to compare with that rush of sensation when you were pitting your wits against an enemy just as keen to finish you off. He thought the RAF was the finest in the world, but he had every respect for the German airmen too, having been brought up on tales of the Red Baron and his daring exploits in the First World War. This mutual respect for the enemy was something no woman could be expected to understand.

He didn't hold with these fiendish new weapons the Germans were spilling over London now, though. Pilotless aircraft seemed to Glenn to be the lowest form of warfare, commanding no skill other than the ability to aim at a distant target. And that target seemed to be mostly the civilian population. As daylight faded, there was no time to ponder on the ethics or otherwise of such things, because his squadron was on high alert to make its nightly raid over Germany, and as usual he felt the blood racing around his veins long before they were scrambled, and his aircraft took to the air.

This was what he had been born for, he thought elatedly, as they soared into the night sky, this comradeship against the forces of evil, and this rush of power in the machine beneath him that was almost orgasmic. There was acute danger in flying in the daylight hours, as all pilots knew, together with the dread of suddenly seeing an enemy aircraft screaming towards you out of the sun before there was time to change course or even pray to your God. Many pilots boasted that they revelled in the danger; Glenn preferred night flying, especially when the sky was a sheer, beautiful indigo except for a myriad of stars, and where the sense of space was infinite. Whatever God you believed in – and he had his own private views on that – never was the sense of believing in something in a wider universe more potent than when there was nothing between you and infinity.

They were flying in formation now, the roar of the accompanying aircraft in his squadron a pleasantly comforting sound – comrades in arms and all that rot, or rather, comrades in wings, he always thought with a grin. They were still above the clouds, but they were shortly about to descend to where they knew their target would be, a heavily protected railway depot in a key German border town.

As if in robotic unison, the squadron made the rapid descent, to be met by the expected barrage of anti-aircraft fire from the ground below. The planes rocked mercilessly as they were buffeted by the blasts, but the gut-need to blow this railway depot out of existence never wavered, even when they were caught in the glare of German searchlights, ready to be picked off like fleas on a dog.

Glenn felt no sense of imminent doom. It was fatal to feel that way. It was one of the lessons you learned. You had to believe you were invincible. You didn't dare falter in your mission. You had to go on blasting away at the enemy until one or other of you emerged triumphant, and the one thing you dared not let yourself imagine was the poor devils who would be blasted to kingdom come. It was a case of them or us. You thought of nothing else – not home nor family nor loved ones. There was just this intense need to do the job and get the hell out of there.

He had known this mission was going to be ultra-successful. When the last of the bombs had been dropped, he looked down at the burning railway depot below and felt a sense of glorious achievement. The entire scene was like something out of hell. Flames shot into the air as machinery and buildings exploded from the aerial onslaught, and the acrid smell of burning oil filled the air.

Within seconds, Glenn was aware of a very different feeling. The noise was so catastrophic all around that the gun-blast on the tail of his plane went almost unnoticed. He was only aware of a strange sensation of lightness in the aircraft; then there was a stomach-churning tipping, a diving, followed by a burning sensation that had nothing to do with elation, but more to do with the fact that the rear of his plane had been ripped away by the anti-aircraft fire.

Flames were shooting towards him from all angles now – above, below and behind – and his crew were staggering forward – those who still had the ability to stagger. There was blood everywhere, and the sickly smell of burning flesh…

"Bale out, skipper," somebody screamed. "For Christ's sake, bale out while you can. We're done for…"

Before he could gather his wits to put the words into action, the plane, silvered and made beautiful by search-light, received another direct hit. Glenn felt the hot, sweet blood coursing from his neck, his eyes, his mouth. The fire shot up his legs, white-hot and fuelled by his own engines, shrivelling his skin in seconds, devouring him, until the agony that filled him turned to blackness as the plane disintegrated, taking him with it.

Chapter Fourteen

Daisy tried hard to stop giggling with her patient about the messages on the plaster cast on his leg. The walking wounded, as they called them, had been writing the most outrageous things they could get away with on it, and some of them were certainly saucy enough to arouse the wrath of Sister.

"You'll get me shot if Sister sees some of these things, Corporal Hodges," Daisy told him. "Not that I understand half of the jokes, of course!"

"Go on wiv you, nursie, I bet you weren't born yesterday, not like that stiff-arsed sister," he chuckled. "A lovely-looking gel like you has more than one young man panting over her, I'll bet. If I wasn't tied to my old missus, I'd give 'em a run for their money!"

"You need a dose of something in your tea, Corporal Hodges," she went on, laughing. He was the joker in the ward; he kept everybody's spirits up, and it was pointless being offended, because he'd only get more outrageous if she did. Besides, she knew he was harmless, and she'd already seen the photo of his wife and the two young sons he kept in his locker. He wasn't all bad, even if Sister frowned on him. In Daisy's opinion, every ward needed a Corporal Hodges.

"I reckon that one shoulda been a nun. I can just see her in one of them habits, covering all her bits," he was saying now. "What do you say, Daisy-bell?"

"I say you'd better keep quiet before she appears with the doctor on his rounds," she said. "And rub some of those naughty words off your plaster."

She knew he wouldn't. She also knew that the doctor and most of the staff were reasonably broad-minded. They had to be, even if Sister was not. Still, it didn't hurt to shock the old dear once in a while.

Daisy caught sight of her hovering behind the glass door at the end of the ward and composed her face. She didn't particularly want to be hauled over the coals when she was still in a happy frame of mind after the outing with Glenn four days ago. She still glowed with the memory of his kisses, and the necklace he had given her was comfortingly warm against her skin beneath her nurse's uniform.

She glanced up again and saw Sister talking with Naomi. From the seriousness of their faces, she presumed Naomi was in trouble again. Daisy sighed. No matter how Naomi tried, there were still times when her cushioned background reared its sophisticated head, and she found it hard to cope with the harsh realities of hospital life. It only made Daisy admire her more for her gritty determination to do her bit.

A few minutes later, Naomi walked down the ward towards her, her face flushed and distressed.

"What have you done now?" Daisy said, hiding a grin.

"Nothing. It's not me. It's…Daisy, there are some people to see you. They're in Sister's room, and she said you can speak to them there. I said I would tell you."

"What people? What's all the mystery?" Daisy said, starting to laugh. Then the laugh faded as she saw the stark misery in her friend's eyes. "Something's happened, hasn't it? Is it Immy?"

She couldn't have said why her thoughts flew to her oldest sister – unless it was some basic instinct to ward off the worst thought of all. In those fractured moments when she wasn't really thinking sensibly of anything at all, she didn't even consider anything happening to her father, or Elsie, or Aunt Rose. It was Immy she first thought of, who was probably somewhere in France right now, in the thick of it.

"You'd better come, Daisy," Naomi said in a strangled voice.

She probably had no idea who the people were, or why they wanted to see her, Daisy thought generously. You'd have thought someone like Naomi was well used to dealing with people in authority, whether it was bishops or kings…

She opened the door of the ward sister's room and her heart leapt as the two men in RAF uniform stood up, their faces grim and taut. She was aware that Naomi had come into the room as well, closing the door behind her and standing very close by, as if to catch her when – if – she fell. She felt her hands curl into her palms, her nails digging grooves in her flesh as she stood rigidly, waiting for the words she knew were about to come.

"Miss Caldwell, please sit down," the first officer said gravely.

"I prefer to stand," she said. "Whatever it is, please tell me quickly."

The men glanced at each other, as if each was loth to be the one…

"I'm very, very sorry, Miss Caldwell," the second one said, "but I'm afraid we have some bad news about Flight Lieutenant Fraser. As he was a personal friend, we offered to come here to tell you ourselves."

Well, of course it was bad news. What else could it be? Why else would they be here, looking so young and awkward and embarrassed, and devastated too? She felt a strange compassion for them, having to do this. Having to tell someone their lover was wounded – or worse. The calm hit her as suddenly as the fear.

"Is he dead?"

As Naomi caught her breath, the two officers glanced at one another again.

Oh, for God's sake, Daisy wanted to shriek, *can't you get the words out?* But the shrieking remained inside her, and she was still deathly calm, like a robot, not really capable of reacting to the words, because they couldn't really be true. Glenn always said he'd come back to her like a bad penny, and she believed him. He would never let her down. The necklace he had bought her burned like a flame against her throat. None of this was true, and she was sorry for these young men for believing it; but just as if they were all acting out the scene in a play, she knew she had to go along with it, pretending, just as they were.

"He bought it over Germany several nights ago," the first one went on. "At first we couldn't identify who – which of our planes – had gone down. There was always the chance that some of the men had bailed out, you see, or that the planes had gone off course. We had to be sure. But eventually…well, I'm so sorry, Miss Caldwell. So awfully sorry."

"So you believe he's dead?" she repeated.

"Daisy," she heard Naomi say in a low voice, "you have to believe it too."

"We've brought some of his things that you may wish to have," one of the officers went on, glad to have something to do. "We have left the official communication with the ward sister, since you are his fiancée. It will also be sent to his family, but presumably you'll want to write to them privately as well."

"No. I will not wish to do that," Daisy said in a clear, harsh voice. "Nor were we officially engaged, so his family won't expect to be hearing from me. I prefer that all communication is made through official sources."

They were clearly shocked by this vehement reaction, and so was Naomi, biting her lip and shaking her head slightly behind Daisy's back.

"I'm sorry, but I can't do as you ask," she went on. "Please arrange for Glenn's belongings to be sent to his family. I'm sorry."

She turned abruptly and went out of the room, leaving Naomi to offer what explanation she could for a reaction none of them understood.

A while later, a shocked Naomi found Daisy laughing and joking with Corporal Hodges again. The doctor's rounds were over, and Sister was accompanying him to the next ward.

"Daisy, what the hell are you doing? Do you understand what you've just been told?" Naomi hissed, appalled.

"What should I be doing? I'm doing my job, of course, and don't you have anything else to do but follow me around like a shadow?"

Naomi grabbed her arm and spun her around, uncaring of the curious interest of the patients. "Daisy, darling, those officers came to tell you that Glenn has been killed," she said brutally. "They've given Sister an official document with all the details, as far as the RAF know them, and you must read it and understand it."

"I don't want to read it, and I won't read it. I won't believe it either."

"Good Gawd, Daisy-bell, is she telling you that young airman of yours has copped it?" Corporal Hodges said hoarsely, earwigging as usual.

"Well, that's what she says, but I know it's not true, and we don't want to hear any of that gloomy stuff, do we?" Daisy said brightly. "Let's concentrate on rubbing out the worst of the jokes on your plaster instead."

As Daisy continued to pooh-pooh the idea that Glenn had been killed, Naomi's mouth seemed to be permanently hung open, and in desperation she rushed out of the ward to find Sister.

Sister Willmott had always thought Naomi Tyler-Smythe the wrong type to work in a hospital, even in a secretarial capacity, but she had to admit the girl had shown some grit recently, helped on by that gutsy Caldwell girl. Right now, however, as Naomi tracked her down on one of her busy ward rounds, she could see that the girl was quaking. Probably finding it difficult to take the news that her friend had had to hear, she thought, wishing she had been able to see Nurse Caldwell right away. But duty always came first here, and there were others in need of her who still hovered between life and death.

"Have you sent Nurse Caldwell to her room for the rest of the day, as I suggested, Nurse Tyler-Smythe?" she asked, once Naomi captured her attention.

"I didn't get the chance," Naomi gasped. "She nearly bit my head off just now. I expected her to burst into tears at the news, but instead, she's laughing and joking with Corporal Hodges, and she wouldn't even take possession of her fiancé's belongings, nor agree to write to his family. I'm really worried about her, and I really think you should speak to her as soon as you can, Sister."

Nurses didn't normally make such bold requests of a fearsome Sister, besides which she hated having to say it at all, since it seemed like such a betrayal of her friend, but Naomi was too alarmed at Daisy's reaction to do anything else. She had never seen her like this before, and she was totally at a loss.

Sister Willmott frowned. "She shouldn't still be on the ward. Most people need to be alone to grieve until the first shock has worn off, and to be alone to cry. The next thing they want to do is to write that letter to the relatives, which they feel will bring them closer to the deceased. If Nurse Caldwell is refusing to do any of this, then it's clear that for the time being she is choosing to deny the fact that her young man is dead. Would you say that this is a fair assessment of the situation, Nurse Tyler-Smythe?"

God, she was a cold woman, Naomi thought, seething; and yet she knew she had more insight and experience than she ever would in this situation.

"Yes," she said humbly. "And I don't know what to do about it."

"If she still refuses to leave the ward, I would like you to keep an eye on her for the next hour. If she is still working by then and seems to be making no attempt to come to terms with what's happened, please ask her to come and see me in my room at once. She needs to read the report the officers gave me, and then perhaps it will sink in."

"Yes, Sister," Naomi said, and fled.

She found Daisy still busy on the ward. Furiously busy, in fact, as if she had been taking some kind of stimulant. She laughed and joked with the men who needed cheering up, and sat and held the hands of those who had no strength for it. She had always been a good nurse, but right now she simply wasn't the Daisy that Naomi knew. She knew that grief took people in many different ways, and she ached for her friend, knowing the reaction had to come eventually.

After an hour had passed, she went to her and told her she had to report to Sister Willmott.

"What for? I haven't done anything wrong, have I?"

"Darling, you know what for," Naomi said in a low voice, noting the brilliant eyes and flushed face. They were the only indications that her mind had received a terrible shock, but Naomi knew her so well, and could recognise the grief that was so far so well contained. "Sister has some documents for you."

"All right, and you can carry on entertaining my chaps, providing you don't sing to them." She grinned at the patients, who gave a small cheer, then shook her head at them. "Don't encourage her to sing, or you'll be sorry."

When she had gone to see Sister, Corporal Hodges called out to Naomi, who wanted nothing more than to get back to her mundane secretarial duties.

"Hey, Smythie, is it right that her RAF bloke's bought it then? She don't exactly seem too upset by it."

"I don't want to talk about it," Naomi said, "and if you'll take my advice, you'll forget you heard it."

"If you say so, but it's a bleedin' funny way of carrying on if you ask me."

"I didn't," Naomi said rudely, and stalked away.

"Sit down, Nurse Caldwell," Sister Willmott said kindly. "Now then, my dear, you do understand what's happened, don't you?"

"Of course I do. I'm not stupid."

"So why don't you tell me then? Tell me why those RAF officers came to see you, and what they told you."

Daisy sighed, recognising the psychology in the question. Nothing was real until it was said aloud and, if necessary, repeated a hundred times. The more you said it, the more real it became.

"I know why they were here. They came to tell me that my fiancé, Flight Lieutenant Glenn Fraser, had been killed in action. I know that. I heard them."

"And do you accept it?"

"I accept what they said."

She spoke like an automaton. Of course she accepted it. The RAF didn't make stupid mistakes. Glenn was dead. Her darling, her beloved Glenn had been killed in action, which was the way they dressed it up, when what they really meant was that he had probably been blown to bits. In Glenn's mind that would have been preferable to the future faced by many of the poor devils living with half their faces burned away. She knew that too, so how could she possibly grieve for him, when he had gone the way he would have wanted? The way they all wanted: to die a hero, if they had to die at all. Doing what they wanted most.

"I have the official report for you, Nurse Caldwell, and I want you to take it and read it and understand it thoroughly. Flight Lieutenant Fraser died for his country and for that you can be proud."

"I was always proud of him," Daisy said sharply.

"And you'll write to his family? They would appreciate it so much, and I know you've written many compassionate letters for other servicemen…"

"No. I won't do that. The news should reach them through an official source, not me. I don't know them, and they don't know me, and I won't do it."

Sister tried to hide her surprise. "May I ask why? I thought it would have been some comfort to you."

"My reasons are personal. And if there's nothing else, Sister, I think I should get back to the ward."

"And I most definitely do not. You are in a state of shock, Nurse, whether you realise it or not, and I don't want a sudden collapse in the ward. You will take the rest of the day off and report to me again tomorrow, by which time I will have arranged for a brief leave for you to see your family."

"If you do, I'll refuse to take it. I don't want to talk to any of my family. I just want to do my work."

By now, Sister Willmott could see there was no shaking her resolve. She could see it in the mutinous set of her jaw, and the way her hands were clenched together. The girl was a time-bomb of emotions, but so tightly held in that she knew she had to release them in her own time and her own way.

"Then take the rest of today off, and I don't want to see you on any of my wards until tomorrow morning, Nurse."

"Yes, Sister," Daisy said, and went out of the room with her head held high, the envelope containing the official news of Glenn's death tucked away in her pocket.

–

"Daisy, I simply don't understand you," Naomi said, two weeks after the news had come through.

Naomi was totally bewildered by then. It was as if nothing had happened. Daisy hadn't cried a single tear, nor behaved in any way differently from the way she always behaved. Nor had she mentioned Glenn again. It was as though he had never existed, and to Naomi's certain knowledge she hadn't opened the envelope to read the official notice of Glenn's death.

Soon after the officers had come to the hospital, Naomi had telephoned the RAF station and managed to have a word with them. She had learned that there could be no burial service for any of the crew, because the aircraft had been blown out of the sky over Germany, and there had been no survivors. Just as with her brother Baz, they couldn't even say goodbye properly. She hadn't dared to tell any of the details to Daisy, sure that she would have refused to listen to the grim realities.

"What is there to understand?" Daisy said, applying a trace of lipstick to her pale lips before starting her evening shift on the wards. "I'm the same as I've always been, aren't I?"

"That's just it, and you shouldn't be the same. And darling, if nobody else has the guts to tell you, then I'm doing it: Glenn is dead, darling."

"I know that."

"So why aren't you contacting his parents and telling them how much he meant to you? Give them some comfort, even if you don't want any yourself."

Daisy's eyes took on that feverish, brilliant hue that Naomi was starting to recognise now, as she turned on her friend.

"Because I've done it once before, and much good it did me. I went through all this when my first young man died: writing to his mother and getting a tragic letter back and having to relive it all over again, and I'm not going to do it a second time. I'm not going through the agony of it again. I don't want their sympathy, and I don't want my family's sympathy either. That's why I'm not telling them."

Naomi was stunned at the brittleness in her voice, and not only that. "You mean you haven't told them? But Daisy, that's not normal! You always said what a loving family you've got, so why are you shutting them out?"

"Because I have to deal with this in my own way, that's why, and I'll thank you not to keep questioning me like this. I'm tired of having your eyes following me around the place too, if you must know, as if you're expecting me to crack at any minute."

"Well, aren't you?"

Daisy didn't answer, and simply walked out of their room.

Towards the end of July, Quentin Caldwell received a letter. He didn't recognise the handwriting, and when he glanced at the name at the end of the letter before starting to read it, he wasn't sure he recognised that either. It was such a mouthful he said it aloud to his womenfolk.

"Naomi Tyler-Smythe!" Rose echoed. "Well, isn't that the name of Daisy's well-to-do friend at the hospital, the one whose family has a posh house somewhere in Hertfordshire?"

"Well, if it is, why would she be writing to me?" Quentin said, frowning. "I know we haven't heard anything from Daisy lately, but that's nothing new with the way things are these days. Young people don't have the same thoughts for their relatives as they used to."

"They could just be busy helping to win a war, of course," Rose said tartly, defensive of Daisy, as always.

She looked sharply at her brother, noting how his voice faded away as he began to read Naomi's neat handwriting.

"What is it?" his wife asked quickly, seeing his change of expression and the way his face blanched.

"Oh my Lord, not that," he said hoarsely.

"Quentin, for heaven's sake," Rose exclaimed in alarm. "Are you going to tell us what's in the letter or not? Daisy's not ill, is she?"

He wished he didn't have to tell them. He wished he could keep the ghastly news from them for a little while longer, knowing that what must have devastated Daisy would affect them all. In that instant he was unknowingly in complete accord with his youngest daughter, but seeing the growing dread in their faces, he knew there was no way he could dress it up to make it seem any less tragic.

"It's Daisy's young airman, the Canadian fellow. This friend of hers says he was killed shortly after D-Day."

Rose and Mary gasped with shock while he quickly read more of the letter, becoming more and more disturbed at what Naomi had to tell him.

"Oh, that poor girl," Mary was saying tearfully; and then the delay in the timing began to sink in. "But why on earth hasn't she told us herself? It's nearly two months since D-Day."

"And why hasn't she come home?" Rose was blunt as usual. "Surely such a circumstance would have merited a few days' leave with her family, at least."

"If you'll both just listen, I'll tell you," Quentin said, thankful that the younger members of the household were out this particular afternoon. "This friend of hers is very worried about Daisy. It seems that, although she accepts that her young man is dead, she hasn't reacted in the way anyone would expect at all. She insists on working every shift at the hospital that she can and is the life and soul of the party when the patients want cheering up. She hasn't even cried, as far as Naomi knows."

"How on earth can she behave like that?" Mary asked in bewilderment. "We've all known bereavement in our time, and it's just not natural."

"I'm just reading the letter, my love. Naomi says the ward sister has offered her some leave, but she refuses to go anywhere. She has also stubbornly refused to write to Glenn's family. She didn't want us to know any of this, but Naomi thought we had a right to know."

"Of course we did!" Rose said, outraged and distressed at the same time. "The girl's obviously going through some sort of crisis, so why can't the medical people see it and do something about it?"

"I daresay they've got their hands full with their patients, Rose, and as long as the nurses do their job efficiently..."

"And how long do you think Daisy's going to do her job efficiently with all this boiling up inside her?"

The same thought struck them all, and it had clearly struck Naomi too. He continued reading the letter out loud.

"'I do worry for her, Mr Caldwell,'" he read slowly. "'This situation can't go on indefinitely, and at some stage I know she's going to crack. The reason I've written to you now, even though I know she'll hate me for it, is so that you can let her know that you know what's happened to Glenn and beg her to come home. Being among so many seriously wounded patients here is doing her no good at all, even though she can't seem to see it.'"

He folded the letter carefully, more disturbed than he could say. His beautiful Daisy, who could cope with anything, was in danger of falling apart.

"I'll telephone her tonight," Rose said forcefully, "and you must do the same, Quentin. We must get her home so she can recover from this."

"I don't think that's a good idea, if you don't mind my saying so," Mary said quietly. "She's obviously not ready to talk to any of us about it yet, so the last thing she'll want is people phoning her out of the blue, when we're not supposed to know anything. I think we should all write to her – and suggest to Imogen and Elsie that they do the same, since they'll need to be told. But Daisy won't thank us – or her friend – if we all bombard her with phone calls."

She stared at Rose, expecting a clash on this, but for once, Rose saw the sense in it and didn't argue. She nodded slowly.

"You're absolutely right, Mary. So we'll all write as tactfully as we can, and let her know we're all here for her, and that we want her home."

"And for the present we say nothing to Vanessa and the boys," Quentin added, "though I think it might be an idea to let that other friend of Daisy's know, Rose. You know her mother, I believe."

"Alice Godfrey's mother – yes, I'll do that," Rose said. "It's as well for her to be forewarned before Daisy comes home."

She had every intention of asking Freddie to write to Daisy too. Freddie would know the right words to say: it was part of a vicar's job. Rose grieved for Daisy so much, but already she was wondering what on earth she could say to her darling niece that could possibly ease the heartbreak of having lost two sweethearts in this terrible war.

Chapter Fifteen

"There are some letters for you, Daisy," Naomi told her a week later. "I've brought them up."

Her heart beat erratically, guessing that two of the letters would have come from the same household as a result of her impassioned and well-meaning letter to Daisy's father. She couldn't guess who the third one was from.

Daisy was still working feverishly on the wards and refusing to mention Glenn at all now. She took the letters from Naomi with a word of thanks. There was nothing unusual in receiving letters from home. Everyone wanted to use the telephones when they got the chance, so it was often impossible to speak to family and loved ones at the times you wanted to, and Daisy hadn't wanted to talk to anyone from home recently.

She ripped open the first envelope and read it quickly. Naomi tried not to look at her, but it was impossible not to miss her friend's gasp of fury as she threw the letter down on her bed and ripped open the others. She barely glanced at the contents before turning a blazing face towards her friend.

"How could you do this!" she said in a choked voice. "How could you betray my confidence in this way? Writing to my *father*, when I expressly told you I didn't want any of my family to know about Glenn until I was ready to tell them myself! I trusted you, Naomi!"

She was shaking with rage now, her eyes dark with anger, her face burning. Naomi's heart thumped as she tried to seize her hands and was firmly rejected.

"I did it because I love you, Daisy, and because your family loves you too, and I thought they had a right to know the torment you're going through."

"Whatever torment I'm going through, I'm going through it in my own way – or I *was* until you interfered," she said shrilly. "What gave you the right to go behind my back like this?"

"The right of friendship, Daisy darling, and because I can't bear to see you like this. It's just not natural. I haven't even seen you cry."

"Maybe that's because I'm doing all my crying inside, but I suppose that's never occurred to you."

Naomi swallowed, hating to see her like this. "And how many times have you advised your patients to cry if they want to, telling them to release all their emotions and not to hold them in? How many times have you held the hands of grown men and waited patiently while they cried their hearts out?"

"That's different…"

"No, it isn't, Daisy. You should think of yourself as the patient now. You've suffered as deep a shock as any of them. It may not be physical, but…"

"But what? You think I'm going crazy – is that it?"

"I just think you should take some time at home and not drive yourself the way you are. You're denying what has happened, and when the pain really sinks in, it will be all the harder to bear."

"So you're a psychology student now, are you?"

"No. I'm your friend, and I love you, and I can't bear to see you like this."

Daisy didn't answer and ripped open the letter she hadn't seen yet. She scanned it quickly and threw it on the bed with an expression of fury.

"Well, that's all I need. I've got the vicar writing to me as well now, as if he'd know anything! And this is down to Aunt Rose. You see what you've done now? I'll probably get Uncle Tom Cobley and all writing to me before long."

"Daisy, I'm really sorry…" Naomi said in distress.

"So you should be. Just leave me alone and stop interfering in my life. I don't need you. I don't need anyone."

Wisely, Naomi decided it was time to leave her alone, but since Sister Willmott was keeping a close eye on the situation, she knew she had to report this latest happening. She felt like a sneak for doing so, but by now she was starting to get really fearful for Daisy's sanity.

Sister Willmott sent for Daisy that afternoon.

"Nurse Caldwell, you are relieved from duty as from now, and you are to take a week's leave, starting tomorrow morning."

"I don't want to take any leave, Sister."

"I'm not asking, Nurse Caldwell, I'm telling you. I don't want to see you back on the ward for a week, so you may use today to make your arrangements." Her face softened momentarily, even if her voice didn't. "It is for your own good, my dear. Go and see your family. Go home where you belong."

There was no use in protesting when Sister Willmott's mouth resumed its usual firm line, and Daisy knew it. She turned and left the room, still incensed with Naomi, and knowing that her interference had provoked all of this, because the last thing she wanted was to go home.

Her thoughts shot ahead, knowing the reaction she would get from everyone. Her father and stepmother would smother her with love and sympathy. Aunt Rose would want her to go to see Vicar Penfold to hear his pious views on why God took one person and not another – or, in her case, why He had taken the two young men she had loved. Vanessa would be openly curious, and Teddy and Harry would want to know more ghoulish details than she ever wanted to know herself. It was impossible.

Daisy caught her breath on a sob. She couldn't bear to go home, but nor could she stay here now that Sister Willmott had given her the ultimatum. She knew that if she asked, Naomi would offer her home as a refuge for as long as she needed it, and that her parents would welcome her, but that too, was not an option. There was only one place.

Before she left the hospital, she swallowed her pride and asked Naomi to forgive her for taking out her black moods on her. Then she nearly dissolved into mush as Naomi uncharacteristically hugged her.

"For pity's sake, Daisy Caldwell, what are friends for, if not to bear the brunt of bad times as well as sharing the good?" she said with a choke in her voice.

–

Elsie Preston frowned as she looked out of the farmhouse window at the sound of the taxi drawing up outside. She didn't know anyone who would take a taxi to come this far into the Dales. Local people either came visiting by farm carts or their own cars, or simply walked. Coming by Shanks's pony was what they called walking, though she had never quite fathomed out why.

Then her mouth dropped open as she saw the pale-faced figure with the shock of red hair emerging from the taxi. She put the baby down in the playpen Joe had made for her and rushed to open the front door.

"Daisy, what on earth are you doing here?" she gasped. Then there was nothing more to be said as her sister gazed at her mutely, her eyes strained with misery, and fell into her outstretched arms.

"I didn't know where else to go," she choked, once she had been drawn inside the cosy parlour. "I couldn't bear to go home, with all of them knowing, and creeping around me. I know they would all mean it for the best, but I couldn't bear it. You must think I'm going crazy, Elsie, when you don't even know what I'm talking about."

"Of course I know, darling," Elsie said quietly. "Do you think Daddy wouldn't have got in touch with me the minute he'd got the letter from that friend of yours? I didn't write to you, because I simply didn't know what to say but if you think I don't feel for you, then you don't know me at all."

"I know, but I felt that sympathy would be diluted here, Elsie, instead of swamping me. That sounds awful, doesn't it? I just mean that it won't be *all* of them at once, just you and Joe – well, and your in-laws as well, of course."

She had forgotten them. She had forgotten the other branch of the Preston family as well – Owen Preston, who had bought out her father's shop all those years ago, and his odious son Robert, who lived in York. They were family now, as far as Elsie was concerned, and would probably have heard the news that poor little Daisy had lost another young man...

"Mother Hetty is a practical Yorkshire woman, Daisy, and she won't smother you, any more than I will, but it won't stop us grieving for you all the same." The squeeze of her hand took the sting out of her words.

"Is she here now?" Daisy said dully.

"She's taken Faith visiting, and the men are out working, so there's only me and Dawn here right now, and despite everything, Daisy darling, I'm very glad to see you, and touched that you thought of us as a refuge. That's all I'm going to say about it unless you invite confidences, so I shall go and make us both a cup of tea while you re-acquaint yourself with your niece."

Without waiting for a reply, she plucked Dawn from her playpen and put her in Daisy's arms. The two of them studied one another, the baby's eyes wide and anxious for a moment, and then her mouth broke into a smile, showing the two small new teeth. She was the image of Faith, and the image of all of the Caldwell girls – of Imogen, Elsie, Daisy – and of their mother too. At that moment, there was such a sense of continuity in Daisy's mind that, for the briefest fraction of time, she forgot her own misery and marvelled at how life went on and renewed itself.

"Isn't she gorgeous?" Elsie said practically, returning with the tray of tea. "She doesn't take to everyone right away, but she obviously likes you, Daisy, probably because you and I are so alike."

"She's like all of us, isn't she?" Daisy said. "It's a reassuring thought, and I haven't had many of those lately."

"Drink your tea and I'll show you your room later," Elsie went on. "You must have had a horrendous journey, and I hope you're going to stay a while."

"For a week, if you'll have me."

"Don't be silly. I'd love you to stay for ever, but I know that's not very likely. I'm very happy, of course, but it's so lovely to have someone of my own here, Daisy. I mean someone who talks my language," she added with a laugh. "You'll be surprised when you see Faith again, at how northern she's become. She's a right little Yorkshire lass, according to her grandfather."

"Do you miss home?" Daisy asked, knowing she had to say something, even though this whole situation was becoming bizarre and unreal to her. The long journey here, simply to get away from the hospital as she had been ordered, and her stubborn refusal to go home, was starting to make her feel light-headed. She didn't belong here, but she felt as though she didn't belong anywhere anymore, which was why she had kept on working so relentlessly, to ward off the inevitable pain of facing up to Glenn's death. She wasn't ready for it yet. She would never be ready for it.

"Of course I miss home," Elsie replied as Daisy continued stroking Dawn's soft cheek and making the baby chuckle with pleasure. "But I belong with Joe, and he belongs here."

Elsie had such simple logic, Daisy thought, with a small stab of jealousy. Life had been comfortable for Elsie. She had always known what she wanted, and she had got it, including two beautiful children.

For a second, Daisy's lips trembled, knowing she would never have babies of her own now. Not Cal's babies, nor Glenn's. Falling in love wasn't worth all the anguish when fate snatched it away from you.

The front door opened suddenly, bringing in a fresh waft of the outdoors, and Elsie's comfortable mother-in-law arrived home with Faith running in ahead of her with a bunch of wild flowers in her hands for her mother.

"I picked these for you, Mummy," Faith shouted, and then stopped as she saw the stranger holding Dawn in her arms.

"They're lovely, sweetheart," Elsie said. "Now why don't you give your Auntie Daisy a kiss? She's come all this way to stay with us for a few days."

She explained it all in one smooth sentence for her mother-in-law to hear.

"Is it a holiday?" Faith said, not prepared yet to kiss someone who was a virtual stranger.

Daisy smiled crookedly. "Well, a sort of holiday. I especially wanted to see you and Dawn. That's all right, isn't it?"

"Say of course it is, lass," her grandmother told her. "And right glad we are to see you, Daisy love," she added.

Daisy knew she must be very well aware of what had happened to Glenn. She nodded without answering, handed Dawn back to Elsie and finished her tea. Finally Faith tentatively offered her face for a kiss.

"If you don't mind, I'd like to put my things upstairs now," Daisy said, a little desperately, needing to be alone for a few minutes at least. Whether or not it had been rash to come all the way to Yorkshire she didn't yet know. She had only known at the time that it was the only place left to her. She had toyed with the thought of going to Cornwall, to the places her family had always loved, but although she hadn't felt able to face all of them at home in Weston, she had still felt the need to be part of a family.

"I'll help you, Auntie Daisy," Faith said importantly. "I'm a big girl now."

She was all of four years old, Daisy thought, a clear-eyed, pretty child, with all of life ahead of her, and no clouds on her horizon. If she had been the mother of these children, she would have wanted to wrap them in cotton wool and keep them that way for ever. But life wasn't like that, and if she didn't stop these maudlin thoughts, she would be filling this comfortable household with gloom.

"That would be lovely, Faith," she said, forcing a smile. "My bags aren't too heavy, so you can show me where I'm going to sleep."

Elsie told her daughter quickly, and Faith struggled ahead of Daisy with one of her bags, while Daisy brought the other one. She hadn't brought much – just some civvies so that she could get out of uniform, which might help to make herself feel a mite more human.

Faith watched as she put the bags on the bed and looked around her at the cosy bedspread and matching curtains and the heavy, old-fashioned furniture. The view from the window was of rolling hills and dales, with a big oak tree in the yard, and a wild rocky outcrop above the farm.

One of Daisy's favourite novels was Emily Brontë's *Wuthering Heights* and she was immediately transported there, imagining Catherine running wild across the moors and searching for Heathcliff – a tragic and doomed love affair if ever there was one…

Abruptly, she willed the images away, aware that Faith was staring at her more intently now.

"Auntie Daisy, is your airman dead?"

She felt a ripple of shock at the question, and then realised that the child must have heard Elsie and Joe talking about it, and Elsie wouldn't have had time yet to prime her not to mention it.

"I'm afraid so," she said in a muffled voice.

"Are you sad? Mummy said you would be," Faith persisted.

Daisy made a great effort. "Yes, I'm sad, but I'm sure you can cheer me up."

Faith put her small hand in hers. "I was sad when my rabbit died," she said solemnly. "But my daddy said he'd gone to rabbit heaven and that all the animals are happy there. Is your airman in airman heaven?"

Oh God. Daisy swallowed hard. She hadn't anticipated any of this.

"I'm sure he is, darling."

"I 'spect he's happy then," Faith told her with her mother's simple logic. "Do you want to see my bedroom?"

"I'd love to see it." Anything to get away from the image of Glenn in airman heaven and being happy there, when she knew for certain he would have been blown into a thousand pieces when his plane went down. Either that or burnt to a shrivelling mass of flesh and bone...

Gradually, however, she knew she had been absolutely right to come here and nowhere else. Being with Elsie and the children was like a breath of fresh air, even though the enormity of her loss still overwhelmed her at times, and she knew it would continue to do so.

She watched Joe pushing Faith on the swing he'd made for her on the big oak tree in the yard outside and heard Elsie's voice behind her.

"Joe's mother said he used to sling a rope over the branches of that old tree and pretend he was Tarzan when he was a boy," she said softly. "Which was fine until the rope broke one day and he ended up covered in bruises with his knees skinned. That put an end to it. But I'm glad he's made a proper swing for Faith. It feels like a bit of continuity, although you'll think me daft for saying so."

"No, I don't. You're so lucky, Elsie," Daisy said without turning round to look at her. "You have everything, and I'm so envious. I don't begrudge you a thing, but I just can't help it."

"Darling, things won't always be bad for you," Elsie said, her hand on her sister's tense shoulder. "When this war is over, and things get back to normal…"

"Oh yes? And what then? When the boys come marching home, you mean. That's how the song goes, isn't it? Well, my boy won't, and I'm probably the only person in the world who isn't looking to the future with any kind of hope. I know that's awful, but it's the way I feel right now, knowing that as soon as the war's over, Immy and James will get married, and my friend Alice Godfrey will marry her Yank and go to live in Hollywood. What will I be doing then, I wonder? Being the eternal old maid like some of the women from the last war?"

"Of course not," Elsie snapped, in a most un-Elsie-like way. "I know you're feeling horrible right now, Daisy, and I'm desperately sorry for you, as we all are, but it's not the end of the world for you. I don't mean to sound insensitive, darling, but you're still only twenty-two, and even I never believed that there was only one partner destined for us all. You should know that, since you've already fallen in love with two young men. Father knew it too, and from what that young Vanessa has been hinting in her *very* occasional letters to me, I reckon Aunt Rose and the vicar will eventually tie the knot."

"Good Lord." Daisy's initial reaction to burst out angrily at her sister's pep talk was tempered by this remark. "Do you really think so?"

Elsie shrugged, relieved to see a spark of interest at last in Daisy's clouded eyes. "Why not? He's been sniffing around her for years — if that's not an irreverent thing to say about a vicar."

Daisy laughed — really laughed, in a way she hadn't done for ages, and the sound of her own laughter, however brief, took her by surprise. Elsie confided to Joe later that she thought it was the first real turning point in Daisy's coming to terms with her grief, and accepting the fact that life had to go on, no matter how many vicissitudes were put in your way.

Joe hugged her to him in the warmth of their double bed. "And I think you've swallowed the dictionary, my wise one," he said teasingly.

"I'm not wise," Elsie said, hugging him back. "Just thankful and grateful to God that I've still got you."

On the fourth evening, Daisy telephoned her father, knowing she couldn't put the moment off for ever. Besides, as soon as she left Yorkshire, she knew Elsie would let him know of her visit, and he'd be hurt that she hadn't told him herself.

"It's me, Daddy," she said flatly, hardly knowing what to say to him.

It took him a heartbeat or two before he answered, and she guessed he was feeling just as awkward as she was. "I'm so relieved to hear your voice, Daisy, and I'm not going to ask how you are, because I can guess. Are you still at the hospital? I thought you might have come home for a while."

"I couldn't. I'm sorry."

"Don't be. You don't have to explain anything to me. But you know that your friend wrote to me, and I hope you weren't angry with her for doing so."

"You had a right to know. I just couldn't tell you." She hated herself for sounding so stilted, but she couldn't help it. "Actually, Daddy, I'm with Elsie and Joe. I was ordered away from the hospital for a week, and I decided the best place to come was here. The children – well, they've been a comfort."

She listened to her own voice, knowing she was speaking like a very old, bereaved woman, which was precisely the way she felt.

"They would be," Quentin was saying steadily now. "And you did exactly the right thing, darling. You have no idea what a comfort you all were to me after your mother died."

There. He had mentioned the word now. The word that always seemed such an intrusion into ordinary daily living. The death word. With it, Daisy felt a sudden surge of emotion, and her voice was thick with it.

"Oh Daddy, I miss him so, and the pain won't go away…"

"It will, my love, it will. And you've taken the first step in seeing your own people again and talking to us. Shutting out the ones who love you doesn't help, even though they'll naturally want to smother you and protect you the way we've always done for one another."

Was it easier for him to talk to her like this, from a distance, with a telephone wire between, instead of face to face? Daisy didn't know the answer. She only knew she had rarely heard him speak in so impassioned a manner, and she knew instantly that he was sharing her pain because he had gone through it himself, so many times before.

"I'll be home to see you soon, Daddy, I promise," she said, feeling choked. "If not before, then I'll definitely try to be home for Christmas."

She didn't know why she said it, because Christmas would only bring back the misery of knowing she would never share another Christmas with Glenn, but he was right. When everything else seemed lost, there was always the family who loved her and would always stand by her.

"Do you want to talk to Aunt Rose, Daisy?" Quentin said now, as the silence grew between them.

"Not now. Give her my love, and all of them, and keep plenty of it for yourself. I love you, Daddy."

"I love you too, sweetheart."

She slammed down the phone, but it had been another milestone, even if it felt no more than stepping an inch forward, she thought tearfully. She had made contact with home. Naomi would be proud of her.

She called her at the hospital that evening and heard her cautious voice at the other end of the line.

"You were right, and I've already forgiven you," Daisy said abruptly.

"Oh God, I'm so glad to hear you say that. So when are you coming back? Were the folks at home glad to see you?"

"I'm not at home. I'm in Yorkshire with my sister and her family."

Naomi squeaked into the phone. "In *Yorkshire*? Isn't it horribly freezing cold up there?"

Daisy risked a smile. Naomi's grasp of geography was not good. "It's still summer, Naomi," she said, almost surprised to realise it herself. "And as a matter of fact it's really beautiful here." As sweet and relaxing, in many ways, as the softness of Cornwall had always been to the Caldwell girls.

"Well, you sound better," Naomi said, relieved. "*Are* you, Daisy?"

"Now that's a pointless question if ever I heard one, so I'll choose to ignore it. And have you got a cold or something? You sound a bit muffled."

Her answer came in an ear-splitting, honking sneeze right into the phone, and then she heard Naomi's gasping apology.

"Lord, Daisy, I'm sorry about that. It's my allergy again, and – oh cripes, here I go again – are you laughing at me, you wretch?"

"Oh, Naomi, I do miss you!" Daisy said, laughing out loud now. "You're completely mad, but I love you all the same."

She hung up the phone, aware that it wasn't hers to use, and discovered that she was actually humming as she went back to the parlour where the family was getting ready for the evening meal – humming the song she and Naomi had once tried to perform as a duet until Naomi's unfortunate allergy had turned the occasion into a farce...

Elsie's relief was obvious. "Will you hold Dawn, darling, while I get Faith settled in her high chair?"

Daisy took the infant in her arms, breathing in the sweet baby smell of her, and cuddled her close for a moment until Dawn wriggled in protest. She couldn't help feeling that this was an almost symbolic moment: holding Dawn in her arms...and holding a tentative hope in her heart for a future that wasn't entirely without love, because she already had it in abundance.

Chapter Sixteen

In late August the news that Paris had been liberated was greeted with great excitement in every Allied newspaper and news broadcast, even though London was still suffering badly from the insidious doodlebug attacks.

"It's a comical name, but it doesn't lessen the terrible impact they're having on folk," Quentin Caldwell commented, to be shushed at once by his sister Rose as Vanessa came into the house.

He remembered that the two of them had been in London when one of the attacks had occurred, and it had been a timely reminder that the war was far from over yet, despite all the celebrations in Paris.

He was thankful that Daisy seemed to be coming to terms with what had happened to her young man at last. That nice friend of hers, Naomi double-barrelled, had been thoughtful enough to write to him again recently, just a brief note to say she'd even persuaded Daisy to go to one of the monthly dances with her. Not that Daisy had enjoyed it much, Naomi told him, but it was a start.

Quentin had to agree that it was, and at least two of his daughters were reasonably out of harm's way. Elsie was safely up in Yorkshire, and Jerry didn't seem so inclined to send his doodlebugs over the south coast where Daisy worked but was concentrating on the poor buggers in London.

Then there was Immy. They hadn't heard from Immy for some time, and those who said that no news was good news went around with their heads in the clouds as far as Quentin was concerned. In wartime it just meant that you held your breath until you had some kind of communication, whatever it was.

–

Immy drove the staff car into Paris with a great deal of caution in the middle of the small convoy of British vehicles going into the city. Captain Beckett had warned that there would be crowds, but she hadn't expected this excited near-riot on the streets, nor the occasional burst of gunfire that sent them scattering. Didn't the Jerries know they were supposed to have surrendered! Hidden snipers should still make folk vigilant, but try telling that to these people today.

She couldn't blame them for swarming on to the streets to celebrate their freedom and the arrival of Allied troops that had successfully driven the enemy back. It was exhilarating to be in the middle of such a crazy, happy mood, and she wished James could have been here to share it with her. The French *mesdemoiselles* were ready to embrace every man wearing a uniform, and there were cheers whenever a soldier caught a young girl up in his arms and gave her a hearty kiss. It made Immy long for James, and the normality of such moments.

"It's like everyone's birthday and Christmas all rolled into one, isn't it, sir?" Imogen said with a smile as she steered the car carefully to the building at the end of the square, where their temporary headquarters were to be.

Captain Beckett's voice was tempered with unease. "That may be, but there's still too much occasional sniper fire for my liking."

She agreed, having seen how the groups of people screeched and blasphemed at the sudden rat-rat-rat of machine-gun fire, and how one or another of them would suddenly fall to the ground. It wasn't over yet, not by a long way, not even here, in the middle of all this celebration; but they were nearing the imposing-looking building now, and once inside, they would set up their communications room with their accompanying team.

There were sudden screams from the crowd nearby. A cloud of blue smoke rose from the pavement, and the next moment a woman fell across the bonnet of the staff car. Blood seeped from her back, and Imogen watched with horrified eyes as she sprawled in ungainly fashion over the car.

"Somebody help her," she shouted, but even as several of her countrymen pulled her off the car, Immy knew it was no use. The woman was already dead. It was such a terrible thing to happen when she had been in the forefront of the celebrations that for one wild moment Immy felt numb with shock.

"Get down, Imogen," Captain Beckett shouted, but she couldn't move, couldn't think. It was only instinct telling her she had to steer the car away from the crowd surrounding them, into which it was in danger of ploughing now.

The next second, she felt a searing, stinging pain in her shoulder and a second agonising pain at the side of her head. She slumped forward, still desperately holding the steering wheel before it was wrenched from her grasp. The pain was so intense she felt as if her head was floating above her. The raucous sounds in the square were muffled and distant, becoming ever fainter as if everything was moving away from her at a terrifying rate. The last sound she heard before she fainted was the unusual sound of Captain Beckett swearing profusely.

"Jerry bastards! Picking on innocent women and children certainly cuts them down to size for the bastard pigs that they are. Let's get her inside quickly..."

—

Immy awoke in a sea of pain. There were strangers everywhere, people she didn't know, wearing unfamiliar uniforms. She wasn't even sure if they were uniforms at all, and those strange white caps resembled those worn by nuns. Or maybe they were angels. Maybe she was dead and hadn't recognised the fact yet. Maybe this was how it felt to be dead, this strange numbness in her mind, and such dryness in her mouth that she couldn't swallow, while her body was still racked with the pain. One of the strangers, the angels, was leaning over her now. She was saying something, but Imogen couldn't understand the words.

She couldn't remember words at all. She couldn't get her tongue around them to ask where she was, or who she was...Sudden panic overwhelmed her. She couldn't remember her name. These floating strangers could be aliens from outer space for all she knew, if such things existed outside comic books. She had been taken here, abandoned here...

"Imogen, thank God you've come round properly at last," a man's voice said close by. "You gave us quite a scare, my dear girl."

Wincing at the pain of sudden movement, she turned her head quickly. At least, she thought she did. In reality she moved excruciatingly slowly, like a very old woman. She looked at the anxious face of the man in the soldier's uniform, which she dimly recognised was an officer's uniform, and fought to remember if she had ever seen him before.

"Did I?" she said, through those numb lips that didn't seem to belong to her.

"Do you remember what happened at all?"

She started to shake her head and then stopped. Her head hurt so badly. She raised a limp hand to touch it and felt the heavy bandages there. Shock rippled through her. Had she suffered some appalling accident? Was there some hideous growth on her brain that was depriving her of speech, of her senses? If so, she would rather be dead…

"You were shot twice by snipers' bullets, Imogen," the stranger who seemed to know her, said gently.

"Shot?" she said vaguely.

"He was in the middle of the crowd when we were driving towards the new headquarters. Don't you remember? Try to think, Imogen. Try to remember."

Why should she? She resented the urgency in his voice. She didn't want to remember. It took too much effort. Why didn't he just go away and leave her alone – leave her to die. She was going to anyway. At his persistence, she struggled to think sensibly.

"There was a woman. She was falling on to a car. Was that me?" she asked.

He looked mildly relieved. "No, it wasn't you. It was some poor Frenchwoman who got the first bullet, but you got the next two, my poor love."

The words startled her. She was quite sure she wasn't his poor love. Good Lord, he was old enough to be her father. But he wasn't. She knew that. Her father was at home with his new wife, and Aunt Rose, and Teddy...

"I'm Imogen Caldwell, aren't I?" she said slowly, and the flood of relief at knowing her own name was so enormous that her eyes filled with tears, and she sobbed inside, aware that it would hurt too much to wail out loud.

"Where am I...sir?"

Captain Beckett spoke gruffly. Not for the world would he have had this happen to his charming young driver.

"You're in a French hospital outside Paris, my dear, and I'm afraid you're going to have to stay here for a while longer, though we'll move you to a British unit as soon as we can. The second bullet only grazed your temple, but your shoulder took a nasty blow and will need time to heal."

She was so very tempted to ask why she couldn't be sent home right away, but Daisy always said how dangerous it was to move patients until the doctors said so. Besides, she remembered that she was in the army, and a soldier, even a female one, didn't request such things when she was needed; but a lot of use she would be now, if she had a busted shoulder. Just like that young American who was going to marry Daisy's friend, Alice Godfrey, she remembered, and Daisy had told her it had taken him weeks to heal.

All the same, despite the awfulness of staying here for heaven knew how long, she gave Captain Beckett a wavering smile, simply with the joy of remembering her family and home and coming back to the land of the living. Whatever else happened, she wasn't going to die. She damn well wasn't.

The next days passed with her in a haze of pain, almost comatose with all the medication and painkillers the nurses were pumping into her, and finally waking, clear-eyed at last, to find a familiar face looking down at her.

"Well, thank goodness," James said matter-of-factly. "I was beginning to think I'd lost my fatal charm if even I couldn't wake you."

At her cry of joy at seeing him he couldn't keep up the pretence of calm any longer and gathered her into his arms until she yelled out at the pain of it.

"You've probably put back my recovery by a couple of weeks now!" she said, laughing and crying at the same time. "But I don't even care. It's just so wonderful to see you, James. How did you know — and how did you get here?"

"We moved into Paris a week ago. I got in touch with your CO right away and had the shock of my life when he told me what had happened. He hasn't informed your family yet and didn't know what you would want. Shall I do it?"

"I'm not sure. Isn't it best to leave them in ignorance?"

"It damn well is not. They'll be so proud of you, and you'll probably end up with a medal for bravery as well."

"Don't be daft," she said with a weak smile, but then he astonished her by telling her how she'd somehow managed to steer the staff car away from the crowd just before she passed out, and she realised that he meant it.

"You write to them, James, but don't make a big fuss about it, please. At least it will give them something else to think about instead of poor Daisy's news."

"I always knew something bad was going to happen," Vanessa declared to her best friend. "That day me and Daisy went to see Madame Fifi, she told Daisy there'd be people she couldn't help – people close to her – and she was right, see? She couldn't help her airman bloke, and she couldn't help her sister, neither."

Hilary sniffed. "You're potty, that's what you are. My mum wouldn't let me go near that woman's place. She says they're all weird."

"She may be weird, but she was right. Anyway, Immy's being sent home to Weston General in a coupl' a' weeks, and then she's coming home for good."

Nessa wasn't at all sure how she was going to like that. In the end, she was rather enjoying being the pseudo-big-sister to those annoying little brats, Teddy and Harry; but Immy was Teddy's real sister, and Nessa knew she was going to get her nose pushed out of joint. Of course they were all upset over what had happened to Immy, but all the same...

Still, now that Daddy Quent's shop was up and running, she had left school for good and was working there, and she didn't give a tuppenny toss what her school cert. results were going to be. It didn't matter anymore. She could add up figures at the till, and Mary had commented how much the customers liked her cheery smile and her nonsense. It all came from working down the market stalls, she told Hilary, who looked as blank as if she said she'd worked on the moon.

When Immy came home, she fitted into the routine as smoothly as if she'd always been there, thanks mainly to Rose and Mary's efforts to keep the peace between all and sundry. There was no doubt, though, that the house was filling up again, and when the war ended and Daisy came home for good, it would be quite crowded. By November the place names on the railway stations and road signposts were being restored, and in December the Home Guard was stood down. All the pointers were that this would be the last Christmas of the war.

Daisy knew she finally had to go home too. She had resisted all this time, even when she knew Immy had been hurt, and she had cried so hard on Naomi's shoulder that it had startled her. She had cried more for Immy than she had for Glenn, until it finally dawned on her that she was doing all the crying she had held in for so long.

Christmas leave was due to her, and she was going to take it, to face them all and get over another hurdle. She had already overcome one, by finally writing to Glenn's parents, and had received a sweet letter back from his mother.

–

"It's going to be a proper Christmas this year," Rose told Freddie firmly. "We'll be a real family again, and Immy says her James is hoping to get some leave, and of course you're invited for Christmas dinner," she added, running out of breath.

"Thank you, Rose," he said, and at his tone of voice she looked at him sharply. She knew well enough by now when he had something on his mind and was hesitant about saying it.

"You don't have any other plans for Christmas dinner, do you?"

"Where else would I want to be but with you?" Freddie said simply. "I mean all of you, of course."

Rose felt her face grow hot. She had thought about this for a long time now, and she knew he was a dear sweet man who needed a bit of a push before he would take the initiative. This was such a time.

"No, you don't. You mean you just want to be with me. Don't you, Freddie? Isn't that what you really mean?"

Dear Lord, her heart was fluttering as wildly as that of a young girl now, just because she was being all girlish and inviting him to flirt with her; but she didn't just want a flirtation, not at her age, and he wouldn't want that either.

"I think you know what I want, Rosie," he said quietly.

"Actually, Freddie, I don't. I've never been much of a mind-reader, so don't you think it's time you told me, my dear?"

"I want you to be my wife." He looked startled at having managed to get the words out, and immediately became flustered again. "But I'll quite understand if it's too soon, or if I'm being far too presumptuous in thinking you might be able to care for me...in time..."

Rose put her fingers against his lips. "Freddie, dear, I think it's high time you and I thought about getting married, and that you made an honest woman of me," she said gently, even though she knew any thought of doing anything else would be farthest from his honest, simple mind.

"You mean it?" he asked, barely able to contain his joy.

"Heavens above, how long have you known me, Freddie Penfold? Have you ever known me to say anything I didn't mean?" But her voice was husky, thanking God in her heart for the gift of having had two good men to love in her lifetime.

"There's just one thing," she said, after a very satis-factory kiss. "I don't want to make any announcement until I'm sure how Daisy's going to react. She'll still be feeling the loss of her young man…"

"But perhaps the news of an impending wedding between us two old codgers will be just the thing to cheer up the whole family – don't you think?" he said teasingly, but with more authority than usual, and clearly prepared to put his foot down when necessary.

Rose beamed. They were in for a good run, she thought irreverently, for however long it lasted.

–

Over the Christmas festivities, Daisy took the news with surprising pleasure. It was Vanessa who told her, unable to keep the news a secret, and preening herself on having guessed long ago that Aunt Rose was going to marry the vicar.

"It's going to be in the spring," Nessa told her importantly, "and when Aunt Rose moves into the vicarage, I'm going to live with them."

"Are you?" Daisy couldn't imagine how the vicar was going to take this!

"They don't know it yet," Nessa added uneasily, "but I've thought it all through. When the war's over, and you come back to work at Weston General, you'll be living here, and I suppose Immy will stay here until she marries her James, and I reckon there are just too many women in the house."

"So you've decided to go and live with them where you can be queen bee – is that it?" Daisy asked, seeing through her at once.

Nessa laughed. "Something like that."

She had been busily painting her fingernails with lacquer now she was no longer a schoolgirl, and ostentatiously admired their pale-pink tips.

"Daisy, I haven't said anything before, but I really am sorry about your airman. It must have been awful."

"It was. It is. But I'll survive. We have to in the end, don't we?" Daisy said, touched by her awkward remark.

"Well, just as long as you don't go into a long decline and never think about marrying anybody else. With your looks it would be such a bleedin' terrible waste for the whole male population," she said, with a brief return to her old cheek.

So 1945 rolled in with a feeling of hope riding high on the air. In early April Rose and Freddie were going to be married, and Daisy promised that, come hell or high water, she would be there, and so would Elsie and Joe and the children. This was an occasion not to be missed.

"I do admire her," Naomi told Daisy, when the news was reported to her. "I mean, it's normal for people of our age to fall in love and get married, but when they're older – well, they get stuck in a bit of a rut, don't they?"

"This is my beloved auntie you're talking about, Naomi," Daisy said with a laugh. "If you ever met her, you'd know there's nothing ancient about her! Nor my father either. He was devastated when my mother died, but he's made a very happy second marriage, even though I never thought I'd hear myself saying so."

"That proves it then, doesn't it?"

"What?"

"I think you know what, darling, but if I said it, you'd probably bite my head off, so I'll leave you to think about it instead. Anyway, duty calls."

She swished away, as elegant as ever, her blonde hair sitting beautifully beneath her nurse's cap, and Daisy knew exactly what she was trying to tell her: there was life after Glenn. There was always someone to love, if she dared to take the chance. Six months on, Daisy was prepared to believe it, but certainly not to go looking for it. Love, if it was going to happen, simply happened, but not yet — not until everyone's dreams of peace had come to fruition. There would be time enough then, if it was ever going to happen, and it was a foolish person indeed who tempted fate for a third time. Meanwhile, there was still plenty of work at the hospital to keep her mind and hands occupied. There were people who needed her here.

"You don't remember me, do you?" one of the walking wounded said, a few days into the new year, as the next intake of patients arrived in an ambulance.

Daisy looked at him coolly. Patients often tried this sort of line, but she was sure she'd never seen him before. He was good-looking in a rugged sort of way, but with a hideous gash across one side of his cheek from a shrapnel wound, though there were no other visible injuries apart from a limp.

"Sorry, no," she said cheerfully.

"I was here the night you and another girl did your singing double act."

Daisy blushed bright red at once. If he'd wanted to say something to impress her, this definitely wasn't it! The memory of that night when Naomi's allergy had had her honking like a pig still stuck vividly in her mind. "Really?" she said stiffly.

"Do you remember the party who came in with Miss Penny Wood, the singer? I was one of them — a distant cousin of hers, as a matter of fact."

"Good Lord!" Daisy's embarrassment briefly vanished. She clearly remembered the Cornish singer she had admired so much, who was entertaining the Forces at home and overseas, but she didn't remember this man. She'd had eyes for no one but the girl she was hoping to impress with her own singing, until the awful disaster of Naomi's faux pas, and the humiliating sounds of laughter in the audience. When she had looked around, Miss Penny Wood and her party had gone.

"It's hardly a night I want to remember," she went on, turning away from him and dealing with those who needed her more than he obviously did.

"I remember you, though," the man said, before he was taken into the hospital and out of her sight.

She recognised his accent if nothing else. He was Cornish, like the singer – his distant cousin, if she believed him – though she imagined Miss Penny Wood had had the rough edges of a regional accent well and truly rubbed off by now. She was a celebrity – a national treasure, some said – singing in a nightclub in London before the war began and entertaining the troops ever since.

Daisy sighed. Once, in what seemed like another life-time, it had been such a wonderful dream to try to emulate her and people like her: to be like her delicate and beautiful mother, singing on a stage and receiving rapturous applause. And what had she achieved? Organising small concerts and choirs to sing Christmas carols for the patients in whatever hospital she worked in.

"Are you going to stand there all day, Nurse Caldwell?" she heard one of the other nurses say crossly. "We do have a job to do, you know, and some of these boys are badly in need of the lavatories."

So much for dreaming, then…

Besides, she thought much later, lying sleepless in her bed after an exhausting day of getting patients into bed, dealing with minor wounds and assisting with major ones, it would never have worked out. This was her true vocation, and she might as well get used to it. A stage career was as likely for Daisy Caldwell as chasing rainbows. The best thing of all was the knowledge that it no longer mattered. She was no longer the frittery young girl she had been when her mother died, or when her father had lost his shop and everything he had worked so hard for. She had even learned to cope with the loss of her close friend Lucy Luckwell, who had been only seventeen when she had died of consumption.

In a way, that had been an eye-opener, making her understand and accept that young people could die too; it wasn't confined to the old and sick. It was a truism that had stood her in good stead for what was to come during these years of war, when she had decided to become a nurse, and discovered that it wasn't all glamour and holding someone's hand and gaining their adoring admiration. It wasn't all Florence Nightingale stuff…

"Cripes, am I turning into a bleedin' philosopher now?" she muttered into the darkness of the room she shared with Naomi.

"*What* did you say, darling?" she heard Naomi ask with a laugh.

"I said I think I'm turning into Vanessa Caldwell-bleedin'-Brown now," she replied with a repressed giggle that was half a sob, and the next minute they were laughing uncontrollably, until a bang on the wall of the adjoining room told them they had better shut up and get some sleep.

Chapter Seventeen

Alice Godfrey knew she had been very lax about contacting Daisy when she first heard the news about Glenn. She had felt such a huge sense of guilt at the time that she simply didn't know what to write to her. The fact that it was a useless and unreasoning guilt didn't lessen the feeling at all. It was guilt that her own future was so happy and assured, with a young man who adored her, and was going to marry her and whisk her off to Hollywood the minute the war was over. It was guilt at feeling so happy, when her friend must be going through such misery. It was guilt at hearing her mother talk about Daisy after her weekly meetings with Daisy's Aunt Rose and being unable to confess to her that not until it was nearly Christmas had she found the courage to write to her friend at all.

Only then, when she had had many second-hand reports about how Daisy was faring, had she felt able to sit down and try to explain how she felt. Only at the end of those Christmas holidays, not having been sure whether Daisy would be at home in Weston or not, had she finally summoned up the courage to speak to her. As it was, the meeting had been totally unplanned.

"Daisy!" she said, hugely embarrassed.

Daisy looked up from arranging the bunch of tiny early daffodils on Lucy Luckwell's grave. Her father had grown the delicate flowers in his small greenhouse, and she hoped they would survive the winter. She straightened up at once, her voice a mite remote.

"Well, this is a coincidence, isn't it? This is where we first met, remember?"

Alice nodded. "Of course. You were doing just what you're doing now, and I was visiting my brother's grave."

She hesitated, and then spoke with a huge rush of emotion, her eyes full of remorse, her heart thumping. "Oh, Daisy, I can't tell you how awful I feel for deserting you the way I did. Morally, as well as physically. You can't imagine how guilty I felt, and I know how stupid that must sound to you, but I can't think how else to say it."

Daisy almost felt sorry for her. If this had been a Victorian melodrama, she would surely have been wringing her hands in distress…

"You don't need to, Alice, because I felt the same way after Cal died. Guilt is a very strange emotion. I know it's not quite the same thing as what you're saying now, but I felt guilty at thinking I could have normal feelings ever again when I should be mourning for ever. But nobody can mourn for ever. So I know all about the guilt that keeps you from saying what's in your heart, and it really doesn't matter, Alice. What matters is that we're still friends. We are, aren't we?"

Alice stumbled across the frozen, wintry ground, and hugged Daisy fiercely.

"Of course we are. But good Lord, Daisy, when did you get to be so bloody noble and understanding?" she added in a choked, angry voice.

"Never, and you'd better let me go unless you want to suffocate me," Daisy answered. "And if you think I didn't feel resentment and hurt when you didn't write to me, you'd better think again," she added for good measure.

"I tried a hundred times," Alice said humbly. "My room was littered with screwed-up pieces of paper because I couldn't find the right words to say to you. Whatever I said, it always seemed so trite and useless."

"It would have helped, though. It would have been better than Aunt Rose's Bible quotations, and my father's awkward attempt at sympathy, and the bloody vicar's pious goings-on about eternity and all that rot."

"But you believe it, don't you?" Alice said uneasily. "You've experienced enough weird occasions on the hospital wards to know that there has to be *something* afterwards, haven't you, Daisy? We all have."

"Oh yes, I believe it. Take no notice. It's just me letting off steam as usual. I haven't changed *that* much!"

"Thank God. Then come home with me and have some tea. My mother will be so glad to see you. Please say you will."

"All right. When I've said goodbye to Lucy."

She turned away, because oh yes, she believed in eternity all right. In the silence of the night, when she had held the hand of a dying soldier and heard his whispered avowal of the bright light coming towards him, seen his beatific smile and heard his gasping words of wonder at seeing someone who had gone before, whom Daisy was not privileged to see...how could she not believe it?

How could she not believe that Glenn had gone to a better place? Because if she believed it for Lucy, she had to believe it for him too. After one of Teddy's more ghoulish stories to Harry about people being blown to bits, she had even somehow managed to explain to them that God wouldn't be at all worried if people arrived in heaven in a thousand pieces, because God had the power to put them back together again like a great big jigsaw puzzle...

"It was good to be friends with Alice again," she told Naomi when she returned to the hospital, refreshed after the Christmas break. "Though I don't suppose things will ever be quite the same between us again. Especially when the war's over."

"Why ever not?"

Daisy continued rolling bandages and didn't look at her.

"Because she'll be marrying her Yank and going to live in Hollywood of all places, and I'll still be here, doing this. Or somewhere else, doing this."

Naomi put her hand over hers. "Daisy, you're not getting some foolish idea in your head that you're never going to meet someone and fall in love again, are you? Do you think that's what Glenn would have wanted for you?"

She carried on relentlessly when Daisy didn't answer. "I know he was a wonderful man, but don't put him on a pedestal, darling. There are other chaps in the world who'd love to put a sparkle in Daisy Caldwell's eyes – and don't snap my head off for saying so."

"Would I ever?" Daisy said drily. "I'll just ignore it instead."

It was hard to ignore it, though, when she was constantly dealing with patients on the mend who knew nothing about her and were as saucy as ever, clearly appreciating the pretty nurse with the glorious red hair and velvety-brown eyes that sometimes looked so sad; and she couldn't deny that it gave a lift to her heart when they flirted with her so shamelessly. So she let them get away with it, if only to raise their spirits, but she was honest enough to know it raised her spirits too, and with a small feeling of guilty relief she knew she wasn't actually ready to go into a decline at twenty-two years old…

Glenn's memory would be forever in her heart, but she was young and alive, and the trite words she had said so many times before to a bereaved relative – that time was a great healer – were undeniably true. You didn't forget, but you came to terms with bereavement, because you were the one who had to go on living.

Besides, the Caldwell family had something to look forward to. Aunt Rose was getting married in the spring, and it still brought an incredulous smile to Daisy's lips every time she thought of her and the vicar…

"What's tickling your fancy now?" Naomi asked her. "Or should I say *who*?" she added, remembering how she had been cajoling Daisy into thinking of a future romance. All in good time, of course.

"I was trying to picture my Aunt Rose and the vicar together. You know, married. On their wedding night. Or perhaps I should say I was trying *not* to picture them. Oh Lord! I wonder if he'll ask permission to do the necessary. Of the *Boss Upstairs*, you know, or Aunt Rose. Or if she'll take the initiative."

"Cripes, Daisy, that's a bit saucy, isn't it?" Naomi said, grinning, but mightily relieved that she could talk so casually about such intimate matters.

"If you knew her, Naomi, then you'd know what I mean. She can be a real battle axe, but she's lovely too, and I wouldn't change a thing about her," Daisy said with a chuckle. "I just can't imagine how they'll go on about *it*!"

"Well, she'll know what to expect, won't she?"

"Yes, but he won't. He's never been married before, so he's what you might call a virgin vicar!" Daisy said solemnly, and they both collapsed with laughter at the thought. When they had recovered, she wiped her eyes.

"I remember when Vanessa once asked me about the facts of life, and I gave her some of Aunt Rose's old medical books – I think I told you she was a nurse in the last war – and I just had a quick vision of her taking them on her honeymoon to instruct poor old Freddie with diagrams."

"Good God, Daisy, stop it, or you'll never get through the ceremony on the day if you go on like this," Naomi said, having to pause to wipe her own eyes now. "Where are they going on this honeymoon, anyway?"

After another moment's convulsion, Daisy croaked: "Down to Cornwall. Our family always go there when we want a bit of relaxation. We've always loved it – and funnily enough, Freddie's surname is Cornish. We'll have to get used to thinking of Aunt Rose as Mrs Rose Penfold soon! A lot of Cornish names begin with Pen, Pol or Tre, in case you didn't know," she added.

"I did know," Naomi said.

As Daisy spoke, she felt a tremendous surge of nostalgia for Cornwall and the summer places where her family had always been so happy. She was a Bristol girl and, more recently, a Weston-super-Mare girl, she supposed; but her mother had always said that, for them, the West Country began in Bristol and ended at Land's End, in Cornwall. It belonged to them, and they belonged to it.

It was a remark that had always made the girls smile with delight at Frances's quaint philosophy. It was true, though. Cornwall might not be in their blood, but it was very much in all their hearts, and one day, Daisy knew, she would have to go back there too. It was a need they all shared, and one that Frances had unquestionably put there.

"You've gone all soppy-faced again," Naomi said. "Is the thought of that wedding finally putting the stars in your eyes?"

"Something like that," she said softly, because there were some things you didn't want to confide, even to your best friend.

–

As the new year wore on, the war in Europe was swiftly coming under the control of the Allies, even if the Japanese showed no signs of surrender, and the barbaric practices of the kamikaze suicide pilots continued. Dying for their country was considered as great an honour as it was for the Allies but pointing your aircraft deliberately at a target to kill yourself was a questionable way of doing it, in most British minds.

The army and navy were having great successes in all war zones now, and air attacks on the large German cities were having a devastating effect. Names that most British people had hardly heard of before were suddenly in the forefront of their minds: Essen, Cologne, Dresden…

As ever, Quentin scanned the newspapers for every bit of news.

"How's this for a more shameful piece of information?" Quentin said in disgust. "The Germans are now so desperate for recruits they're even conscripting fifteen- and sixteen-year-olds. They're just babies."

"If the war went on for years, I could be a soldier then," Teddy told him eagerly. "Or a sailor, or an airman like Daisy's boy."

"You most certainly could not," his father snapped. "And you've been listening to too much war news lately, young man. Off to bed with you and Harry now, and Mary will come and tuck you in later."

"I don't want to be tucked in, and she's not my mother," Teddy shouted, angry at the implication that he needed such a thing at his age.

Before his father could explode with anger, Mary put her hand on his arm. "Well, you're not my son, either, Teddy, and I won't tuck you in if you don't want me to. I think you're too old for it, anyway."

"You can tuck me in, Aunt Mary," Harry said slyly, at which Teddy turned on him at once, calling him a slimy little sneak and a mummy's boy as they chased one another out of the room.

"Leave it, Quentin," Mary told him. "They're just boys. They may not understand our feelings about war, but they know how to play off one another."

"I know. It was just Teddy's remark about being a sailor that got me riled. Reminding me of Baz, I suppose."

"You never quite got over the way he ran away to sea instead of wanting to be a shopkeeper just like his dad, did you, my love?" she said with a wry smile. "But he did what he loved best, didn't he?"

"And died for it."

"Well, Teddy won't," she said firmly, seeing how his mood was deteriorating. "The war will be over soon, and people will be wanting new clothes to wear and things to enjoy, and with all your old contacts, the shop will really be thriving. You've got a fine new assistant in young Vanessa, too. As the saying goes, I suspect she could sell ice to the Eskimos."

"She's turned out better than I expected," he admitted. "I never thought she'd turn out so well, almost like another daughter – not that she could ever take the place of one of my own," he added, in case Mary should think otherwise.

"Well, you'll soon have to do without her here, at least, when she moves into the vicarage with Rose and Freddie."

Quentin laughed. "And how the little minx ever persuaded them into agreeing with that suggestion I'll never know."

She pressed his shoulder as she went to the kitchen to make their nightly cocoa. "Don't you? I do. It's called female persuasion, darling!"

She was glad when Rose and Immy and Nessa came into the house a little later, changing his mood with news about the impending nuptials, as Freddie persisted in calling them. Immy looked pale, and she was always going to have one shoulder slightly lower than the other after the surgery that had been performed on it; but as her father always told her, it was better than some of the poor devils, who had no shoulders at all.

"So how go the preparations?" Quentin greeted them.

"Quite well," Immy said cautiously.

"*But?*" he asked, ignoring the way Vanessa sniffed audibly.

Rose snorted. "Freddie's installing his brother and his wife in the vicarage while we're away, and this little madam has got her nose put out of joint, because she thought she was going to have a high old time, playing at being the lady of the house for the week."

"I'm not moving in with *them*," Nessa said, with a toss of her head. "Mr Penfold's brother is a vicar as well, and he'll be trying to bleedin' well convert me the whole time he's there."

"I doubt he'll have any more success than the rest of us," Quentin said mildly. "So does that mean you'll be honouring us with your presence a little while longer then?"

"Well, if you don't want me here..."

"Oh, for heaven's sake, girl, don't you know when he's teasing by now?" Rose said. "Of course he wants you here. Now go and make us some cocoa, there's a good girl, seeing as these two have had theirs."

Nessa went off humming, and Immy smiled at her aunt. "You've really got her tamed, haven't you, Aunt Rose?"

"Oh, she just wanted a firm hand, that's all," Rose said airily. "Now let's tell these folks the finer details of the wedding day."

It wasn't going to be a lavish affair. It wasn't appropriate at their age, or in wartime. Nor could it be a hole-and-corner affair, either, considering Freddie's status in the town. It would be in his own church, of course, with his brother from Devon conveniently officiating, and they were only going to invite family members and a few close friends.

"Even so, that will make quite a number," Rose concluded. "Freddie only has the two relatives – his brother and sister-in-law – so it's all on our side, apart from friends of the church and friendship clubs that we both want to be there."

"I've made a list," Immy went on when she paused for breath. "And we can't get away with calling it a small family affair, Aunt Rose. Our family has expanded quite a bit."

And been depleted too — but she wouldn't have said so for the world.

"Let's hear it, then," Quentin prompted.

"Well, starting at the top, there's the bride and groom, since I'm counting the vicar as being on our side for the moment—"

"For heaven's sake, call him Freddie, girl. You can't go on calling him the vicar, as if he's some remote person you don't know! And as for being on our side, we're hardly at war with him, are we?" Rose said indignantly.

"Freddie, then." Immy ignored the question, though finding it as difficult to use the vicar's Christian name as did her sisters. "So there's you and Freddie; Daddy and Mary; myself and James, providing he can get leave; Elsie, Joe and the girls; and Daisy."

She paused, aware of how lost Daisy would feel at being on her own, compared with her sisters and their loved ones.

"Don't forget me and Teddy and Harry," Nessa said, coming in from the kitchen at that moment. "We'll all be together, and we can look after Daisy."

"Then there's Helen, if she can get leave," Immy went on, touched at Nessa's intuition, especially where Daisy was concerned. "And your friends from the church, Aunt Rose."

"Well, that will include Alice Godfrey's mother, and since Alice is Daisy's friend, we must invite her as well — and her young man. Heavens above, it begins to sound as if we'll have a churchful!"

"The more the merrier," Quentin said, as Immy added the names.

He was more than thankful that Immy was taking such an interest in the proceedings. She had been unusually depressed when she had finally been discharged from the various hospitals she had been sent to – unusual for her, anyway. He was used to seeing her as the pragmatic and practical daughter, but the bouts of depression had been harsh and painful, proving that she could be as vulnerable as anyone. Early in the new year, however, she had taken a secretarial job at the town hall and, as the year progressed, she was hearing more frequently from James, so that it seemed as if she had turned the corner at last.

Then it was the beginning of April, with only the habitual winds of the Bristol Channel to whip up the sands in Weston Bay to mar the lovely burgeoning days of spring. April showers came and went, but it was a lovely morning when Rose Painter awoke to realise that this was her wedding day, a day she had never expected to happen for a second time in her lifetime.

She felt a shiver of nerves. Was this what she really wanted? And would Bert, her dearest Bertie, have thought she was betraying him by marrying another man? She looked at the faded, brown-tinted wedding photo of that other day, so long ago, ran her finger over his smiling face and kissed his memory in her mind.

She knew Bert would never have wanted her to live alone, even though they had never spoken of such an eventuality, but even surrounded with a large and loving family, a person could still be alone, and Rose knew she had been alone for a long time now.

There was a knock on her bedroom door, and she replaced the photo on the dressing table as her brother put his head around the door.

"Ready, Rose?" he said. "The others have all gone, so there's just you and me in the house – and I must say you look a picture."

She gave a shaky laugh. Ridiculous for a woman of her age to feel nervous, she told herself, or to have doubts. She had always been so strong…

"I felt just the way I suspect you do, my dear," Quentin said unexpectedly. "But I can assure you that marrying Mary was the best thing I ever did, and I know you'll find just as much happiness with Freddie. Bert would have been happy for you, just as I know Frances would have been happy for me. We must all go on, Rosie, so don't waste time in having second thoughts."

"Are you a mind-reader now?" she said, with a catch in her breath, because he was saying exactly what she had been feeling.

"No," he said with a smile. "Just a brother who loves you and knows you very well, and since I doubt that I'll ever say such a thing again, are we going to set out for the church, or are you going to give Freddie a heart attack by thinking he's been left standing at his own altar?"

She hugged his arm, and asked him in her more usual brusque manner what the dickens they were waiting for then?

It was intended to be a very quiet ceremony as befitted the dignity of their age and standing, but they had forgotten the impact on local people of hearing the banns read out in church on the previous three Sundays, and the charm of knowing it was their own vicar who was to be married. So the church was full of well-wishers as well as family and friends.

Daisy, and all of them, thought how lovely Aunt Rose looked in her powder-blue dress, carrying a white-leather prayer book instead of a bouquet. She had always been a woman of great and unwavering faith, and it was so fitting that in the end she had married a vicar. If Daisy felt more than a pang at the way things had turned out so well for everyone except herself, she was determined not to show it. James had managed to get leave, and Immy was looking more like her old self now, after the shock of her injuries. They hadn't been nearly as severe as those suffered by so many others, but she knew they had left her mentally scarred for a time. And Elsie and Joe, with their two adorable children, were such a complete and happy unit. Alice was there with her Yank. Quentin had Mary by his side, no doubt reliving their own vows as Rose and Freddie made theirs.

As the ancient words of the service were concluded, Daisy swallowed the lump in her throat, and then felt someone's hand squeeze hers.

"Cheer up, old girl, we've still got the bleedin' bunfight to go to yet," Vanessa whispered, just loud enough for Daisy to hear, and for Teddy to snigger and try to hide it by a cough.

He was given a kick on the ankle by Nessa and shushed up, but it had been enough to relieve the sudden anguish Daisy felt at that moment, missing Glenn with a physical pain, but knowing she had to put it all behind her and look to the future, as they all did, because it was a future that was looking ever more positive and hopeful now that the end of this awful war was surely in sight.

None of them were going to think about that today, and Quentin had ordered that any mention of it be banned when they all went back to the family home for what Nessa called the bunfight.

The wedding cake looked magnificent, until the cardboard covering was removed to reveal the small sponge cake inside it and made them all laugh. It didn't matter.

This was the celebration of a marriage, a happy occasion that brought family and friends together.

The bride and groom had planned to spend their wedding night in a hotel in Wells, then leave for Cornwall the following morning; but before they left the reception at the house, there was one last poignant moment when Rose went back to her old bedroom to collect her things, and Daisy found her staring motionless out of the window.

"You're not having regrets already, I hope, Aunt Rose?" she said teasingly.

"Of course not. I was just savouring this house, that's all."

"Well, you're hardly going to live miles away from it, are you? It's only a good walk away from the vicarage."

"I know, but your father and I were brought up in this house, Daisy. It has so many memories, not just of me and Bert, but of our parents and our childhood too. I've never lived anywhere else, but you're right," she said determinedly. "It's only a walk away, so what am I lingering here for?"

They hugged one another, two women who had both known sorrow, but for one, that sorrow had turned into joy and a new beginning.

—

The house remained full to overflowing for the next few days, and once the excitement of the wedding was over and the boys became fractious and a bit resentful of all the attention Elsie's children were getting, Daisy decided it was time to get away. She loved being at home, but she knew, too, that through all the years of the war, she had grown away from it.

Now that Rose and Freddie would be living in the vicarage, incredibly taking Vanessa with them, this was Quentin and Mary's home. There would always be a place for her here, but she felt oddly rootless, even stifled. For a moment she envied Rose and Freddie so much, not just for their happiness, but for being in Cornwall, in those lovely open spaces they had all adored so much as children. They had always called it a land of magic and mystery where anything could happen, and often did. Frances had perpetuated that belief, Daisy thought nostalgically, instilling in them all the love of nature and all things wonderful.

Now, back on the overcrowded train to Chichester to resume her duties, and being pushed and shoved about by heavy-footed servicemen, she thought crossly that what she longed for most of all right now was a bit of privacy and a hot bath. Dreaming about sea and sand of the Cornish variety could wait for another day.

Chapter Eighteen

"After the war" was the phrase on everyone's lips now. It was as if, just by saying it, the time would be brought ever closer and become a reality. In fact, everyone believed it might be only weeks away now. Anticipation was high, saddened by the news that President Roosevelt, who had played such a major part in reaching the end, along with Churchill and Stalin, had died in his sleep on the 12th of April.

While James Church had been home on leave for Immy's aunt's wedding, he had also been thinking of the future. He had serious discussions with his father and with Immy, since she would be a major part of that future, and he needed her to be in full agreement with his plans.

"My father always wanted me to follow the law with him," he said as they walked along Weston sands on a cool, sunny morning just after the wedding. "He raised no objections when I chose the army instead, but I think I've had my fill of it now, and Father's getting older, so I've been seriously wondering—"

"James, you know I'll be happy to be a soldier's wife or a lawyer's wife. Just as long as I'm *your* wife," she said quietly, her hand held loosely in his.

He squeezed it tightly. "That's what I hoped you'd say, darling. Not that I'd go in as a fully-fledged lawyer, of course – rather as a junior member of his chambers. I know that. But Father says the chances are there and I want to take them. We'd also need to live in Bristol again when we're married, but I'm sure we can find a house to suit us."

And one where we'll have gorgeous babies, just like Elsie's, Immy thought, without really being aware that she had wanted such a thing, until now, when the possibility of a life without fear of bombs and privation stretched so invitingly ahead. A life of peace such as none of them had been able to dream about for six long years.

"Tell me it's what you want too, Immy," James was saying urgently. "If you're settled here in Weston, please say it now."

"Of course I'm not settled here. This was only ever a temporary arrangement after I left the ATS. Marking time, if you like, until we could be together. Bristol is where we both belong, and the sooner the better."

He put his arms around her and kissed her, oblivious to the amused glances of the other walkers along the sands. Neither of them cared, because they were both remembering the stolen times when they had shared blissful nights in each other's arms, knowing that, when they did so again, it would be as man and wife, and for ever.

–

Rose Painter, now Penfold, was not slow in writing to Daisy after her honeymoon to tell her that Cornwall was as wonderful as ever, and that she and Freddie had visited a garden centre near Marazion and discovered to their amazement that the owner's brother was someone called Kenneth Harris.

"Good heavens!" Daisy said out loud.

"What? Has your aunt been made a saint already for marrying the vicar?" Naomi said with a grin.

"No, idiot. When we lived in Bristol, Immy used to work for a house agent called Kenneth Harris, and when the war started, he went to live in Cornwall to be near his brother and started a bed and breakfast establishment. I've stayed there myself. And his brother is the one who owns the garden centre that Aunt Rose and Freddie visited."

"Small world, then. What was he like, this Kenneth Harris?" Naomi said. "Did you fancy him or something, if you've stayed at his place?"

Daisy laughed out loud, folding up Rose's letter to peruse properly later. "I certainly did not! He was round and pink and forty if he was a day. I think he once had a soft spot for Immy, but if you'd ever seen her James, you'd know why dear old Kenneth never stood a chance."

She was smiling as she went back to her ward duty. Aunt Rose was always so forthright in her views, and now she was so clearly enamoured of Cornwall. The idea she was outlining to Daisy in her letter was that, when the war was over, she should take a long, long holiday there, if only to get the smell of disinfectant out of her lungs and breathe some of God's good clean air.

Daisy leaned over the half-conscious patient in her care now and resisted the urge to throw up at the distinctly unclean and unpleasant smells emanating from the poor wretch. The war might be nearing its end, but its legacy would continue for years to come, she thought. She didn't even know if she could bear to continue doing this job, or if her life might take a completely different direction. Nobody knew that, and she wasn't going to think about it until the time came.

Her mother had always believed in omens. Daisy believed in them too, and if some new opportunity came her way, it would be a foolish person who didn't take what fate offered so generously.

–

April was a month of varying hopes, fears and horror. A friend of Alice Godfrey's brother was killed on one of the last missions over Germany, and the dread of a War Office telegram arriving at anyone's door was still a very real possibility. The two older Caldwell girls gave up frequent and silent thanks that their own men had been spared, while knowing how hard it must be for Daisy now, and that it would be even harder as the armistice came nearer; because then she would really know that she was alone. The pain of losing Glenn would be all the sharper, seeing everyone else rebuilding their lives in a peaceful world. Her romantic vision had been to marry Glenn and to live happily ever after in Canada. As it was, it was clear to the family that she was merely drifting through the days now and doing her job like an efficient automaton.

"I worry for Daisy more than I let on," Quentin had told Rose, on their return from Cornwall. "You write to her, Rose, and try to keep her spirits up. You'll know what to say far better than I do." Which was why Rose urged Daisy to take a long, long holiday when the war ended, back in Cornwall where her spirit would revive. She would never go as far as to say that in time she would meet someone else. She wouldn't be so crass as to do that, and besides, it wouldn't be well received.

As Rose herself knew, you had to find that second chance in your own time – or even your third chance, she thought, remembering Cal – and nobody else could hurry it; but Daisy was too young and beautiful to remain on her own for ever, and the more she could be gently steered towards thinking the same way, the better.

Rose had very soon become integrated into the role of vicar's wife and revelled in it. She had always shared Freddie's interest in the church, so it was no more than a matter of wearing a different cardigan, she thought with satisfaction. However, towards the end of the month the news broke that the Allies had made the terrible discoveries at Buchenwald, Belsen, and Auschwitz; and although Freddie preached impassioned sermons for forgiveness, which she could hardly stomach, she defiantly led her women's groups in prayers for all the victims and their families.

She certainly couldn't feel the slightest regret when it was learned that Adolf Hitler had committed suicide. If she felt anything at all, it was only the savage wish that he had been shot by machine-gun fire and strung up by his heels for all to see, like his despicable Italian pal, Mussolini. Now the war in Italy was officially over, with the unconditional surrender to Field Marshal Alexander.

Unable to be as forgiving as Freddie, Rose was enraged that Hitler had cheated the world of revenge by hiding in his bunker like the coward he was, and then taken the easy way out. Quentin agreed with her views, even though Freddie couldn't approve of such hatred; and her feelings were only strengthened by learning what the terrible concentration camps had done to their victims.

To Rose's mind the knowledge that such atrocities had existed far outweighed any thoughts of forgiveness and was another reason for grasping life by the scruff of the neck and making the most of what you had, because you never knew when it might end. However, the subject was wisely no longer mentioned between them.

"It surely can't be long before the end comes now," she said to Freddie and Vanessa, when the early days of May brought the welcome news that the Germans had surrendered in Austria, Holland, Denmark and Norway. "Like everyone else, I'm anxious to see my family safely home again."

"But they won't be, will they, Rose?" he said reasonably. "Not here, anyway. Daisy will presumably resume nursing at Weston General, but Immy will live in Bristol when she's married, and I doubt that Elsie will leave Yorkshire now. Nothing will be as it was before, my love, and we must all face that."

"Well, I'll still be here," Vanessa put in, precocious as ever.

"So you will," Rose said tartly. "My cross to bear, may God forgive me for saying so!"

Nessa had got too used to her now to take offence. She laughed airily. "Now don't go pretending you don't want me around, Aunt Rosie dear. I'm the daughter you never had, remember?" Without warning, she put her arms around Rose and hugged her, and Rose went decidedly pink at this unusual display of affection.

"Oh well, then, I suppose you'd better stay," she said, mock-grudgingly, but her smile belied the harshness of the words.

–

At last, at the end of that tense first week in May, came the formal news that the Germans had signed the instrument of total surrender. The war was over, in Europe at least, and as the US forces continued relentlessly to bombard the Japanese cities, it surely couldn't be long before they capitulated as well.

The whole country had licence to go wild, and so it did. Lights blazed out from towns and cities as blackouts were torn down, with no more fear of alerting enemy air attacks. Spontaneous victory celebrations went on everywhere, well in advance of the more organised ones by town councils and civic bodies. People simply thronged the streets and hung bunting, waved flags, brought out their hoarded rations for street parties, kissing and hugging strangers, forgetting the so-called British stiff upper lip in a frenzy of goodwill to everyone they met. It was a time of delirium, of not looking back, or even forward, but of living for the moment.

"Lord knows what it's like in London, but I plan to find out!" Naomi said excitedly to Daisy, a few days later. By then, the hospital was bedecked with all the bunting and old Christmas decorations that could be found to brighten up the wards, and they had been kissed and hugged by practically every member of staff at the hospital, and most of the patients too. "I haven't told you before, Daisy," she went on uneasily, "but my father's already arranged my early discharge and I'm leaving at the weekend. I'm meeting my parents in London and we're all set for a whacking great party with all the champagne money can buy, black market or not! Why don't you come too? It'll be no trouble to book in an extra person with us at the hotel. We can share, just as we do now, and it'll be tremendous fun!"

"You're leaving so soon?" Daisy echoed, unable to grasp anything else.

"Well, you'll be going too, won't you? You'll want to be transferred back to Weston, I'm sure, and besides, I reckon you're due for a hefty spot of leave. It must have been piling up, and you've only taken those few days' leave for your aunt's wedding since Christmas. You should take it, Daisy, relax properly and give yourself time to sort out what you want to do."

"And what do *you* intend to do?" Daisy asked. "Or is that a question one doesn't need to ask a rich man's daughter?"

"I don't know what I shall do yet, darling," she said coolly, ignoring Daisy's scratchiness. "Get out of this beastly uniform and have a good time for a while, that's for sure. I'm certainly not rushing into anything."

She didn't need to, of course, not with her daddy's money and the prospect of inheriting that stately pile – and a probable marriage to some chinless wonder in the near or distant future.

"*So?* Are you joining us in London or not?" Naomi demanded. "For pity's sake, get rid of your prejudices about money, Daisy. They're all old hat now, anyway, and honestly, I'd love to have you with me for the celebrations. We're going to be there for the thirteenth when Mr Churchill broadcasts to the nation at three o'clock. Do come, Daisy. I'd hate to lose touch after all this time."

Daisy shook her head, willing the silly moments of envy away. "Thanks all the same, and I know it sounds marvellous, but I'm sure we'll hear the speech on the wireless, anyway. I just think I should go home as soon as I'm given my marching orders. I want to spend some time with my family and get to know them all again, and London's not really for me."

"All right, but I'm really going to miss you, Daisy."

"I'm going to miss you too," Daisy said, and then they were hugging one another fiercely, because, like everyone else who had been thrown together in unusual circumstances, they both knew it was going to end.

It was two more weeks before Daisy was given the extended leave she was due, and by then Naomi had gone, so, despite the bustle of the hospital, she felt oddly alone. Even so, leaving where she had spent so much time now was an emotional day. She had received letters and phone calls nearly every day from one or another of her family; she knew they were planning a special celebration for her when she got back to Weston, and that Rose and Freddie would be there too.

"Weston has gone every bit as wild as London," Immy had told her excitedly. "I was hoping James would get back when you do, but he has a while longer to go yet. Never mind, we'll have a great time, darling."

Teddy came on to the phone then, and she had to hold the receiver well away from her as his voice blasted into her ears. Teddy could never talk quietly, and he bellowed that he and Harry had been given loads of sweets and chocolates by the Yanks they had met at the Saturday-morning pictures, and that they were organising a fireworks display on the beach lawns as a thank-you to the town.

Daisy spoke to her father next, and finally put the phone down, the smile leaving her face as soon as she had done so. Quentin and Mary were so looking forward to having her home. Teddy was in his element, crowing over his association with the Yanks, and Immy sounded so happy. Alice Godfrey would be excitedly thinking about Hollywood too, and both of them would be planning their weddings now that peace was here.

She would be obliged to listen to all of it and be happy for them – which she *was*, of course, but nothing could take away the fact that she had no one to share the victory celebrations with. No one of her own. And the last thing she wanted to do was to put a damper on any of them when the entire world was celebrating. Well, most of it. She doubted that the Germans were, and the latest news was that many of them had been assigned to the concentration camps, to clear away the remains of the rotting corpses.

Daisy shuddered, desperately sorry for those who received such orders, as if Hitler was still dictating what his subjects did from the grave and knowing she simply couldn't ever have done such a thing. She willed the dreadful images away.

The plan that hurtled into her mind then was so clear-cut and obvious that she didn't give it a second thought. Her hands were shaking when she finished making the telephone call, and then she made another one to Aunt Rose, sure that she would be able to explain her decision to her father with less emotion than Daisy herself.

"I think you're absolutely right, Daisy," Rose said briskly. "You've got the rest of your life to think about what to do, and you don't need to spend time with us old fogeys."

"You know I never think about you like that," Daisy protested.

"I know, dear," Rose said, softening. "But for what it's worth, you have my blessing – and Freddie's too," she added.

Daisy smiled. "You can speak for him, can you?"

"Naturally," Rose said.

A few days later, having been given her discharge papers, and knowing she could report to be reinstated at Weston General whenever she chose, Daisy left the hospital for the last time. She didn't look back as she went to Chichester railway station and joined the throngs of people travelling to all parts of the country, all wearing cheerful smiles on their faces now, instead of the gloomy air of despondency that had been rife for so long.

She had done more travelling on trains than ever in her life before, she thought, as she was jostled good-naturedly by servicemen going home on leave, or those who were out of the services for good. She felt as if she had travelled the world – or at least, the small part of it that led down to Chichester and up to Yorkshire – and now she was going where her heart always took her in times of stress or happiness. She was going to Cornwall.

It had either been inspirational on her part to think of booking a room at Kenneth Harris's bed-and-breakfast place for a week or two, or it had been something Aunt Rose had said in her less than subtle way. Whatever it was, Daisy had done it, and it was going to give her a proper breathing space, enjoying the bliss of walking the sands at Marazion in her bare feet, and maybe crossing the causeway to St Michael's Mount at low tide. The pleasure of almost forgotten memories soared in her mind, blotting out the awful truths that were coming out of Germany now. Aunt Rose always said that if you could do something about a problem, you should do it. If you couldn't, you shouldn't have nightmares about it.

Now that she had made the decision, she knew she *needed* to be alone, at least to be away from her family for a while. They would always be there, supporting her, smothering her…

She managed to get a seat on the crowded train and dozed fitfully for most of the long and tiring journey. She was hungry and thirsty by the time the train pulled slowly into Marazion station, and she stepped out of it, stretching her legs, feeling thankful she was able at last to be wearing a cool summer frock and not the nurse's uniform she had worn for so long. It was wonderful to be in civvies again, and to know that if she ever went back to nursing, it needn't be at a military hospital. Her thoughts brought her up short with a little shock. *If* she ever went back to nursing? She wasn't aware there had been any doubt – until now, when she had a choice.

A number of people were getting out of the train at the same time as she was, and she knew she should go straight to the boarding house and let Kenneth Harris know she was here. But not yet – not until she felt that sand between her toes and knew that no German planes were going to disrupt the lovely peace. And the beach was so near…

"Can I leave my bags here for a while and collect them later?" she asked the station master impulsively.

"Course you can, me dear," he said in his rich voice. "They'll be quite safe here with me. You'll be going on to Penzance, no doubt, and 'tis all excitement there, of course. But maybe you'll be wanting to join in the festivities here too."

He smiled at the pretty young woman with the lovely red hair he had seen before on numerous occasions. Then he forgot about her as he stored her bags away safely in his office and attended to other duties.

Daisy didn't enlighten the station master that it wasn't excitement she was looking for, not right now. She'd had enough of that in one way or another. She left the station and walked the short distance towards the beach, feeling her heart lift with every step, and her breathing deepened as she took in the reviving, tangy salt air.

She felt her mouth curve into a smile, remembering how her mother often said that, after it had been washed by the tide, this lovely stretch of beach was as fresh and pure as if God had just created it.

Aunt Rose had approved of such a statement, of course, just as if it defied those who thought Frances Caldwell's balletic dancing in the beautiful, floaty, gossamer gowns she favoured could be construed as being in any way erotic – unless it was in the minds of the audience.

She sang and danced like an angel, Daisy had always thought reverently, and there had been a time when she had so wanted to be like her…The bright Cornish sunlight danced on the sea and dazzled her eyes in her first glimpse of it, and she could almost imagine she was in another time, another place, and that an adoring audience was applauding and cheering her mother…

She blinked as she stumbled a little, and then gasped as she rounded a corner and came fully within sight of the sea. Offshore, the elegant, soaring St Michael's Mount complemented the long, stretch of sand in the bay that went all the way to Penzance and beyond, and the beach should have been empty, welcoming her to her special place.

Instead of which…She gasped, knowing now what the station master had meant about the festivities here too. The noises in her head were the excited chattering of children, and the adults with them were laughing and chattering just as loudly, trying to calm them down as a great cloud of coloured balloons was sent flying into the air, caught by the breeze as they soared into the sky to the sound of the children's wild cheers.

Abruptly, Daisy stood perfectly still for a moment, taking in the scene. Long trestle tables were set up along the sands, covered in paper tablecloths and loaded down with food that must surely have been hoarded for weeks or months to provide such a feast. They always said Cornwall had a slower, more leisurely pace of life, which was one of its many charms, and this children's victory party was certainly later than most. Or maybe the festivities were just lasting a while longer, because victory wasn't just for a day, but for ever.

Her thoughts became a mixture of nostalgia and confusion, and Daisy knew that if this had all been happening some years ago, she and her sisters might have been among those excited children now, enjoying the generosity and hospitality of local people, determined to give them a good time after being so long without. It was like a huge extension of the picnics she and her family had so enjoyed on this very beach, so long ago...She closed her eyes for a moment, imagining herself as a five-year-old, sitting on a blanket on the sands, eating blancmange and jelly and fishpaste sandwiches...

She became aware of the sound of cars pulling into the car park nearby, and more helpers spilling out of them, carrying more food in cloth-covered baskets, more lemonade drinks, to make this party seem never-ending. As she was bumped from behind, she automatically turned to apologise, close to tears and feeling like an intruder.

"Good God, what are you doing here? It *is* Nurse Caldwell, isn't it? Or is it just *Miss* Caldwell now?" said a voice she didn't recognise, except for the accent.

She squashed the sudden pangs in her heart at the feeling that all her dreams were of yesterday, and that she didn't really belong here after all...

"I'm sorry," she said vaguely, and then the man laughed, and as his face widened, she couldn't miss the jagged scar down one of his cheeks. She sought to remember his name and couldn't. There had been so many.

He went on talking easily. "I'll have to remind you then. We had a few laughs at your hospital. I'm Josh Tremayne. I told you I was at the Forces' Club with my cousin's party the day you and your friend did your singing double act."

His smile became a grin now, and Daisy squirmed with embarrassment. Oh yes, they had had a few laughs – well, he certainly had, remembering her and Naomi's disaster; but it suddenly seemed so futile to waste this glorious day on being embarrassed over something that was long past.

"Of course I remember you," she said at last.

His blue eyes gleamed in mock-surprise, clearly appreciating her summery appearance in the fresh, lemon-coloured dress she was wearing instead of her nurse's uniform.

"I'm impressed. Patients always fall for their favourite nurse, but you don't expect her to remember every patient – especially the prettiest one I ever met!"

"Stop it," Daisy said, laughing now. "And you weren't my patient for that long, so you certainly never fell for me!"

She realised her heart was jumping as she said the words, knowing she was being provocative, and that they were practically flirting with one another, right here on a Cornish beach in broad, glorious sunlight, with the scent of the sea in her nostrils, and seabirds wheeling overhead, waiting to catch the scraps of food left over from the children's feast.

"Maybe not," Josh went on teasingly, "but there's no reason why we couldn't put that right, is there? I don't know what brought you here today, Miss Caldwell with the lovely red hair, but there's a very special party going on for these kids, and some of them will have no fathers coming home to them, so how about putting your tender loving care into action, and helping out?"

He put out his hand and, after a second's hesitation, Daisy put her hand in his and felt his fingers curl around hers, and they crossed the soft sands together towards the cheering children.

Daisy didn't know what had brought her here today either, except a sense of coming home, of intuition, of putting everything right in her world — and a strange certainty of knowing that, oh yes, it was just as her mother had always insisted in that fey, faraway manner of hers. Cornwall was a place of magic and mystery, where anything could happen, even when you least expected it.